MURDER AFTER HOU[RS]

As usual when working, I lost all [...]
Thaddeous and Joleen had long since lost interest in what I was doing and even Richard's eyes were starting to glaze over when we heard the shot. Or rather, when everybody but me heard it. I was so deep in Joleen's files that it didn't register.

There was a second shot, and even I heard this one. "What was that?" I asked.

"It came from upstairs," Thaddeous said. "We better check it out."

No one spoke as we rode the elevator slowly up to the fourth floor. The hall was dark, but a light showed from the open door to Burt Walters's office. Thaddeous held up one hand for silence, but there were no sounds other than our breathing. Then he slowly stepped out.

"Wait a minute," I said and stepped up next to Thaddeous. I felt Richard's hand on my shoulder, just letting me know he was there. Then, as a group, we stepped forward.

There was a sharp smell in the air. "Gunpowder," Thaddeous said. He stepped ahead just a bit so he could peer into the office ahead of us. "Mr. Walters? Is that you?"

I was just behind him, and looked to the left as he looked to the right, so I saw it first. A man was lying face down on the plush carpet.

An ugly puddle of red flowed out from under his body.

* * *

"Toni Kelner deftly captures both the fishbowl and the fun of small-town Southern life — where everybody knows everything about everybody . . . or do they? DEAD [...] blends romance and violence with long-buried [...] then adds a dash of humor for a mystery that goes [...] smoother than a glass of sweet iced tea."

Margaret Maron, author of Edgar winning
BOOTLEGGER'S DAUGHTER

DEAD RINGER

Toni L.P. Kelner

ZEBRA BOOKS
KENSINGTON PUBLISHING CORP.

DEDICATION

My father once toasted my husband and me with these words: "May you always stay in love, but more importantly, may you always stay best friends."

This book is dedicated to my best friend, Stephen P. Kelner, Jr.

ACKNOWLEDGEMENTS

I want to thank:

- *Stephen P. Kelner, Jr., Michael Luce, Daniel Schaeffer, and Elizabeth Shaw for reading drafts, offering suggestions, and not minding it when I ignored them.*
- *Brenda Perry Holt, Peggy Perry, William Perry, and Robin Perry Schnabel for reminding me of how people from North Carolina talk.*
- *Joan Brandt and John Scognamiglio for taking care of me.*
- *All of the above plus the following for enthusiasm above and beyond the call of duty: my co-workers at BGS Systems, Alice Cannon, Tony Cannon, John Holt, Amanda Holt, Elizabeth Green, Judith Kelner, Bill Kelner, D'Arcy Kelner, Kathe Kelner, Tamsin Kelner, Stephen P. Kelner, Sr., Kate Mattes, Virginia Raines, Karl Schnabel, Jennifer Schnabel, Derek Schnabel, Michael Schnabel, Kyle Schnabel, Sarah Smith, Bill Spencer, Connie Perry Spencer, Karen Spencer, Kristi Spencer, and the Ward family.*

Chapter 1

I do love the fall in Byerly. Some Bostonians I know say that leaf-peeping in New Hampshire is wonderful, but as far as I'm concerned, the colors in North Carolina are just as pretty. I almost wished it was a longer walk to the church.

As Richard and I crossed the stretch of grass that separated Aunt Maggie's house from the Byerly First Baptist Church, I saw that the parking lot was already half full and the door to the hall was wide open. Half a dozen people turned to smile and nod as we walked by, and a woman called out, "Hey there! How are y'all doing?"

"Who was that?" Richard asked in a low voice as we passed.

"I haven't the slightest idea," I said, smiling and nodding back at the folks.

"You are sure that we're at the right family reunion, aren't you?" Richard said.

"Fairly sure," I said, wondering if it would be possible to wander into the wrong gathering. Then I caught sight of a familiar face. "We must be in the right place.

There's Yancy Burnette. You remember him, don't you? He spoke at Paw's funeral."

We exchanged nods with him, but I don't think he knew quite who Richard and I were, so we kept going.

"Why don't you wear name tags?" Richard asked.

"I suggested that once," I said, "but Paw said there wasn't any need. What difference does it make who's who? We're all family, one way or another."

"There will be people here we actually know, won't there?"

"You know doggone well there will be." My so–called immediate family included five aunts, two uncles, eleven first cousins, three second cousins, and two cousins by marriage. It was just that my grandfather's brothers and sisters had all been prolific, meaning that there were lots of more removed cousins to keep track of.

It had been a few years since I had come to the annual Burnette reunion, but when this one was scheduled during Boston College's fall break so Richard could take time off, I thought that it would be a good time to come down.

"Shall we go inside?" I asked.

" 'Once more unto the breach, dear friends, once more,' " Richard quoted. "*King Henry V,* Act III, Scene 1."

"Richard, you're not going to quote Shakespeare all day, are you?"

"Who? Me?"

"These people already think you Yankees talk funny, and a college professor is particularly suspect. Let's not encourage them."

"Perish the thought," he said innocently, and we went inside.

8

As Aunt Maggie would have said, the people were so thick that you couldn't have stirred them with a stick.

"What a crowd," Richard said. "I didn't know there were this many people in Byerly."

"They don't all live in Byerly," I said. "Some are in Dudley Shoals or Granite Falls or Saw Mills. A few moved up to Hickory."

"All the way to Hickory?" Richard asked, sounding amazed. "Goodness gracious."

"The kitchen is over there," I said, ignoring his sarcasm. "Why don't you go drop off the lasagna?" He was carrying the pan that was our donation to the upcoming feast.

"I don't mind if I do. It's getting heavy." He made his way through a crowd of women clustered around the doorway.

I looked around to see who else was there, but didn't see anybody I knew. Then a voice made itself heard over the roar of conversation.

"Laurie Anne? Is that you?" my cousin Vasti squealed.

I managed not to wince. "Hi, Vasti."

"Hi? Is that the way people act up North? You come give me a great big hug."

As hugs went, it was no great shakes, but then Vasti had to be sure that her dress didn't get wrinkled. "What a pretty outfit," Vasti said, "but I think it's missing something." She reached into her pocketbook and pulled out a bright red button with white letters that said BUMGARNER FOR CITY COUNCIL. "Let me put this on."

I obediently stood still for her to pin it to my dress. "How's the campaign going?" I asked.

"Pretty good, but I'm still worried about Big Bill Walters. He hasn't endorsed Arthur yet and it's only a little over two weeks until the election! I don't know why he won't go ahead and formally approve Arthur. Everybody knows that he'll do a wonderful job."

"I imagine it will work out, Vasti."

"I sure hope so." She turned and saw someone coming in the door. "Aunt Nora!"

"Hey there, Vasti," Aunt Nora said, and gave her a quick hug. "It's awfully good to see you, Laurie Anne. Just let me hug your neck."

I hugged her neck, and the rest of her besides. Plump and an inch or so shorter than I am, Aunt Nora looked like the stereotype of an aunt. She was just as nice as she looked, and right much tougher.

"When did you and Richard get into town?" Aunt Nora asked. "I was hoping to see you at church."

"We didn't get to Aunt Maggie's house until after eleven last night, so we had to cook this morning." Actually, Richard had made the lasagna while I watched, but that was close enough.

"I've got something for you, Aunt Nora," Vasti said, reaching into her purse for another button.

"Thank you, Vasti," Aunt Nora said, "but I've already got a button on. See?"

"So you do," Vasti admitted. "I think it's so important for all of us to support Arthur as much as we can."

"Where is the future city councilor?" I asked.

"Arthur had some campaigning to do, but he'll be here shortly."

"What about your mama? Daphine is coming, isn't she?" Aunt Nora asked.

"Of course she's coming," Vasti said. "She's just running late. Look, there's Uncle Ruben and Aunt Nellie. I

10

haven't given them their buttons yet." Vasti clattered away.

"Why wouldn't Aunt Daphine come?" I asked Aunt Nora.

"I just hadn't spoken to her lately, and I wasn't sure," Aunt Nora said.

"Why not?" I asked. My four aunts usually talked to one another at least once a day. "You two aren't feuding, are you?"

"No, nothing like that. She's just been acting kind of funny lately. Not like herself."

"Really?" Aunt Daphine was one of the more stable personalities in the family. "Is something wrong?"

"I'm just not sure, Laurie Anne." She looked around the crowded room. "We'll talk about it later, all right?"

I nodded, feeling uneasy.

"I haven't seen Aunt Maggie," Aunt Nora said. "Didn't she come with y'all?"

"She said she wasn't ready yet, so we should come on without her. Where's the rest of your crew?"

"Willis and Buddy are outside somewhere, but Thaddeous had to go get his date."

"A date? Really? You know what *that* means."

Surprisingly, Aunt Nora did not look pleased. "You don't believe that old tale, do you?"

"It's always happened that way before. Vasti brought Arthur, Linwood brought Sue, and I brought Richard. Plus all of your generation brought their boyfriends before they got married. If a Burnette brings someone to the reunion, they end up married."

Aunt Nora shook her head. "I don't know that it would be a good idea this time. Thaddeous barely knows Joleen and they've only gone out once before now."

11

"One date and he's bringing her to the reunion? She must be something special."

"Just wait till you meet her," she said, still shaking her head.

Richard finally made it out of the kitchen and came to give Aunt Nora a hug.

"What took you so long?" I asked.

"Comparing recipes. The ladies in there had to have a taste of the lasagna when I told them that I made it myself, and then they wanted the recipe." He looked terribly smug. "I don't know if there will be any left by the time lunch is served."

"Then I better go get myself a bite right now," Aunt Nora said. "I'll see y'all later." She headed for the kitchen.

"So who else is here that I know?" Richard asked. "I don't want to miss out on any hugs."

I looked around the room. "There's Aunt Nellie and Uncle Ruben," I said, and we started walking in their direction.

" 'This is the short and the long of it. *The Merry Wives of Windsor*, Act II, Scene 2," Richard said.

"Now stop that," I said, but he just grinned. Admittedly, Aunt Nellie was a full head taller than Uncle Ruben, just as her shiny black hair and dark eyes were a sharp contrast to his light brown hair and pale blue eyes, but I didn't think that it was polite to mention it.

We exchanged greetings and hugs, and Uncle Ruben said, "I hear the water isn't too good up there in Boston. The harbor filled with garbage and all."

"It is pretty bad," I admitted. "We buy bottled water ourselves."

"It's a big health concern these days. Have you ever

considered a water filtration system? It could save you a lot of money in the long run."

Now I knew what money–making scheme they were involved in this time. "Actually," I said, making up an excuse as I went along, "our lease forbids us from doing anything with the plumbing."

"This doesn't go on your plumbing," Aunt Nellie said. "You screw it onto your faucet."

"Well," I said, trying to think of something else. "I don't think—" Then a trio in red, blue, and yellow arrived to save me.

"Mama! Stop trying to sell those filters. This is a family reunion, remember?" Carlelle said. At least I thought it was Carlelle. With the triplets, sometimes I wasn't sure. They all had the same buxom builds, hazel eyes, and brown hair curled into the same elaborate hairstyle. They usually dressed alike, too, although at least they were in different colors today.

"You too, Daddy," Odelle chimed in. "Laurie Anne and Richard did not come all the way to North Carolina to talk about dirty water."

"We just thought they might be interested," Aunt Nellie said. "What with the fluoride in the water, and all."

Idelle said firmly, "I'm sure they'll call you later if they want to talk about it." Then she relented a bit, seeing that her parents looked so disappointed. "Let's us go see Cousin Herman. His trailer isn't on city water, so maybe he'd want one of your filters."

"Is that right?" Uncle Ruben said. "Then maybe I should mention it to him. We'll see y'all later." Idelle led the two of them away.

"Sorry about that," Carlelle said. "You know how they are when they get started on a new project. Some-

13

times I think they're more like the children and we're more like the parents."

"Thanks for rescuing us," I said.

"That's all right. We were in such a hurry to distract Mama and Daddy, that we didn't even say hello like we should."

That meant more hugs, of course. I was glad the sisters were wearing different colors so I wouldn't hug one more than she was entitled to.

Richard asked, "Was setting them after Cousin Herman altogether kind?"

Odelle grinned. "I never did like Herman."

"Did you hear Thaddeous is bringing a date to the reunion?" I asked.

"Really?" the two sisters said in unison.

"I didn't know he was dating anyone serious," Carlelle said.

"Aunt Nora said he and Joleen had only gone out once before now," I said.

"Not Joleen Dodd?" Odelle said.

"I don't think Aunt Nora mentioned her last name."

"You don't suppose it could be Joleen Dodd, do you?" Carlelle asked Odelle.

"I know he's been mooning after her ever since she started working at the mill, but I didn't think she'd give him the time of day," Odelle replied.

"I don't know why not. She'll go out with anything else in pants," Carlelle said.

"If he's got enough money to suit her, that is," Odelle said. "And Lord knows a wedding ring doesn't stop her."

Richard finally broke in to ask, "Who is Joleen Dodd?"

"She's the receptionist at the mill," Carlelle said.

14

"I assume from your reaction that she is not a nice lady," Richard asked.

Odelle snorted. "Not any kind of a lady, if you ask me."

"Trouble looking for a place to happen," Carlelle added.

"She doesn't sound like Thaddeous's type," I said doubtfully, "but I know he wouldn't bring just anyone to the reunion."

"Maybe it's not the same Joleen," Richard said.

"I don't know of another Joleen in Byerly," Carlelle said. "We'll go track down Aunt Nora and ask her. Bye now."

They moved off quickly.

"Why all the fuss about Thaddeous bringing Joleen Dodd to the reunion?" Richard asked.

"Don't you remember the Burnette tradition?" I asked. "Every time one of us brings a date to the reunion, that person ends up married into the family."

"How could I have forgotten?"

"I should think you'd be scarred for life from the first time I brought you to the reunion." Uncle Buddy had wasted no time in telling Richard that he was destined for the altar. Richard had turned white as a sheet, and didn't quote Shakespeare for the rest of the day.

"You could have warned me ahead of time," Richard said mildly.

I grinned. "My mama didn't raise no fool. I knew a good thing when I saw it." It seemed an appropriate time for a kiss, and Richard evidently agreed.

"Look at the lovebirds," Vasti's unmistakable voice said, and I looked up to see her and Arthur. "Still acting like they're on their honeymoon after all this time."

"Thou—," Richard began, but when I glared at him,

he changed it to, "Hello Vasti, Arthur. Or should I say Councilor Bumgarner?"

Arthur grinned his best politician grin. "Just Arthur will do fine. No call to put on airs around here. Besides, I haven't won the election yet."

"But everybody knows you're going to win," Vasti said. "Oh! I haven't given Richard his button yet." She pulled out a badge from her bag and handed it to him.

"Thank you," he said, pinning it on. "I'm just sorry I can't help stuff the ballot box on your behalf. What's the opposition like?"

"There isn't any," I said.

Richard raised one eyebrow. "Then why the concern?"

"Because of Big Bill Walters," Vasti said as if it were the most obvious thing on earth.

"Byerly's town council doesn't have a set number of members," I explained. "If somebody wants on the council, he just runs on a yes-or-no ballot. The trick is that if Big Bill Walters doesn't want you on the council, you're not going to make it. And you have to campaign to make sure he knows you're sincere."

"I see," Richard said, though I could see that he thought it was strange. I thought so, too, but that's the way it was done in Byerly.

"These small town elections probably don't seem very important to someone from Boston," Arthur said.

"On the contrary," Richard said. "It's the local politicians that really make a difference in this country. When you need something done, you should always start in your own town."

"I hear that," Arthur said approvingly.

I grinned. I had been a little worried the first time I brought my Northerner boyfriend to meet my family, but he had charmed them all. "Just plain folks," had been the final verdict.

"So how are things up your way?" Vasti asked. "Are you still teaching school, Richard?"

"Richard doesn't just lecture," I said sharply. "He's also writing articles. His paper discussing the third murderer in *Macbeth* was just accepted for publication."

"Is there much money in that?" Arthur asked.

"Not a penny," Richard said.

"Scholarly journals don't actually pay," I added. "You write papers for the prestige and to get noticed. That's how you get tenure and research grants."

"Not to mention the spread of knowledge," Richard said.

I sighed inwardly. When would I learn not to get so defensive when I was in Byerly? "It's a very important paper," I said lamely.

"Isn't that interesting?" Vasti said, but her expression said plainly that she wasn't the least bit interested. "Have y'all seen Thaddeous yet? I hear that he's bringing a date."

"News does spread quickly," I said. "I don't think they're here yet, but I'm getting pretty curious."

"Curious?" Vasti said. "That's not the half of it. If he brought her to the reunion, he must be planning to marry her."

"Now don't you go telling that poor girl about the Burnette curse," Arthur said. "You'll scare her off."

Vasti frowned. "It's not a curse—it's a tradition. It worked out all right for you, didn't it?"

"I'm not complaining," Arthur said quickly.

"You know," Richard said speculatively, "I've been thinking about this tradition. Now the way I understand

17

it, if a non–Burnette comes to the reunion, he or she ends up married into the family. Right?"

"That's how it works," I said.

"Do they always marry the one that brought them, or do they get to pick and choose?"

Arthur hooted. "Pick and choose! That's a good one." He slapped Richard soundly on the shoulder. "Richard, you're all right for a Yankee."

"I've always thought so," Richard acknowledged.

Just then Vasti gasped. "Oh my goodness!"

"What?" I turned in the direction she was staring. Our Great–Aunt Maggie had arrived, and she had dressed to impress. In her own way, that is. She was wearing her usual blue jeans and a plaid flannel shirt, but her sneakers were the really impressive part of the ensemble. They were hot pink high tops with purple tiger stripes.

She came over. "Hey there, Vasti. Now isn't that a pretty outfit you've got on."

"Why thank you, Aunt Maggie," Vasti said, but she just couldn't make herself pronounce the return compliment that good manners demanded.

"You look very nice, too," I finally said.

Aunt Maggie snickered. "Laurie Anne, your mama taught you right, you know that. I was going to wear a dress but I couldn't find not one thing in my closet that was fitting to wear, and I didn't see the point of buying something I wasn't going to wear but the once."

I couldn't argue with that.

"I love your shoes," Richard said, and darned if he wasn't serious.

Aunt Maggie held up one foot so he could get a closer look. "They got a whole batch of them down at the Thrift Store, brand new, and they only charged me four dollars for them. I couldn't pass that up. What's your shoe size, Richard? I could see if they've got a pair that will fit you."

"I wear a ten," Richard said.

I could just see him wearing shoes like that to lecture on Shakespeare at Boston College. He was never going to get tenure at that rate.

"How about you, Laurie Anne?" Aunt Maggie said.

"No, thanks. I just bought a new pair of sneakers." Then, to change the subject, I asked, "Have you been here long?"

"Nope, just got here. I swear I don't see hardly a soul that I recognize. I don't know why I come to this thing anyway. I have to pay rent for my booth even if I don't show up." Aunt Maggie usually spent her weekends at the local flea market, selling paperback books and all kinds of knick-knacks.

"I'm sure folks will be glad to see you," I said.

"If they're so all fired glad to see me, why don't they come visit instead of waiting until the reunion to hug onto me. Besides, I didn't bring anything to eat, and I shouldn't show up empty-handed."

"There's plenty of food here already. And no matter how much you fuss, I know you enjoy the reunion."

"Well, I guess you're right," Aunt Maggie admitted. "It is right nice to see all of us in one place. Those of us that are left, anyway."

I nodded, knowing she was thinking about her brother, my grandfather. The last time I had come to Byerly was when Paw was in the hospital, the victim of a brutal attack. When he died, Richard and I had set about finding out who killed him.

"Well," Aunt Maggie said, "I think I'll go see if there are any other old folks around. I'll talk to y'all later."

Then she said to Vasti, "Have you got any more of those buttons for Arthur? I forgot to put mine on."

I know Vasti was trying to decide whether or not she wanted Aunt Maggie to wear a button with those sneakers, but she smiled and said, "Of course. Here you go, Aunt Maggie."

Aunt Maggie pinned it on, winked at me, and headed into the crowd.

Once she was gone, Vasti said, "Arthur, if I ever start dressing like that, I want you to lock me up in the nut house and throw away the key."

I said, "Vasti, you know she only wears sneakers like that to get a rise out of people. If you'd quit noticing, she'd quit wearing them."

"How on earth could I *not* notice those shoes?" Then Vasti gasped again, even more dramatically, and said, "And would you look at *that!*"

"Now what?" But this time, I couldn't blame her for her being taken aback. Our cousin Thaddeous, as usual the tallest man in the room, had just come inside the hall with a woman on his arm. And what a woman she was.

"Can you believe what she's wearing?" Vasti said in a shocked tone.

Obviously Thaddeous had not told Joleen what people wore to the reunion. The men were in suits, and other than Aunt Maggie, who was old enough to make her own rules, the women were wearing nice dresses. In contrast, Joleen had poured herself into a pair of blue jeans and wriggled into a bright red tube top that didn't look like it was quite up to the strain. The only thing that kept the outfit decent was the thin cotton shirt she had put on over the tube top. Though it was unbuttoned, it was tied around her waist and at least covered some of her freckled pulchritude.

"Does she really think she's fooling anyone?" Vasti asked. "Her hair has got to be dyed."

Dyed or natural, her red curls were impressive, especially the way she had teased them up several inches above her head.

I guess Thaddeous saw us watching, because he smiled and came our way. He was smitten all right. I could tell from the way he was walking that he thought this lady was the best thing since sliced bread.

"How's everybody doing? Good to see you two in town," Thaddeous said, and exchanged hugs with me and Richard.

"Joleen, I want you to meet my cousin Laurie Anne Fleming and her husband Richard."

"Just Laura," I said, knowing that it was a losing battle.

Thaddeous went on. "And this is my cousin Vasti Bumgarner and her husband Arthur. This is Joleen Dodd."

"Hey," Joleen chirped.

"Nice to meet you, Joleen," I said, and Richard said something comparable.

"Joleen," Arthur said, drawing the name out. "That's an awful pretty name. Wasn't there a Dolly Parton song about a lady named Joleen?"

"I believe there was," Vasti said sweetly. "The Joleen in that song was a homewrecker, wasn't she?"

"I guess that song was before my time," Joleen said, smiling just as nicely as Vasti was.

It wasn't a nice thing to say, but I couldn't really hold it against Joleen. Vasti did tend to bring out the worst in people.

"Vasti, it looks like you've fallen down on the job," Arthur said. "Thaddeous doesn't have a button."

"You are so right," Vasti said, and produced yet another one.

"And how about one for Joleen?" Arthur added.

"I don't think Joleen has anyplace to put one, Arthur," Vasti said.

"That's all right," Joleen said. "I'll pin it onto my pocketbook strap."

Vasti had to hand her one after that.

We chatted for a few minutes, and then Thaddeous said, "Well, if y'all will excuse us, I want to go introduce Joleen to some of the rest of the folks." He strutted off, Joleen on his arm.

Arthur said, "Come on, Richard. I bet these two want to have a little girl talk."

"Then let us make an honourable retreat."

That sounded suspiciously Shakespearean to me, but at least Richard omitted the attribution as he and Arthur retreated.

I wish I could say I was above idle gossip, but I wasn't. I wanted to talk about Joleen nigh about as much as Vasti did.

"Can you believe that?" Vasti said. "I have never seen *anything* like that at the Burnette reunion. I'm pure ashamed for her to be wearing one of Arthur's buttons."

"Well, every vote helps," I said. "I just can't imagine Thaddeous dating a woman like that."

"When it comes to women, men don't have the sense God gave a milk cow," Vasti said with far more cynicism than her age allowed for. "They think with what's in their britches, not with their heads." She shook her head ruefully. "I don't know if I can ever call that one 'Cousin.'"

22

"Come on, Vasti. We've just met her. She may be very nice. I mean underneath it all."

"Laurie Anne, with what she's wearing, there's nothing underneath that we can't see."

I resisted the impulse to giggle. "Besides, we don't know that Thaddeous is serious about her."

"Then why did he bring her here?"

I had no answer for that. Thaddeous knew the family tradition as well as we did. No wonder Aunt Nora was concerned.

"Look!" Vasti said. "She's going to the bathroom. Come on!"

I'd like to be able to say that I only went along because of the death-grip Vasti had on my elbow, but to tell the truth, I was fairly curious myself.

Joleen was in one of the stalls by the time we got in there, so Vasti and I killed time by pulling out brushes and working on our hair. After a minute, Joleen joined us and somehow managed to tease her bangs into standing up just a little bit higher.

"I just cannot get my hair to do right today," Joleen said. "It won't stand up worth a flip."

Actually I thought Joleen could teach a few things about hair to the punks who stood around Harvard Square, but knowing that this would not be considered complimentary, I settled for saying, "I know what you mean."

I was counting on Vasti to subtly bring up the subject of Joleen's relationship with Thaddeous, and I didn't have long to wait.

"So Joleen," Vasti said, "have you and Thaddeous been dating long?"

That was about as subtle as Vasti ever got.

Joleen said, "Not really, but I've had my eye on him

for a while now. I finally got him to ask me out this weekend, and when he told me about your reunion, I let him know right quick that he could bring me along if he wanted to."

I was impressed. I couldn't think of anything that would induce me to come to someone else's family reunion. Coming to my own was bad enough.

Joleen plucked one last hair into place, and said, "You know Laurie Anne, I hear you and I have something in common."

"What's that?" I asked. It certainly wasn't our figures, I thought ruefully. Hers was much bigger than mine in all the favored places.

"Computers. You know about computers, don't you?"

"I'm a programmer, mostly database management stuff." I modestly refrained from mentioning my degree from MIT.

Joleen went on, "I use a computer in the office up at the mill."

"No kidding. What kind of system are you working with?"

"Just a little one. What do they call it? A PC? Mr. Walters has me type up his memos with it."

"Those are nice," I said politely. Trust Burt Walters to buy a computer and then use it as a glorified typewriter.

"Sometimes I think it's more trouble than it's worth. Always crashing and stuff, and then I have to start all over again."

"They can be ornery," I agreed.

"You know, Laurie Anne," she said in a confidential tone, "I've been having a little trouble with my computer. Maybe while you're in town you could come by the mill and take a look?"

"Maybe," I said vaguely.

She put her comb away. "Well, I better go find Thad before he thinks I've run out on him."

"Thad?" I said to Vasti as soon as Joleen was gone. I had never known Thaddeous to allow anyone to call him anything short of his full name. But then, I had never known him to date anyone quite like Joleen before.

Vasti shrugged her shoulders. "Men are *so* stupid," was all she said.

Once out of the ladies room, we spotted our husbands in a cluster of other young men. As we approached, I heard someone saying, "Pick and choose? I'd sure like to pick and choose!" There was some hearty male laughing, which dwindled when they saw me and Vasti. Vasti gave me a look that said as plain as day, "Didn't I tell you that men are stupid?"

Richard extricated himself from the group and joined me while Vasti went to pull Arthur away and hand out more buttons. "Having a good time?" I asked.

"Very nice. How about you? Have you obtained any information on Joleen yet?"

"Not much yet, but give Vasti another hour or so."

"You are, of course, above such concerns."

I stuck my tongue out at him in reply. "Who shall we mingle with now?"

"Actually, I think they're about to start serving lunch," he said.

Sure enough, women were trotting to and fro placing platters and bowls on a line of tables down the center of the room. A line of eager Burnettes was already starting to form, and we took a place at the end.

Though everybody insists that we Burnettes get together each year purely for companionship and that the meal is only for convenience, the amount of time that goes into preparing the food tells the real story. Though there is no formal competition, I've heard more than one aunt crow when her dish was the first one emptied and others looking crestfallen when they had leftovers to take home.

Richard and I did our best to make sure nobody felt left out. I loaded my plate with ham, fried chicken, pulled pork barbeque, macaroni and cheese, snap beans, mashed potatoes and gravy, cole slaw, a hunk of cornbread, and one of Aunt Nora's biscuits. The lasagna Richard and I had brought was gone before I could get any.

"I guess I'll have to come back for dessert," I said once my plate was stacked as high as I could manage.

"You've got to be kidding," Richard said, looking at his plate.

"You can suit yourself, but I'm not about to pass up Aunt Daphine's apple cobbler." I looked around at the rapidly filling tables. "Tell you what. Give me your plate and I'll find us a place to sit while you go get us some iced tea."

Richard agreed, handed me his plate, and I snagged the last empty table. I wasn't alone for long, because Vasti appeared almost instantly.

"I found out all about Joleen Dodd," she said triumphantly.

"What did you find out?" I asked.

"Joleen and her mama only moved here about three months ago. They're from somewhere in South Carolina, but they left town in a hurry because the mama is in the middle of a nasty divorce. Her third husband, by the way, and not Joleen's father. Burt Walters hired Joleen right away and made her receptionist even though there were three local girls applying for the job. I think we can guess why." She raised her eyebrows significantly. "Everybody is surprised that she's dating Thaddeous, because the men she's been dating up to now have all had a whole lot more money than any Burnette." She tried to look modest when she added, "Except for me and Arthur, of course."

"Maybe that means she really likes him," I ventured. "Thaddeous is an awfully nice fellow."

"Laurie Anne, I don't think 'nice' is what Joleen Dodd is looking for. In three months she's already made herself quite a reputation."

"You found all that out in a hurry," I said, pretty impressed.

"Actually, I knew part of it already. I just didn't realize who Joleen is because of her last name. Joleen's mama is Dorinda Thompson, who works for my mama down at the beauty parlor. And with these two, like mother, like daughter."

"Dorinda can't be too bad," I said, "or Aunt Daphine wouldn't have her working for her."

Vasti just shrugged. "Mama hasn't been feeling too well lately."

Richard arrived with our iced tea right about then.

"Is it terribly crowded over by the drinks?" Vasti asked him. "I am so thirsty, but I haven't been able to get anywhere near there."

"Why don't you—" Richard began to say.

I nudged him under the table and interrupted with, "Why don't you go check, Vasti? I'm sure the crowd will have died down by now."

"I suppose I'm going to have to," she said, giving Richard another chance to offer her his iced tea. By now Richard had taken my hint, and took a long swallow himself. "I guess I'll see you two later," she said and headed for the side of the room away from the drinks.

"I could have given her my drink," Richard said once she was gone.

"I know you could have, and with just about anybody else I would expect you to, but you know how Vasti is. If you got her a drink, then she'd want you to go get her food. If she had her way, she'd never have to tend to herself."

After that, we dedicated our attention to our plates. Vasti eventually wandered back over with her own plate, and then complained that all the good stuff was gone by the time she got there. I would have been more sympathetic if I hadn't seen her talking to half a dozen different people before going to serve herself.

"That was wonderful," I said, sopping up the last bit of gravy with the last piece of biscuit and popping it into my mouth. "Now I'm ready for dessert. Vasti, which end of the table did Aunt Daphine put her apple cobbler on?"

"Mama didn't bring any this year."

"She didn't?"

"She said that she hadn't had time to bake, so she bought an apple pie at the grocery store."

"Really?" I was going to have to track down Aunt Daphine after this. I couldn't imagine her not having time to make apple cobbler for the reunion. Where was she anyway? I hadn't seen her yet.

Despite my disappointment over Aunt Daphine's cobbler, I managed to console myself with helpings of pecan pie and chocolate cake. Richard, despite his earlier protests, also managed to squeeze in a couple of desserts.

After everybody had eaten enough to bust a gusset, Yancy Burnette stood up to make the announcements of family news he had been gathering all year. The Burnettes had seen three marriages, one divorce, four

28

births, and two deaths over the previous year. There was a moment of silence for the two we had lost: Paw and a third cousin.

Then they gave out prizes for the youngest and oldest attendees and for the attendee who had come the furthest. Aunt Maggie, after much protestation, accepted the designation of oldest and her prize of a shawl, but refused to put it on over her jeans. Richard and I got the prize for coming the furthest, which was no big surprise. Our only competition would have been if my cousin Augustus had gotten leave from the Army to come home from Germany. Our prize was a set of glass ash trays.

"But we don't smoke," Richard said in a low voice.

"I know," I whispered back. "We'll give them to Aunt Maggie to sell."

After that, a couple of musically–inclined Burnettes took turns playing the guitar and singing gospel songs. Richard and I sat and listened for a little while, but then decided to go visit some more. I still wanted to see what was going on with Aunt Daphine.

We finally found her at a corner table with Aunt Nora.

"Well!" I said in mock exasperation. "It's about time you showed up."

I expected her to respond in kind, but all she said was, "Hey there. How are you two doing?"

"Just fine." We hugged, and Richard and I sat down at the table with them.

Aunt Daphine asked the usual questions about work and life in Boston, but even though she listened politely, I could tell that her heart wasn't in it. She didn't look good, either. Not exactly sick, but there were dark shadows under her eyes that hadn't been there the last time

I had seen her and her cheekbones, usually her most striking feature, jutted out as if she had lost weight. Even her hair, usually a shiny brown, looked listless and indifferently styled. That was a bad sign for the owner of a beauty parlor.

Aunt Daphine quickly ran out of questions, and excused herself to go to the restroom.

"Aunt Nora," I said once she was out of earshot, "what's the matter with Aunt Daphine?"

"I wish I knew, Laurie Anne, but she won't tell me a thing."

Now I was really worried. If Aunt Nora didn't know what was going on, something had to be bad wrong. "Hasn't she spoken to Vasti?" I asked. Even if she had told Vasti something in confidence, Vasti wouldn't have been able to resist dropping hints.

But Aunt Nora shook her head. "She won't talk about it to anybody. Ruby Lee, Nellie, Edna—all of us sisters have been taking turns with her, but we might as well be talking to a stone wall. I was hoping that maybe you could try to get something out of her if you're going to be in town long enough."

"We're staying a couple of weeks," I said. "I don't know if it will do any good, but I'll try."

"Good," Aunt Nora said. "So, did you two meet Thaddeous's new girlfriend?"

"She sure is something," I said, then hesitated. "They aren't really planning to get married, are they?"

"Lord, I hope not," Aunt Nora said, and then looked embarrassed. "I shouldn't say that. I barely know the girl. It's just that she's not the kind of girl I expected Thaddeous to bring home."

She started to rise from the table. "I better head on into the kitchen and help with the washing up."

"Aunt Nora," I said, "you have been helping with the washing up at every reunion for as long as I can remember. Don't you think it's somebody else's turn?"

"Shoot, it doesn't take but a few minutes." She started toward the kitchen, but turned back with a grin. "Besides, you hear the best stories over the dishes."

"Do all Burnette women gossip?" Richard asked.

"No more than the men," I retorted. "Besides, it's not gossip if you're really interested in the people you're talking about."

"I think Webster would have a few questions about that definition," Richard said.

I ignored the comment. "Come on. I'm sure there must be a neck around here that we haven't hugged yet."

I guess I wasn't really looking where I was going, because I nearly ran into a man coming our way. It was my cousin Linwood. He stopped short and gave me a fierce look.

"I might have known that you'd be here," he said.

"Hello Linwood," I said as evenly as I could. Even though Linwood was more heavyset than his late father had been, that straw-colored hair and the expression on his face made him look an awful lot like Loman.

"Planning to get somebody else shot?" he asked, but before I could answer, he added, "I suppose you made sure that they didn't mention my daddy when they were telling who died this past year."

"Shut up, Linwood," Linwood's wife Sue said as she came up behind him. He glared at me with those nearly colorless grey eyes for a long couple of seconds, then stomped away.

"If looks could kill," I murmured, grateful for the arm Richard put around me.

"Don't mind him," Sue said. "I tried to talk him out of coming today, but he said that he has a right to come and he was going to. I'll make sure that he doesn't say anything else to you."

"Thanks, Sue," I said. "I know it's awkward for Linwood, and for you, too." Linwood's father Loman had been involved in Paw's death, and he ended up dead, too. Linwood had it in his head that it was my fault, and there didn't seem to be anything anybody could say to change his mind.

Sue shrugged, and pushed a stray piece of sandy blond hair back from her face. "Shoot, there ain't nothing nobody can say that can bother me. Linwood's just touchy these days, especially since he lost his job."

"I didn't know the mill was laying people off."

"It wasn't no layoff—Burt Walters fired him," Sue said matter-of-factly. "It was Linwood's own fault, too. People around town are willing to forget about Loman, but Linwood's not. He picked one fight too many, and Walters told him to take a hike."

"That must be tough on you two, what with the new baby and all." Crystal had just been born in September, and they already had Jason and Tiffany.

"We're doing all right," Sue said. "I wanted to thank you for that outfit you sent the baby. It's right pretty."

"Where is Crystal, anyway?" I asked. "We haven't seen her yet."

"Edna's showing her off," she said, referring to Linwood's mother.

"Sue!" Vasti squealed as she appeared from somewhere. "You're not wearing a button." Without waiting for permission, Vasti pinned a badge onto Sue's dress. "That's a real pretty dress you're wearing. You can hardly tell that it's a maternity dress."

32

I winced. Sue never had been a thin woman, but with Crystal only a couple of months old, I would have thought that Vasti could have resisted teasing her just this once.

"Hey there, Vasti," Sue said unenthusiastically.

"The Retort Courteous," Richard said under his breath.

"How do you like *my* new outfit?" Vasti asked, preening. "I think it matches my eyes real well."

"The Quip Modest," Richard said. Neither of my cousins seemed to hear him, but I nudged him anyway.

"Since when are your eyes striped?" Sue said.

"The Reply Churlish," from Richard.

"I mean the dress sets off my eyes nicely," Vasti said.

Richard said, "The Reproof Valiant."

Vasti went on. "After all, some of us do try to color coordinate our wardrobes."

"The Countercheck Quarrelsome," Richard said. I nudged him again.

"Maybe you can come coordinate my clothes sometime," Sue said.

"The Lie with Circumstance."

"Now you don't need me for that, Sue," Vasti said. "You always look real nice."

"The Lie Direct," Richard said with glee.

"What was that, Richard?" Vasti asked.

"Nothing," I answered for him. "Come on, Richard. Let's go say hello to Aunt Ruby Lee."

Undaunted, Richard said, "As you like it."

Aunt Ruby Lee was still legally married to Conrad Randolph, but since he was in jail and the divorce was in the works, her ex-husband Roger Bailey saw no reason to waste any time in trying for a second chance with her. He had his arm around her shoulder, just like old

33

times, which led me to believe that he just might succeed. I couldn't blame him. With her blond hair, blue eyes, and generous figure, Aunt Ruby Lee was the prettiest of my aunts.

"Laurie Anne! Richard!" Aunt Ruby Lee said. "I am so glad you two could come." She hugged us both, and then Roger hugged me and shook Richard's hand.

"How are you doing these days, Roger?" I asked.

"Mighty fine," he said with a big smile. "Spending time with Ruby Lee has reminded me of what I've been missing. Let me tell you, Richard. A good woman is the most important thing you can have in your life, and that's a fact."

"You'll get no arguments from me," Richard said.

"You two boys just cut that out," Aunt Ruby Lee said. "You're going to have both me and Laurie Anne blushing in a minute."

"And what's wrong with that," Roger said. "Laurie Anne, I've been trying to talk your aunt into letting me make an announcement this afternoon, but she's being shy."

"Oh?" I said innocently. So they *were* talking about getting married again.

Aunt Ruby Lee shook her head firmly. "It's too soon to make that kind of announcement, Roger. How would it look, when things with Conrad aren't official yet?"

"I don't give a hoot about how it looks! I'm in love with the prettiest woman on this earth, and I want everybody on earth to know it."

"If you don't lower your voice, everybody in Byerly is going to know about it," Aunt Ruby Lee scolded him, but I could tell that she didn't really mind. She was in love again, too. After her last marriage ended the way it had, I was glad to see her so happy.

We chatted a little longer before drifting off to visit with more cousins. The festivities were starting to wind down when Thaddeous came over.

"Laurie Anne? Can I talk to you for a minute?" Thaddeous said.

"Sure. What's up?"

"I need a favor."

"Name it." I meant it, too. After my last trip to Byerly, I owed Thaddeous more than any favor was going to repay.

"Actually it's for Joleen. She just told me about it, and she's so worried that she started crying on my shoulder. She's in a lot of trouble at work, and I was hoping you could help her out. Somebody must have done something to her computer, and it's not working like it's supposed to. She's afraid that Mr. Walters will fire her if he finds out." He lowered his voice. "Walters has been trying to make time with her, and he was right put out when she told him that she isn't that kind of girl. He's been looking for an excuse to get rid of her ever since."

"I don't know what kind of system she's got," I warned, "but I'll be glad to give it a try."

He beamed. "I really would appreciate it. Do you think we could go over there today? That way we can get it fixed up before Mr. Walters comes into the office tomorrow morning. I'm afraid Joleen wouldn't get a bit of sleep tonight if she was worrying about it."

"Sure thing. The reunion is about over anyway. Let me check with Richard, and find Aunt Maggie to tell her." I conferred with Richard while Thaddeous conferred with Joleen. After a round of goodbyes and a quick stop at Aunt Maggie's to pick up what I needed for the rescue operation, we piled into the car Richard and I had rented to drive out to the mill.

Chapter 2

So many of the people in Byerly depend on Walters Mill for their livelihood that it always seems to me that the mill building should look more impressive than it does. But then, founder Big Bill Walters had never been one to spend two pennies when one would do the job, and I guess he figured a nearly windowless, boxy build-ing made of mud–brown bricks was good enough. And his son Burt, the current man in charge, hadn't done anything to improve the mill's appearance.

We pulled up to the security booth and Ralph Stew-art, the guard on duty, came out as Richard rolled down the window.

"Hey there! What are y'all doing out here? Didn't I hear that you folks were having your family reunion to-day?"

"We have reunited to our heart's content," Richard said.

Thaddeous spoke up from the back seat. "We wanted to go up to the mill for a few minutes, if that's all right with you." Then he nonchalantly added, "I've got my key." Thaddeous was the youngest supervisor at the mill, and was still awfully proud of his position.

Ralph scratched his chin. "I don't know that I should let you in, Thaddeous. Mr. Walters said that I'm not supposed to let anybody up there after working hours without special authorization from him. Today especially, because Mr. Walters is on the warpath about something or another. He wants me to get all the sign—in books in order right away, and said he'd be over to check them any time now. He'll be awful mad if he sees y'all when he gets here."

Joleen looked alarmed. "He's coming over here tonight?" Then she said, low enough that Ralph couldn't hear her, "What if he tries to use that computer?"

"Look, Ralph," Thaddeous said. "We won't be in there but for a little bit. You know we won't hurt anything."

"Well," Ralph said, "I just don't know."

"I didn't want to bring this up," Joleen said, "but Ralph, do you remember that morning last week when I came in early and you weren't here yet? Remember how I didn't tell Mr. Walters?"

"Everybody's late sometimes," Ralph said indignantly. "I had car problems that day."

"We understand that, Ralph," Thaddeous said. "We all bend the rules every once in a while, and that's all we're asking you to do now."

Ralph was clearly weakening. "I guess it'll be all right, just this once," he said, "but you be sure to get gone before Mr. Walters gets here."

Thaddeous nodded. "We'll park around back, and if he gets here before we leave, call up to the mill and we'll be out of there in a heartbeat."

"Thanks Ralph," Richard called out as we drove to the mill. As Thaddeous had promised, we parked on the

37

far side of the mill, where Walters would be unlikely to see us. Thaddeous let us in by a side door.

The building echoed as we walked through to Joleen's desk, stationed right in front of the elevators at the main entrance.

My heart sank when I saw Joleen's computer. It was at least five years old, which was ancient in computer terms. Papers were stacked on top of the air vents and the screen didn't look like it had been dusted off in a year. This was not going to be fun. "Now what exactly is wrong with your system?" I asked Joleen.

"I don't know," she said defensively. "I was entering in orders like I always do, and all of a sudden it wouldn't do anything anymore. I kept typing, but nothing happened."

The system froze, I said to myself. "What did you do then?"

"I turned it off, and tried to turn it back on, but nothing happened."

"Sounds like a hard disk crash to me," I said speculatively. No one argued with me. "First things first. Joleen, move those papers off of there. If you block the air vents, your system is bound to overheat." Then I pointed to the metal copy holder next to the disk drive. "And keep that away from the computer from now on."

She moved it, but asked, "How come?"

"Paper is held onto the holder with a magnet, right?" I said.

She nodded.

"Well putting a magnet next to a floppy disk or a hard disk is just about the worst thing you can do to it. It scrambles your data." She still looked confused. "Trust me," I said emphatically.

"Now let's see what we can do," I said, pulling up a

chair and switching on the PC. As Joleen had said, an error message told me that she was in deep trouble. "When was the last time you made a back-up?" I asked hopefully.

"What's that?"

"Never mind," I said. "This is going to take a while, so y'all may as well get comfortable." As the three of them found chairs, I went to work. Joleen was lucky I had brought my laptop computer down to show off to the family. The utility software on my hard disk was the only way I was going to be able to save her data.

As it turned out, it wasn't as bad as it could have been. With the help of a couple of utility programs, I salvaged a bunch of files and Joleen showed me which were the latest. That done, I couldn't resist the opportunity to set up a decent file structure and clean up the disk in general.

As usual when working, I lost all track of time. Thaddeous and Joleen had long since lost interest in what I was doing, and even Richard's eyes were starting to glaze over when we heard the shot. Or rather, when everybody but me heard it. I was so deep in Joleen's files that it didn't register.

"What was that?" Richard asked.

"It sounded like a gunshot," Thaddeous said.

There was a second shot, and even I heard this one. "What was that?" I asked.

"Thaddeous thinks it was a gunshot," Richard said doubtfully.

"It came from upstairs," Thaddeous said. "We better check it out."

Joleen looked up nervously. "Shouldn't we call Ralph and let him handle it?"

Thaddeous stood deliberately. "You go ahead and call

him, and Richard and I will have us a look. You two wait here."

"You know me better than that, Thaddeous," I said, following him to the elevator. I pressed the "UP" button, and stepped inside as soon as the door slid open. "Are you coming?" I asked.

"Well, I'm not staying down here by my lonesome," Joleen said, and she took Thaddeous's arm. "Besides, I know Thaddeous can take care of me."

"And Laura will take care of me," Richard said with a grin meant for me alone.

"Let's try Mr. Walters's office first," Thaddeous said, and pushed the top button.

No one spoke as the elevator slowly creaked its way up to the fourth floor. The hall was dark, but a light showed from the open door to Burt Walters's office. Thaddeous held up one hand for silence, but there were no sounds other than our breathing. Then he slowly stepped out.

"Hello," he said softly. "Anybody here?"

There was no answer.

"Hello," he called more loudly.

"I guess everything's all right," Joleen said. "Let's go back downstairs."

"Wait a minute," I said and stepped up next to Thaddeous. I felt Richard's hand on my shoulder, just letting me know he was there. Then, as a group, we stepped forward.

There was a sharp smell in the air. "Gunpowder," Thaddeous said. He stepped ahead just a bit so he could peer into the office ahead of us. "Mr. Walters? Is that you?"

I was just behind him, and looked to the left as he looked to the right, so I saw it first. A man was lying face down on the plush carpet. An ugly puddle of red flowed out from under his body.

I tugged at Thaddeous's sleeve, and he turned and saw the body.

"Jesus!"

"Is he dead?" I asked.

Thaddeous knelt down in front of the man and looked at him closely. "He's not breathing."

I forced myself to kneel on the other side and take the man's wrist. It was still warm, and that helped at first, but made it all the worse when I couldn't feel a pulse. I shook my head, not trusting myself to speak.

"I think I'm going to be sick," Joleen said, as she tottered towards a chair.

"Don't touch anything," Richard said. "We have to call the police. Joleen, go downstairs and call."

"I'm not going down there alone," she said. "What if whoever did this is still in here?"

I had forgotten all about the shots we had heard, forgotten that someone must have shot this man while we were downstairs. I said, "She's right. Joleen, use Mr. Walters's phone, but be careful not to touch anything else. Call Ralph at the front gate and tell him to make sure no one leaves."

Joleen dialed the number, and stood there for a moment. "There's no answer! He got Ralph, too."

"He's probably just making his rounds," Thaddeous said. "Let it ring a while longer."

Endless seconds went by, and then Joleen's face relaxed. "Ralph! Are you all right? Ralph, someone's been shot in Mr. Walters's office. No, this isn't a joke. Ralph, you listen to me!"

"Let me," Richard said. He took the phone, and said, "Ralph? This is Richard Fleming. There's been a shooting. We found a body in Mr. Walters's office." He paused. "We don't know who it is, but the main thing is that whoever did it may still be on the grounds. Call the police, and be sure to watch the gate and make sure no one gets out before the police get here. The four of us will wait up here. Have you got a gun, Ralph? Is it loaded? Well, load it now, just in case." He hung up.

We stood there a minute, not able to take our eyes from the body.

"Who is it?" Joleen asked.

"I can't tell," Thaddeous said. "It's not Mr. Walters."

No, the dead man's coloring was right, but he was both too tall and too thin to be Burt Walters.

"Shouldn't we turn him over and look?" Joleen said.

"I don't think so," I said. "There's nothing we can do for him, and it might disturb the evidence."

We stared a while longer, but I started to feel sick and noticed that the others were looking a little green, too.

"Why don't we wait in the hall?" I suggested. "The police will be here soon."

The others nodded, and we waited by Mr. Walters's secretary's desk. Richard stood behind me and put his arms around me, and I leaned back and closed my eyes. "Are you all right?" he asked.

"I guess so. You?"

I felt his nod. "It shouldn't be too long," he said. No one else spoke while we waited.

Chapter 3

As far as I could tell, we had been waiting for about twenty minutes when the phone on the secretary's desk rang. We all hesitated, but I finally answered it on the third ring. "Hello?" I said cautiously.

"Laura? This is Ralph. Junior Norton and Mark Pope are on their way up. I just wanted to let you know."

"Thanks, Ralph." I hung up the phone and told the others, "The police are here."

A minute later we heard the elevator head down to the first floor, and a minute later it returned. Junior Norton, Byerly's police chief, was a head shorter than her deputy Mark, but there was something about the way she walked that showed you who was in charge. Both she and Mark were wearing their usual uniform of khaki pants with navy blue piping and navy blue shirts, but Junior was wearing battered cowboy boots while Mark had spit–polished oxfords.

Junior said, "What's the trouble here?"

"The trouble is that there's a dead man in there," Joleen said, sounding more irritated than upset. She pointed toward Walters's office.

Junior nodded, showing no more surprise than if

Joleen had pointed out a cat stuck in a tree. "I better check it out."

Junior probably wasn't gone more than a minute before she stepped back out. "He's dead all right. Do any of you know what happened?"

"Of course we don't," Joleen said indignantly.

Junior held up one finger. "I'm not accusing, I'm only asking. Mark, I want you to take these folks downstairs and find them someplace they can sit for a spell. Then call the county office and ask for some help. Tell them that an unidentified man has been found dead, and remind them to get a hold of the coroner. Then call Ralph and tell him not to let anyone but the county police in. Then call my mama and tell her that I'm going to be late for dinner."

Mark took in most of the instructions without looking bothered, but he didn't look pleased at having to call Junior's mother. "What about Burt Walters? Do you want me to call him, too?"

Junior grimaced. "I'd best call him myself."

Mark nodded, and started to usher Joleen, Richard, Thaddeous, and me into the elevator.

"On second thought," Junior said, "I want Laurie Anne to stay up here with me for a minute."

Richard didn't look happy about it, but I pushed him toward the elevator.

"I'd offer you a seat," Junior said as soon as they were gone, "but I don't want the crime scene folks to fuss at me."

"That's all right," I said.

"Laurie Anne, why is it that I only see you in Byerly when there's been a murder? If I didn't know better, I'd think you were some kind of jinx."

There wasn't much I could say to that. The last time

44

I had been in town, I had insisted that my grandfather had been murdered, despite the lack of evidence, and then proved myself right by catching the murderer.

"So what happened?" she asked.

I explained how I had been drafted to rescue Joleen's hard disk, and that we had been downstairs at her desk when we heard two gunshots. I assured her that we hadn't touched anything on this floor other than the telephone. "And the dead man's wrist to make sure he was dead," I added.

"How long did it take y'all to get up here?"

"Maybe two or three minutes. No more than that."

"And no one could have taken the elevator down without your seeing him?"

"No. Joleen's desk is right there at the elevator."

"I don't suppose you thought about someone staying downstairs to watch the door."

"We didn't know anyone had been shot yet," I said defensively. "Besides, Ralph was out there. Why didn't he see anything?"

"No offense to Ralph, but sneaking by him wouldn't take a whole lot of effort. Even if he was paying attention, that booth isn't placed for him to see everything he ought to see. I think we can assume that whoever it was went down the stairs when he heard you coming up the elevator, and snuck out. Did you see or hear any signs of anyone else being in the building before you heard the shots?"

I shook my head, and then asked, "Do you think it was murder?"

Junior gestured at the body. "I don't see any gun, so unless he hid it after he shot himself twice, he had some help."

"Right," I said, feeling foolish.

"How come you didn't turn him over?"

"I didn't want to disturb anything until you got here."

"Good thinking."

That made me feel better.

We heard the elevator rising again. "That must be the help I asked for," Junior said. "Head on back downstairs with the others. I hope you haven't got any plans for this evening, because I expect you're going to be here for a while."

When I got downstairs, Mark asked me to join the others in the mill's break room. I did so, hugged Richard soundly, and said, "I told Junior what happened. She said we may be here for a while."

"I don't know why," Joleen said. "We don't know what happened. We don't even know who it was who got killed."

Thaddeous patted her hand. "Junior's just doing her job, honey. I'm sure she'll let us go as soon as she can."

"Well, it better be soon," Joleen said. "I've got a—I've got plans for tonight."

After what Vasti had said about Joleen, I had a nasty suspicion that Joleen's plans included a man other than Thaddeous. Why was she going out with Thaddeous, anyway? It was darned convenient for her to start dating a man just before his cousin the computer programmer came into town. Had she invited herself to the reunion just as a way to get to me?

That sounded conceited, but the fact was that there weren't a whole lot of folks in Byerly who would have known how to repair her hard disk. If Joleen hadn't enlisted me, she'd have had to tell Burt Walters. Paying an expensive consultant to do what I had just done would not have pleased Burt Walters.

It was a good thing we had eaten heavily at the reunion, because we spent a good two hours in that break room. Every once in a while, a police officer would wander in to get a Coke from the vending machine, but no one spoke to us. Richard, Thaddeous, and I talked about nothing in particular for a while, but eventually we ran out of things to say. Finally Mark came back in and said, "We can take your statements now."

"It's about time," Joleen said, and flounced out. The rest of us followed more calmly. A county police officer took us aside one at a time, and questioned us. He didn't ask me anything Junior hadn't, and I gave him the same answers I had given her. Then Mark took us back upstairs to Mr. Walters's office.

Police officers were busy measuring and photographing everything in the office while Junior watched. The body had been moved onto a stretcher and covered with a sheet, and the place where he had been was outlined with tape.

"We got their statements," Mark said.

Junior said, "I'm going to need y'all to come down to the station tomorrow and sign a copy of those statements." We nodded, and she went on. "Now that we've got the body turned over, I want you to take a look and see if you recognize him."

I swallowed hard, and Richard took my hand and squeezed.

Junior gently lifted the sheet over the body, and folded it down below his chin. Fortunately he didn't look particularly grisly. If I had seen him under other circumstances, I might have thought that he was just sleeping.

"I don't know who it is," Joleen said and turned away. "Can we leave now?"

"Let the others look for a minute," Junior said. "Thaddeous?"

He looked hard at the man, but then shook his head. "He's a stranger to me."

"Richard?" Junior said.

Richard said, "I don't think I've ever seen him before."

"Laurie Anne?"

I started to shake my head. Then I said, "I'm not sure."

"Take your time," Junior said, and I studied him for a while longer. "Do you think you know him?"

"No, but ... He does look awfully familiar, Junior. Something about the chin, and the nose. I just can't place him."

Junior waited patiently while I kept looking at him. "I just don't know." I looked up, meaning to take a minute to stare into space and try to remember. Instead I looked down again, and then back up. "I don't believe it."

"What?" Junior asked.

"Look!"

Junior followed my gaze to the life–sized portrait of Big Bill Walters, hanging over Burt's desk as if to constantly look over his shoulder. "Junior, am I crazy, or does that man look like Big Bill Walters?" I said.

To be specific, he looked *a lot* like Big Bill had when that portrait was painted. I knew that Big Bill's hair had gone from salt–and–pepper to solid grey a long time ago, and that he had just a bit a of paunch now, but if it had been twenty years earlier, I would have sworn that the dead man was Big Bill Walters.

Junior looked for herself, and said mildly, "He does favor Big Bill, doesn't he?"

"Favor him?" Thaddeous said. "I'd say that he was a dead ringer."

Chapter 4

"Has Burt Walters seen him yet?" I asked Junior.

She shook her head. "I called him right after we got here, but he was out somewhere and couldn't be reached."

I would loved to have stayed around to see Burt's reaction when he got there, both because of the aggravation of a murder in his office and to see if he knew who this man was, but Junior didn't need us for anything more.

She did ask us to keep quiet about the dead man's resemblance to Big Bill until she could talk to the Walters family, but we both knew that it was a losing battle. Several other police officers had heard me when I realized it, and the word was going to get out pretty quickly.

After that, Junior thanked us politely for our time, reminded us to come in sometime the next day to sign our statements, and firmly bade us farewell.

It was just as well. Joleen was chomping at the bit to leave, and asked Richard and me to drop her off at her house rather than go back to the church for Thaddeous to get his pickup truck and drive her home himself. She did thank me for helping with her computer, and even kissed Thaddeous goodbye, albeit briefly.

"Ain't she something?" he said as we drove off.

"She sure is," I answered.

Thaddeous went on to describe Joleen's charms until we left him at his car. Then he said, "I appreciate your helping out with the computer, but I sure am sorry about getting y'all into that mess."

"It wasn't your fault, Thaddeous," I said. "We'll talk to you later this week."

"What do you think of Joleen?" I asked Richard, once Thaddeous was out of earshot.

"She sure is something."

"That's what I thought, too. Poor Thaddeous."

The phone was ringing when we came in the door at Aunt Maggie's. She stopped on her way to answer it, and said, "You may as well get it yourself. It's probably for you."

I picked up the receiver. "Burnette residence."

"Is Laurie Anne Fleming there?"

"This is Laura Fleming," I said.

"Mrs. Fleming, this is Hank Parker at the *Byerly Gazette*. I was wondering if I could ask you a few questions about the body you found at Walters Mill this evening."

"That was fast."

"We regularly monitor the police bands." He proceeded to ask the same set of questions that the police had, and I gave him the same set of answers. I did fudge about why the four of us had been at the mill, saying only that Joleen and I had been comparing computer techniques. After all the trouble I had gone to to save her data, I didn't want her to lose her job now. Not while Thaddeous was still smitten, anyway.

Parker pushed hard when asking if I knew who the

body was, even asked for a description, but in deference to Junior's request, I pleaded ignorance. I suspected he already knew something and was just hoping for confirmation. Finally I told him goodbye and hung up.

"That was Hank Parker from the paper," I said.

Aunt Maggie nodded. "That's the fourth time he's called looking for you."

"How did he find out about the shooting so quickly?" Richard wanted to know.

"He said he heard it on the police radio," I told him.

Aunt Maggie snorted. "He heard it from his mama, is what happened. Mark Pope's mama is Hank Parker's mama's sister. So he gets all the news right quick."

"I don't know what he's in such a hurry for," I said. "The *Gazette* won't come out again until Wednesday."

"He's just nosy," Aunt Maggie said. "Working at the paper only gives him an excuse."

"Did he tell you what happened?" I asked.

"He gave me the short version, and I heard you tell him the rest. They don't know who the dead man is?"

"Not yet," I said. "But between you, me, and the gate post, he looked an awful lot like that portrait of Big Bill Walters that's hanging on the wall. Burt is an only child, isn't he?"

"Only living child, anyway. His brother Small Bill died in Vietnam."

I remembered hearing that, now that she mentioned it. William Walters, Jr., known in Byerly as Small Bill, had been Burt's older brother.

Aunt Maggie went on, "Now it wouldn't surprise me none if Big Bill had sowed himself some wild oats. He was quite the ladies man a few years back." She grinned.

"It sounds like you have reason to know," Richard said.

She grinned even wider. "Maybe I do, and maybe I don't."

The phone rang. "Now who?" I asked as I reached to answer it.

I should have known it would be Vasti. I gave her as quick a rundown as I could get away with and finally got off the phone. It promptly rang again.

"Let it ring," Aunt Maggie advised. "Or better yet, leave it off the hook. If you want to get any sleep to-night, that is. It's after ten, and people don't have any business calling this late."

"Do you think it would be all right?" I asked doubt-fully. "I don't want to hurt anybody's feelings."

Aunt Maggie reached over, picked up the phone, hung it up, and then laid the receiver down beside the phone. "There," she said. "If anyone fusses, you can tell them that it was me who done it."

My conscience was soothed by her taking responsibil-ity, and since Aunt Maggie said that Richard and I looked like we were worn to a frazzle, we headed up to bed.

Chapter 5

Not surprisingly after such a long day, Richard and I slept late the next morning. By the time we got up, Aunt Maggie was gone on her daily trip to the local thrift stores to see what she could find to buy and then sell at the flea market. That was one of the best parts about staying with Aunt Maggie. She went her own way and expected us to do the same. And since the house was the Burnette home place and I had lived there with Paw after my parents died, I felt nearly at much at home there as I did at my apartment in Boston.

Aunt Maggie had left us a bag of sausage biscuits from Hardee's for breakfast, and Richard heated them up in the toaster oven while I tried to find a news show on the radio.

"Checking the weather?" Richard said innocently.

"You know doggone well what I'm looking for," I said. I heard the word "shooting" and turned up the sound.

We already knew most of what the radio announcer had to say, but he concluded with the part I was interested in. "Chief Norton says that the victim has been identified, but the police are withholding his identity pending notification of the family."

"Rats!" I said.

"Come eat your biscuit before it gets cold again," Richard said.

Enjoying the treat of sausage biscuits kept me quiet for a little bit, but after I finished my second, I said, "I wonder who that fellow was. I swear he looked just like that picture of Big Bill."

Richard said, "I'm sure Junior will get everything squared away."

"I suppose so," I answered. "Anyway, you and I have our own mystery to deal with. What's going on with Aunt Daphine?"

"Are you sure that something is wrong? Everyone has off days."

"Not like this. She's not talking to Aunt Nora and she didn't have time to bake for the reunion."

"Well, when you put it that way," he said with mock seriousness.

"I mean it, Richard," I said. "Her acting like that is like you not reading Shakespeare. Or like me not programming."

"I concede the point," Richard said. "Something is wrong. But do you really think that she's going to tell you anything when she hasn't told her sisters or her own daughter?"

"Maybe not, but I feel like I should at least try. And it won't hurt for us to invite her out to lunch."

"We just ate," Richard said.

"Richard, sometimes you have to make sacrifices for your family." Even if it meant eating that wonderful country-style steak at Woolworth's lunch counter.

Richard agreed that desperate times call for desperate

measures, so we showered, dressed, and drove over to the strip shopping center that included Aunt Daphine's beauty parlor.

The bell hung over the door to La Dauphin jingled as Richard and I walked inside. A woman with bright red hair was buffing her nails at the front counter.

"Hi," I said.

She didn't look up.

"Excuse me," I said politely, "but is Mrs. Marston in?"

"Do you have an appointment?" the woman asked without looking up.

"No, but—"

"Mrs. Marston only works by appointment."

"I'm not here to get my hair fixed. Mrs. Marston is my aunt."

She put the nail file down and squinted at me. "You must be the one from Boston."

It wasn't really a question, so I didn't feel like I needed to answer. "Is Aunt Daphine here?"

"Uh–huh. You were there at the mill last night when my daughter found that body, weren't you? I hear you're pretty tight with that lady police chief. Did she tell *you* who it is?"

"No, sorry. Can you tell Aunt Daphine that I'm here?"

She was opening her mouth, probably for another question, when I saw someone I knew behind the curtain of colored beads that separated the waiting room from the rest of the shop. "Hi Gladys," I called out.

"Hey there Laurie Anne," the dark–haired girl called back. "Daphine, look who's here!"

Aunt Daphine looked in our direction, smiled and

waved. "I'll be there in a minute, just as soon as I get Mrs. Hart's hair combed out."

Gladys came on out, waving her fingers around to dry a fresh coat of nail polish.

"Have you met Gladys?" I asked Richard. "She's the manicurist now."

They exchanged hellos.

"Dorinda," Gladys asked the woman at the counter, "why didn't you tell Daphine that Laurie Anne was here?"

"How was I supposed to know who she was?" Dorinda asked sulkily. "She didn't tell me her name."

True enough, I thought, but she had known exactly who I was.

"While you're here, Gladys, watch the desk so I can take my coffee break." Dorinda grabbed her purse and scooted toward the back of the shop before Gladys could say a word.

"So that's Dorinda," I said as soon as she was gone.

Gladys grimaced. "Sweet, isn't she? I keep thinking that Daphine will fire her, or at least tell her off, but so far . . ." She shrugged.

If the way Dorinda had greeted me and Richard was any indication of her performance, I couldn't imagine why either. Though Aunt Daphine wasn't a difficult woman to work for, she didn't usually stand for any nonsense.

"So what are you two doing up here?" Gladys asked. "Are you going to get your hair cut, Laurie Anne? Or how about a new hair color? We got a new batch of French hair colors, and there's a real pretty blond."

"Not today," I said. "We just stopped by to see if we can talk Aunt Daphine into coming out to lunch with us."

Gladys shrugged her shoulders again. "Well, maybe *you* can. I haven't been able to get her to go out for lunch in I don't know how long. She brings herself a little old sandwich some days, but most of the time she says she's not hungry and works right through lunch. She schedules appointments all day long and into the evening. I just couldn't believe it when she said she wanted to open the shop on Mondays."

"That's right," I said. "She always used to take Monday off."

"For years, nothing could make her change that. Don't you remember that time Dorcas Walters had a party on a Monday night? She wanted Daphine to open up on Monday so her guests could get their hair done that day, but Daphine wouldn't do it. They all had to get their hair done on Saturday afternoon and hope for the best. I don't know what happened to change her mind." Gladys shook her head. "The way Daphine's been acting lately, I think she'd open on Sundays if the town council would let her."

"She wouldn't do that," I said, but I wasn't so sure.

The phone on the counter rang just then. Gladys said, "I better get that. Why don't you go on back and talk to Daphine?" She reached for the phone.

"You stay out here," I told Richard. "Aunt Daphine's customers hate to be seen by a man while in the process of beautification."

"Surely they don't think that anyone believes hair comes that way naturally?"

"I don't know, but I don't want to be the one to destroy their illusions."

Richard sat down in one of the pink vinyl–covered chairs, reached for the latest copy of *People* magazine, and muttered, " 'Here are a few of the unpleasant'st words that ever blotted paper.' *The Merchant of Venice*, Act III, Scene 2."

I pushed my way through the bead curtains and wrinkled my nose at the pungent smell that meant someone was getting her hair dyed. No doubt it was one of the French colors Gladys had recommended.

Aunt Daphine was just finishing up with her customer. I waited until the woman left, then gave my aunt a hug. "Hey there."

"Hey sweetie," Aunt Daphine said. "What can I do for you today?"

"Richard and I were out wandering," I answered, more or less truthfully, "and we thought we'd take you out to lunch."

"That would be real nice, Laurie Anne, but not today. I'm booked up all day."

"You have to eat sometime," I protested.

"After yesterday, I don't think I'll need to eat for a week."

"I know what you mean," I said, but I had seen her plate at the reunion. She hadn't eaten half of what she usually would have. "What about supper?"

"I can't. I've got a couple of late appointments."

"Richard and I can wait until you're done."

"That's all right. I wouldn't want to hold you up."

If I hadn't known better, I would have thought she was trying to avoid us. "Lunch tomorrow?" I asked.

"This whole week is pretty busy," she said vaguely.

Aunt Daphine's next customer arrived before I could suggest another time, and Aunt Daphine said, "I'll call you before you leave town, don't you worry."

"All right," I said. There wasn't a whole lot else I could say. Gladys was still at the front desk when I went out.

"Any luck?" she asked.

I shook my head. "I guess we better leave before Dorinda shows up and starts interrogating us about what happened yesterday."

"I don't suppose it would be polite for me to ask about it, then," Gladys said with a grin.

"To tell you the truth," I said, "the way gossip travels around here, you probably know more than I do. We heard the shot and found the body, but that's all."

"Is it true that the dead man looks like Big Bill Walters?"

I nodded. I guessed that that detail had already become common knowledge despite Junior's efforts. "Maybe he was a cousin."

"There aren't any close cousins," Gladys said. "Big Bill was an only child."

"I didn't know that. See, I told you that you know more than I do."

Gladys lowered her voice. "Some people are saying that Big Bill must have had himself a woman on the side, and got caught. Maybe this fellow found out how much money the Walters have, and wanted his share. Maybe Big Bill told him 'No!' in the worst way he could."

It was a nicely convoluted story, but I had to shake my head. "I don't think so. The rug in Burt Walters's office is ruined. If it had been Big Bill, he'd have put papers down first to keep from staining it."

We were giggling over the idea of Big Bill trying to place an intended victim somewhere where it wouldn't make a mess when Dorinda reappeared, carrying a red leather change purse.

"Look what I found in the back. Gladys, do you know who this belongs to?"

"That's Clara's ring bag," Gladys said. "She puts her ring in there when she's working with hair color so it won't get stained."

"Are you sure?" Dorinda asked, not very convincingly. "Let me just make sure that it's in here." She opened it and pulled out a very nice diamond solitaire ring. "Now where on earth did Clara get a ring like this?" she asked.

"Her husband gave it to her, of course," Gladys said. "You better put it back."

Dorinda continued to hold it up. "It sure is a big stone. Must be nearly half a caret. I wonder how it would look on me."

"Dorinda . . ." Gladys said warningly, but Dorinda slipped it onto her finger anyway.

"Doesn't it look nice?" she asked, admiring it. "Maybe Clara will let me borrow it."

"I don't think so," Gladys said. "You better put it back."

"I'm not hurting it," Dorinda said, continuing to preen.

That's when Clara McDonald walked up behind her, and for the first time since I had known Clara, I saw strong emotion on the little woman's face. Even so, all she said was, "Dorinda, I'll thank you to take my ring off."

Dorinda looked startled, but quickly said, "I was just looking at it. It looks right pretty on me, don't you think."

"I want my ring back."

"Oh come on, Clara. I've got a hot date tonight, if you know what I mean. Can't I borrow it for just the one night? I'll bring it back tomorrow?"

"No. Give it back now."

"Oh pooh." Dorinda pulled half-heartedly at the ring. "I think it's stuck."

"Dorinda, stop fooling around," Gladys said nervously.

"I'm not fooling," she insisted, pulling harder. "It's stuck."

"Take it off," Clara said.

Dorinda said, "My fingers always swell right before lunch. If you let me wear it tonight, I'm sure it will come off in the morning."

"No!" Clara said, not quite yelling.

"Why don't you try using some soap," I said.

"That's a good idea," Gladys said. "Soap suds will get it off." She pulled Dorinda over to a sink, and reached for some shampoo.

"Not that stuff," Dorinda protested. "That'll dry out my skin."

Gladys ignored her, poured a dollop on the be-ringed finger, and started rubbing vigorously."

"Stop up the sink in case it falls off," I said.

Gladys put a stopper in the sink before continuing to make suds.

"You're hurting me," Dorinda said. "You don't have to rub so hard."

"I've almost got it," Gladys said.

"It hasn't moved a bit," Dorinda contradicted her. "I think we're going to have to cut it off."

I could have sworn there was a low growl from Clara. I had a hunch that as far as she was concerned, if anything got cut, it wasn't going to be her ring.

"There!" Gladys said triumphantly, finally pulling the ring off. She rinsed it off, and then handed it to Clara, whose eyes had never left the ring.

Clara slipped it back into place, then held it close to her face to examine it.

"I didn't hurt it none," Dorinda said indignantly, and stomped back to her stool. She wasn't quite out of ear-shot when she muttered, "I bet it's not even real."

Clara was still staring at her ring. Her hair was dark brown today, which suited her as much as any other shade she had ever tried. I had never been sure whether she changed her color so often because she was the shop's unofficial colorist and felt honor-bound to test each product, or if she really expected to find a color that would make her prettier. I kind of hoped it was the first reason, because with her ears and nose, nothing was going to make her pretty.

"Is your ring all right?" I asked her.

She nodded slowly, and the angry color started to fade from her cheeks. "I guess so. I shouldn't let Dorinda get to me like that, but sometimes she makes me so mad."

"I don't blame you, Clara," Gladys said, "Not one bit. I think you should tell Daphine about it."

"No," Clara said, shaking her head. "There's no need for that. I'll just be sure to keep it with me from now on. I better get back to work." She went back toward her station, and I noticed that she stayed as far away from Dorinda as possible.

"Can you imagine trying to borrow somebody else's engagement ring?" Gladys asked me indignantly.

I shook my head, and looked at my own diamond protectively, thinking that I'd like to see Dorinda try to make off with it.

Gladys went on, "And to pull that now, when Clara just lost her husband a few months ago."

Now that Gladys mentioned it, I remembered Aunt

Nora telling me that Ed McDonald had died. "How's Clara been taking it?"

"As well as could be expected, I guess, but you think that Dorinda would have a little respect." She snorted. "I should know better by now. Dorinda gets on everybody's nerves. I don't want to say anything against Daphine, but I just don't know why she puts up with it."

Aunt Nora was right, I thought to myself. Something was bothering Aunt Daphine, something bad. "Well, we better get going. Take care, Gladys." I got halfway to the door before I realized that Richard was still reading a magazine. "Richard?" There was no response. "Richard!"

He jerked up. "What? Where's Aunt Daphine?"

"She can't come. What were you reading so intently?"

"Nothing," he said, closing the issue of *People* quickly.

Not quickly enough. I saw the page he had been looking at. "The Brady Bunch: Then and Now?" I asked.

"I didn't notice," he said haughtily.

"Stop back by before you go back up North," Gladys said. "I could show you some samples of that new hair color. Richard, don't you think Laurie Anne would look pretty with blond hair?"

"Her hair shall be of what colour it please God," Richard replied. *"Much Ado About Nothing,* Act II, Scene 3." Then he took my arm and grandly escorted me out.

Chapter 6

"So what's up with Aunt Daphine?" Richard asked as we climbed into the car.

"I don't know. Like Aunt Nora said, she's not saying. I tried to set up a time to talk with her, but she kept wriggling out of it."

"Now what?"

"I suppose we might as well go by the police station and sign our statements for Junior."

"And perhaps find out about any new developments in the shooting?"

"I *am* curious. After all, it's not every day that we find a dead body."

Junior was on the telephone when we walked into Byerly's tiny police station, but she gestured for us to sit down. After a few more minutes, in which she didn't get a chance to say a word, she said, "Yes, sir, I certainly will try to track down that leak. Thank you for calling." She hung up the phone quickly.

"This has been a day and a half!" she said. "It's just now lunch time and I'm already worn slap out."

"The murder investigation, I assume," Richard said.

Junior nodded. "That was Big Bill Walters on the

phone. Word has gotten around that the deceased bears a definite resemblance to him, and he's more than a little irate at the suggestion that this person could be related."

"Have you found out who he is yet?" I asked.

"Finding out who he was was easy," Junior said. "He had a wallet with credit cards and a driver's license. Plus his car, including registration, was found parked on the road that runs back behind the mill. His name was Leonard Cooper, and he was an architect from Richmond, Virginia. He was a widower with a nice house, a twenty–year–old son, and a dog named Frisky. I've found out his bank balance, the church he attended, and the grades he made in college. I just can't find out what he was doing at Walters Mill yesterday afternoon!"

"Was he staying with somebody in town?"

Junior shook her head. "No such luck. We found a hotel key in his pocket for the Holiday Inn on Highway 321, and the manager there identified him from his driver's license. She wasn't sure, but she didn't notice him having any visitors. We searched the room, but didn't find anything but a suitcase with the stuff anyone might have to spend the weekend away from home. With one exception: he had last Wednesday's *Byerly Gazette*."

"Does that mean something?" I asked.

Junior threw up her hands. "How should I know?"

"What about the son?" Richard asked. "Doesn't he know why his father might have come here?"

"Michael Cooper didn't even know his father was out of town until the police tracked him down this morning. He'll be here to identify the body later today. He's studying at NC State in Raleigh, as it happens. He's never heard of Byerly and was certain that his father

65

had never lived here and fairly sure that he had never visited here. A neighbor was watching the dog, but all he knew was that Cooper was going out of town for a few days. He was supposed to be back by this morning at the latest. I've got the Richmond police talking to everybody else Cooper knew to try to find out if he told somebody something useful."

"And he's not related to the Walters family?" I asked.

"Not as far as I can tell. Big Bill was an only child, and Burt is his only surviving son. No one knows of any Coopers from any branch of the family, and besides which, Cooper was born in Tennessee. Big Bill assures me that he has no relatives in Tennessee. In fact, he quoted me his entire family tree from the Civil War to the present day to make sure that I understand that this man could not possibly be related to him."

"Not legitimately, that is," I said, thinking of Gladys's idea.

Junior looked exasperated. "Not you, too. I've had a dozen calls this morning from people who think that Big Bill has been leading a double life with another family somewhere else. As much as that man was always on my father's case, and has been on mine since I took over, I feel sure that he never had time to look after another family."

I started to say something else about the idea, but Junior held up one hand to stop me. "Don't worry, I'm checking into the possibility, just in case. It's pretty far-fetched, but even that's better than what one woman told me. She thinks that the man was the ghost of Small Bill Walters, risen from the grave to claim his birthright. I was foolish enough to ask her how you could shoot a ghost and why a ghost would have Leonard Cooper's

66

belongings, and she started in on reincarnation or crystals or something like that." She shook her head again.

"They say that everyone has a double. Maybe the looks are just a coincidence," Richard said.

"Maybe they are, but I'd be more likely to believe that if the man hadn't died in Walters Mill. Anyway, enough of that. I assume y'all had some reason to come down here, other than to hear about my troubles."

"You wanted us to sign our statements from last night," I reminded her.

"So I did." She rummaged in the stacks on her desk until she pulled out two typewritten sheets. "Just look these over, and make sure that you didn't leave anything out."

Richard, the fastest reader I've ever met, read his twice and had it signed before I was finished. I was about to sign my own when I remembered something. "This probably doesn't mean anything, Junior," I said, "but when we got to the mill yesterday, Ralph said that Burt Walters was supposed to come over that evening."

"Is that so? Walters didn't mention it, but like you said, it probably doesn't mean anything. Big Bill, Burt, and Burt's wife were at a barbeque at the time Cooper was shot."

"If that's really when he was shot," Richard said speculatively.

"Y'all did hear the shots," Junior said.

"We thought we did," Richard said, raising one eyebrow meaningfully. "What if it was a recording, and the man was actually shot earlier?"

"Richard, the body was still warm when we got up there," I said. I didn't care much for that particular memory.

"And unless you think the murderer kept the victim

warm in the microwave in the break room," Junior said with a wide grin, "I think we can assume that you heard the actual shots."

"I suppose so," Richard said reluctantly.

"I hope I don't have to remind you two not to get involved in a police investigation," Junior said sternly.

"We did catch two murderers last time," I said.

"And nigh about got shot in the process," Junior said.

"Don't worry," Richard said. "I'll keep Laura out of trouble this time."

"Uh–huh," Junior said. "And who's going to be keeping you out of trouble?"

The phone rang again, and Junior answered it with a look of distaste. We took that as a hint, and left her to her business.

Chapter 7

Richard and I spent the rest of the afternoon visiting folks a bit more thoroughly than the reunion had allowed for. First there was a stop at Aunt Ruby Lee's house. She played a tape of a song her son Clifford had written, and pulled out her photo albums so we could look at the latest family pictures. Ruby Lee's daughter Ilene was looking more and more like her mother, but unfortunately, Ilene was all too aware of how pretty she was.

Next was a visit with Aunt Nellie and Uncle Ruben. They showed us their water filters, and gave us a stack of printed material to take home.

We only made a short stop at Aunt Edna's. I knew she didn't blame me for her husband's death, but I felt uncomfortable all the same. Besides, she had a prayer meeting to attend.

Finally we ended up at Aunt Nora and Uncle Buddy's house, just in time for dinner. This was not accidental. Aunt Nora is the best cook in the family, and always makes enough for an unexpected guest or two. We tried to refuse her invitation for the sake of politeness, but were soon seated happily at her table.

"I wish I had known you were going to be here for dinner," Aunt Nora fussed. "I'd have fixed something special."

I looked at the platters of pork chops and fresh biscuits, and the bowls of snap beans and macaroni and cheese in disbelief. "Aunt Nora, I don't think you could have fixed anything that I would have wanted any more than this."

"I second that," Richard said.

Conversation was sparse, as it always was at Aunt Nora and Uncle Buddy's table. For one thing, food that good deserved one's full attention. For another, Aunt Nora was too busy filling plates to talk, and Uncle Buddy and my cousin Willis never spoke two words when a grunt would do. Thaddeous was more talkative, but he had long since grown used to quiet at the table.

Only when the dishes had been cleared, and we were lingering over generous wedges of apple pie did Aunt Nora ask what Richard and I had been up to.

I said, "We went to see Aunt Daphine this morning, but we may as well not have bothered. I could not pry her out of that shop for love or money."

Aunt Nora shook her head. "She's been like that for nigh onto three months. At first I thought she was depressed about Paw, because some people don't make their peace with a death right away. But I don't think that that's it. Daphine always could handle things like that. When Mama died, she was like a rock. Not hard like a rock, mind, but strong for the rest of us. When your mama and daddy died, she was just the same."

"I remember," I said.

Aunt Nora said, "That's how she's always been. Shoot, she lost her own husband when she was only nineteen years old, and I think she spent as much time

70

comforting her mother–in–law and father–in–law as she did being comforted."

"If she was so strong then," I said, "what can it be that's got her so down now?"

"Money," Uncle Buddy said.

"Daddy thinks it's something to do with money," Thaddeous elaborated. "He heard that Aunt Daphine's been taking money out of the bank, and even looked into taking out a second mortgage on her house."

"I thought that the beauty parlor was doing well," I said. "It's always packed to the gills when I go by there."

Aunt Nora shrugged. "It's doing fine, as far as I know. And her car hasn't needed any work, and she hasn't had any medical bills. I just don't know what it could be."

Conversation turned to more pleasant family news after that, and we chatted for an hour or so until the phone rang.

Aunt Nora answered it. "Crawford residence. Hey there, Daphine. What can I do for you? Yes, she's here. Hold on for a minute." She held her hand over the receiver and said, "I guess her ears were burning. She wants to talk to you, Laurie Anne."

I took the phone from her. "Hey Aunt Daphine. What's up?"

"Laurie Anne, would you mind coming over to my house? Right now?"

"Sure," I said, trying not to sound too enthusiastic at her change in attitude. "We'll be right over."

"Do you mind not bringing Richard? I'd like to talk to you alone, if that's all right."

"I don't see why not. I'll be over there directly." I hung up the phone. "She wants me to come over there to talk."

"Hallelujah!" Aunt Nora said. "She's got to talk to somebody soon or she'll just bust."

"Richard, she wants to see me alone. Do you mind?"

"Of course not," he said.

"Shall I take you back to Aunt Maggie's?" I asked.

"Why don't you stay here for a spell, Richard?" Thaddeous suggested. "Monday Night Football will be on in a minute. I'll ride you over to Aunt Maggie's when you're ready to go."

"Sounds great," Richard said.

Since I knew that Richard has no use for football, I was impressed by his devotion to family. I kissed him goodbye, hugged the rest of the folks, and left for Aunt Daphine's.

Chapter 8

Aunt Daphine's house was a lot like her. It had a lot of character, and was so well cared for that it looked a lot younger than it was. Aunt Daphine didn't come to the door when I rang the bell. Instead, I heard her call out, "Come on in."

She was on the couch in the living room, with a large photo album across her lap. She was crying, and for the first time I realized how rarely I had seen her cry. Once at my parent's funeral and once at Paw's—that was it.

"Aunt Daphine?" I said.

She smiled, and blew her nose into a tissue. "I'm all right. Just remembering the old days. Did I ever show you these pictures of my John Ward?"

"Yes, ma'am," I answered as I sat down beside her, "but you know I love looking at family pictures." I wasn't sure why she had called me over to look at photos, but I knew that she must have a reason.

"This was his high school graduation picture," she said, pointing to a carefully posed picture of a serious young man wearing a mortarboard. "This is him later that day, at the party Big Bill Walters threw for Small Bill." This time the young man was smiling, with a beer in one hand and his arm around a young Aunt Daphine's waist.

"That was some party. Big Bill wanted to keep it formal, but Small Bill showed up in shorts and ordered cases and cases of beer. He got the dance band so drunk that they couldn't find their instruments, much less play them, so we danced to records instead."

"I didn't know you were friends with any of the Walters," I said. The line between mill owner and mill worker was pretty sharp, mostly because of money. People in Byerly had long memories, and the local strikes had been pretty bad.

"Oh, Small Bill wasn't anything like his father," Aunt Daphine said. "He always wanted to be one of the gang. John Ward was his best friend, you know."

I hadn't known, but I nodded anyway.

She turned the page. "This was taken the day John Ward went to Vietnam. He looked so handsome in that uniform. So grown-up."

He didn't look grown-up to me. He looked painfully young to be going off to war.

"I don't think of him that way, anymore," Aunt Daphine said. "I've been kind of aging him in my mind all these years, imagining what he'd be like if he was still alive. I talk to him, you know, late at night when I'm alone. I loved him so much, Laurie Anne." Her voice caught a little.

I patted her arm awkwardly, and thought about how I would feel if anything ever happened to Richard. We had already had more time together than what Aunt Daphine and Uncle John Ward had shared.

Aunt Daphine tenderly closed the album. "Laurie Anne, I'm going to tell you something I haven't told a living soul since the week I found out that John Ward was dead." She didn't say anything for a minute, and I guessed she was wondering where to start. Finally she said, "You know about what happened when John Ward went to Vietnam, don't you?"

"Yes, ma'am." I had heard it often enough when growing up, and it still sounded awfully romantic. After Uncle John Ward finished basic training, he had to go through Norfolk, Virginia on his way to Vietnam. He was only there for a couple of days, and they wouldn't let him come home, so he called Aunt Daphine to say goodbye to her. After she got off the phone, crying her eyes out, Paw handed her the keys to his truck and some money for gas and told her to go say goodbye for real. She drove all night to get there, and they got married at a justice of the peace that day. After a two-day honeymoon, he left for Vietnam and died there, never knowing that Aunt Daphine was already carrying Vasti.

"The way you've always heard it isn't the way it really happened," Aunt Daphine said. "You see, the day I got to Norfolk was Washington's Birthday. That's a federal holiday, so the justice of the peace had the day off."

It took a minute for her meaning to sink in. "If the justice of the peace wasn't around, then how . . . ?"

"How did we get married? We didn't."

You could have knocked me over with a feather, and I guess it showed on my face, because Aunt Daphine started talking faster, as if to get the rest of it out in a hurry. "We were going to, I swear that we were, but when we found out that we couldn't, we decided to go to a motel and tell them that we were married. I felt like John Ward was going away to do a man's job, and he deserved to be treated like a man." She looked down at her hands. "And I guess I wanted it, too.

"Afterwards I went home, and waited for his letters. I hadn't gotten but a few of them when we got the telegram from the Army saying that he had been killed. His being gone was bad, but I felt even worse when I realized that my period was late. I told Maw the whole story."

"Was she upset?" I asked.

Aunt Daphine shook her head. "She wasn't mad at me, if that's what you mean. Maw knew that I wasn't the first girl it had happened to, and I wasn't going to be the last. She was just worried about how I was going to get by. They didn't call babies illegitimate then, they called them bastards, and what they called girls like me was even worse.

"Anyway, she and Paw and I talked it all out, and I guess it was Paw who came up with the idea. We'd just tell everybody that John Ward and I really had got married. That way, the baby could have his name."

For a minute, I was surprised that Paw had been the one to suggest Daphine's lying. He had always been such an honest man. But then again, he had always said that it wasn't the letter of the law that mattered, it was the spirit.

Aunt Daphine went on. "Of course we had to tell John Ward's parents the truth. I was dreading what they would think of me, but I should have known better. You see, they had just lost their only child and were feeling awfully alone. It's hard on people, losing a child. Then I come tell them that they're going to have a grandchild. They were tickled to death.

"I didn't like lying to everybody like that," Aunt Daphine went on, "but I had to think about Vasti. I didn't want her to suffer for my mistake."

"Didn't you tell anybody else? Didn't you even tell

Mama?" I knew that Aunt Daphine had been particularly close to my mother.

Aunt Daphine shook her head. "I'll tell you, it was hard not to tell Alice the truth. I knew I could trust her, of course, but I was pure ashamed to tell her. There she was with her husband in that pretty little house they had. And there you were, such a sweet baby. I just couldn't tell her what I had gone and done."

"Oh Aunt Daphine," I said helplessly. "You don't think Mama would have thought anything less of you, do you?"

"I suppose not," she said, but she didn't sound convinced. She rubbed her bare finger and said, "Maw wanted to get me a wedding band to wear, but I told her not to. I said I could use John Ward's name and pretend like we were married for Vasti's sake, but I wouldn't wear a ring he didn't give me."

"He would have married you if he had lived, you know that."

"I guess so."

"Of course he would have."

She nodded, and said, "I imagine you're wondering why I picked now to tell you all of this."

Actually, she had caught me so much by surprise that I hadn't thought that far ahead, but I said, "Yes, ma'am."

"Well, like I said, I haven't told anybody about this in all these years. I know Maw and Paw wouldn't have, and the Marstons wouldn't have either. But somebody found out."

"Who?"

"I don't know who, Laurie Anne, but whoever it is has been asking me for money for the past three months, and I just can't pay any more."

I stared at her. "Blackmail? In Byerly?"

She nodded. "I didn't believe it myself when I got the first letter, but it's true." She went over to a table, opened a drawer, and pulled out several sheets of notebook paper. "Look at these."

The blackmail demands looked like something out of a Nancy Drew mystery. The letters were cut out of newspapers and magazines and pasted together into words. I read the first one.

I know that you weren't married to John Ward Marston. Does your daughter know? Do you want her to read about it in the *Gazette?* I've got proof! If you don't want me to tell, put $200 cash in an envelope and leave it under the flower pot on John Ward's grave Sunday morning. Don't try to look for me, or I'll tell.

There was no signature.

"Did you leave the money?" I asked.

"I was afraid not to. If this came out now, Arthur would be sure to lose the city council election and Vasti would never forgive me."

"You haven't told her?" I didn't mean the blackmail—I meant about her father.

"No." She looked down at her hands again. "I wanted to, lots of times, but I just couldn't. This would just kill her."

My first inclination was to discount the idea of anything bothering Vasti, but I knew that I wasn't being fair. How would I feel if I found out something like that about my parents?

I looked at the other notes. They all said pretty much the same thing, except that the amount of money kept rising. "This adds up to $2400," I said. "Where in the world have you been getting that kind of money?"

"I used my savings at first, but I can't get to the rest without the bank asking all kinds of questions. I've been taking money from the shop, but I'm afraid that the tax people are going to find out. I've worked as many hours as I can, but there are only so many heads of hair to cut in Byerly."

"Why didn't you tell somebody?" Only I knew the answer to that. She had been ashamed.

"I suppose you know that I've been feeling pretty low ever since this started. Then I got an idea. Laurie Anne, I want you to help me find the blackmailer."

"What?"

"Everybody at the shop today was talking about the dead man at the mill, and wondering if Junior Norton was going to ask you to help because of how you found out what happened to Paw and Melanie Wilson."

"Junior doesn't need my help," I said.

"I know that, but it got me to thinking that maybe you can help *me*. If you can find out who the blackmailer is, we can make him stop somehow."

"Aunt Daphine, I'm not a detective. The stuff with Paw was mostly dumb luck. You should talk to Junior."

"I can't," she insisted. "The letters said not to or he'd tell the newspapers everything."

"How would he know? Junior wouldn't tell anybody."

Aunt Daphine shook her head. "He'd find out somehow. Byerly is too small a town for him not to. I know Junior is a good police chief, but if she starts asking questions, people are going to notice."

"What about a private detective?"

"Laurie Anne, do you really think that some stranger could come to Byerly and ask the kind of questions he'd have to ask without people wondering why? Besides, I couldn't have afforded one before this all started and I certainly can't afford one now. My sisters would help if they could, but can you see Ruby Lee or Edna trying to find out something like this? And if I tell one sister, the others are bound to find out. You know how they are. I know it's a lot to ask of you, but there's no one else I can ask."

I wanted to say no, I really did, but how could I? After all these years of keeping her secret, Aunt Daphine had trusted me enough to tell me. "All right," I finally said. I didn't really think I'd do any good, but if I tried for a while and couldn't find the blackmailer, Aunt Daphine would have to call Junior. Then I added, "I have to tell Richard, but I'm sure he'll want to help, too."

Aunt Daphine nodded. "That's all right, you go ahead and tell him. But you have to promise not to tell anybody else."

"I promise."

Aunt Daphine suddenly realized that I had been in her house for nearly an hour and she hadn't offered me anything to drink or eat, and she insisted on bringing me a glass of iced tea.

I could tell from the way she walked to the kitchen that she felt like a load had been lifted from her shoulders. I was glad of that, but uncomfortably aware of the fact that her load was now on my shoulders. She was counting on me to help her, and I didn't know what she'd do if I couldn't.

Chapter 9

After Aunt Daphine brought me my iced tea, I quizzed her for a few details, but I didn't stay much longer because I wanted to talk to Richard. Fortunately he had escaped the perils of Monday Night Football and was waiting for me at Aunt Maggie's house.

"So?" Richard asked. "Did you solve the mystery?"

"Yes and no. Where's Aunt Maggie?"

"Already immersed in sore labor's bath, balm of hurt minds, great nature's second course, chief nourisher in life's feast."

"You could have just said she was asleep."

"But the Bard said it so much better. *Macbeth*, Act II, Scene 2, of course."

"Of course. Now do you want to hear what Aunt Daphine had to say or not?"

"Yes, dear."

It took a while to tell the whole story, because he hadn't heard the original tale of Aunt Daphine's romance as often as I had. When I finished, Richard said, " 'Neither maid, widow, nor wife.' *Measure for Measure*, Act V, Scene 1."

"That's about the size of it."

"I think we need a pad of paper so we can start planning strategy."

I looked at him. "You're taking all of this rather calmly. Aren't you bothered by the idea of trying to track down a blackmailer?"

Richard shrugged. "If you can stand one more quote, 'What's mine is yours, and what is yours is mine.' *Measure for Measure* again, same act and scene. If Aunt Daphine needs help, we'll help. I don't know if we can do any good, but I'm willing to try."

"I knew I had a good reason for marrying you." I kissed him soundly.

After a pleasant interlude, Richard said, "I do have to insist on one thing. You are not to run off to deserted tobacco sheds or anyplace else where you could get hurt."

"Agreed," I said, remembering the time I had done just that.

"Good. Now where did I put my notebook?"

"Let me use my laptop," I said. "That way we don't have to worry about anyone seeing our notes."

"See?" Richard said approvingly. "You're already thinking like a detective."

"I'm thinking like someone whose cousin Vasti found and read her diary every chance she got. Her knowing who I had a crush on was bad enough. I don't want her finding out this particular secret."

I ran upstairs to get my computer from the bedroom, brought it back, and spent a few moments opening a file. "What first?"

Richard put a hand under his chin in his most professorial pose. "The way I see it, there are several categories of people we should look at. One, people who need money."

"Anybody around here could use the money," I said.

"Having a use for the money and needing it badly enough to blackmail someone are two different things."

"What about plain old greed?" I asked.

"Possible, of course. But then they'd fall into my next category."

"Which is?"

"People who have come into money unexpectedly, or who are spending beyond their means."

"Right. What next?"

"People who don't like Aunt Daphine."

"I think we can leave that one out. I don't know of anyone who doesn't like Aunt Daphine."

"What about the woman with big hair at the beauty parlor?"

"Dorinda? As Aunt Nora would say, I can't say what she is but it rhymes with witch. I'd cheerfully consider her as a suspect."

"Now, now, we must remain objective."

"You remain objective. I don't like her."

He shook his head ruefully, but went on. "And our final category, people who know that Aunt Daphine wasn't married to John Ward Marston. This is probably the one we should concentrate on."

"Aunt Daphine said she hadn't told anyone but Maw and Paw, and Uncle John Ward's parents," I objected. "Two of those four are dead."

"What about the Marstons?"

"Still alive and kicking. Vasti was always talking about her rich grandparents when we were growing up, and they did their best to spoil her rotten."

"Do I detect jealousy?"

"A little," I admitted. "They gave her the prettiest dresses and jewelry. Not costume stuff, either."

"If they're that rich, surely they wouldn't need to blackmail Aunt Daphine."

"Well, I don't know for sure that they're rich. Vasti talks like they are, but she has been known to exaggerate. Besides, Mr. Marston is retired now, and they're probably living off of investments and such. Stock market woes could have taken a bite out of their nest egg."

"Would they do something to hurt their only granddaughter?"

"Probably not, but they haven't hurt her, only Aunt Daphine. They could threaten to expose Vasti's illegitimacy all day long without ever having the slightest intention of doing it."

"Right you are. Now assuming Aunt Daphine didn't tell anyone else, what about Uncle John Ward? Could he have told anyone?"

I shrugged. "How can we know for sure? I do know he shipped out for Vietnam two days after they got married. Or rather, didn't get married. He died about a month later. That means the only ones he was likely to have told are his Army buddies. Unless he put it in a letter, and I don't think he'd have done that."

"How likely are any of these Army buddies to have come to Byerly?"

"Pretty likely, to tell you truth. I seem to remember that a lot of Byerly boys went over together."

"Then we have plenty of suspects." Richard thought for a minute. "Maybe we're making this too difficult. Can't we just watch for the blackmailer to pick up the money?"

"We can try," I said, "but unfortunately, the blackmailer is smart. He has Aunt Daphine leave it at the cemetery on Sunday afternoons."

"So?"

"This isn't nice, flat Woodgreen Acres we're talking about," I said, referring to Byerly's newer cemetery, where my parents were buried. "This is the old Byerly Graveyard. Not only are there trees everywhere, making it a wonderful place to hide, but every Sunday afternoon the place is filled with people coming to tend to their family graves. Half the women in Byerly are there on any given Sunday."

"Only women?"

"Men, too, but mostly women. Tending to the dead folks seems to be a woman's job. Aunt Nora used to drive Great–Aunt Patsy over there every month, and they'd drag me and Vasti and the triplets along so we could learn about family history." I snorted. "All I ever learned was that I want to be cremated. Aunt Patsy would tell the most gruesome details about how everybody died and how hard it was to make the bodies pretty for the funeral. Then she'd cry."

Richard was trying not to laugh.

"I'm serious," I said. "I don't know if it's a Southern thing or just an old lady thing. Aunt Patsy would have us pull up the batch of plastic flowers from the last time, trim the grass, and put in new plastic flowers. She'd always say that she'd rather put in fresh flowers, but they wouldn't last for the whole month and she was too old to get there more often. Then she'd look at us kids like we were just horrible for not volunteering to bring flowers every day."

"Couldn't you beg off from going?"

"I tried, believe me, but Aunt Nora would just look so disappointed that I couldn't stand it."

"What about Vasti? Surely such tactics wouldn't work with her."

"Actually, she rather enjoyed it. She wasn't much

help with the flowers, but she liked having something to cry about. Vasti was a very melodramatic child."

"As opposed to how she is now?"

"Anyway, the only reason this was at all bearable was because everybody else in town would be there, too, with their own plastic flowers. The old ladies would find a bench so they could compare messy ways of dying while the kids did the work. Pretty much everybody has relatives there. The Nortons, and the Walters, and the Marstons, and of course us Burnettes."

"So almost anyone in town would have an excuse for showing up."

I nodded. "You know, making Aunt Daphine leave the money *there* is a pretty nasty trick. It really rubs it in that she and Uncle John Ward weren't married." I wasn't sure what we'd be able to do to the blackmailer if we found him, but I hoped it would be something equally nasty.

"I'm still tempted to stake out the place," Richard said, "but since the next payment isn't due until Sunday, I think we can leave that until later."

"Right," I said. "Who shall we start with?"

"The Marstons? We can scope them out, and maybe also check on the fellows who went to Vietnam with Uncle John Ward."

"Good idea. The only problem is, we need an excuse to go over there. I mean I barely know them, and they're not really related to me. We can't just drop in."

"Call Aunt Daphine. Maybe she can provide an excuse."

"Good idea." I reached for the phone and did so. "Aunt Daphine? This is Laura."

"Hey there, Laurie Anne." There was a pause. "You haven't changed your mind, have you?"

"No, ma'am," I said firmly. "Richard and I have been talking it out, and we need your help with something."

"Just ask."

"Richard and I want to go talk to the Marstons tomorrow, but we need an excuse."

"Why the Marstons? You don't think they're the ones, do you? Laurie Anne, I'm sure that they'd never do anything like that."

"You said yourself that they're the only other people who knew. Maybe they told somebody."

"Why would they?"

"They are pretty old. Maybe it slipped out."

"Laurie Anne, things like this don't just slip out."

"Aunt Daphine, we've got to start somewhere."

There was a pause. "I suppose you're right. I don't like thinking that anybody I know would do something like this, but I guess it isn't likely to be a stranger. Let me think for a minute." There was another pause. "Vasti said that the Marstons had volunteered to help do something for Arthur's campaign. Stuffing envelopes, I think. Maybe you could go help them. That would be a good way to talk."

"Perfect," I said. "I'll give Vasti a call."

"You won't tell the Marstons what's going on, will you?" Aunt Daphine asked. "About the blackmail, I mean. It would really upset them, I know it would."

"I won't tell them or anybody else anything about it," I promised. "We'll talk to you later and let you know what we find out."

"She suggests we call Vasti," I told Richard as I hung up and dialed Vasti's number.

"Bumgarner for City Council. Campaign Headquarters," an official-sounding voice said.

"May I speak to Vasti Bumgarner, please?"

"This is Vasti," she said in her usual voice. "Laurie Anne?"

"Hi Vasti. How goes the campaign?"

She sighed loudly. "It's going, but it's *so* much work. I had people putting up posters all afternoon, and Arthur gave a speech for the Elk Lodge this evening, and tomorrow he's going to the Byerly Garden Club. I am just exhausted."

"Poor thing," I said sympathetically, though it sounded like it was other people who were doing the work. "I was thinking that since Richard and I are in town for a while, maybe we could help out. We've got some free time tomorrow if there's something we could do. Like stuffing envelopes maybe?"

"Laurie Anne, you must be a mind reader. I was just talking to Grandmother Marston a little while ago about stuffing envelopes. I took a stack of fliers over there last week because she said she could get them out for me, but she's way behind. I need to get them in the mail by tomorrow, but she said she wasn't going to finish them in time. Her arthritis is acting up, and what could I say to that?" She sighed again, even more dramatically. "Can you imagine what a tragedy it would be if Arthur actually lost because of arthritis?"

"That *would* be terrible," I said, hoping I didn't sound too sarcastic. "Maybe Richard and I could go over there tomorrow and help her."

"Could you? That would be wonderful. I'll call her up and tell her you'll be there at nine."

"That's kind of early," I said, but Vasti wasn't listening. I heard voices in the background, and Vasti called out, "Not like that! Make the picture of me and Arthur bigger. Laurie Anne, I've got to go. Once you get the envelopes stuffed and all, you can bring them over here and run them through the postage meter. Now they have to be in the mail by one o'clock, so I'll expect you here no later than noon. Bye now!"

I hung up the phone and said, "The good news is that we have a usable excuse. The bad news is that we have to be at the Marstons's house by nine and we're on a deadline."

"I think we can manage," Richard said. "Now, since there is nothing productive we can do as regards the investigation, you can shut down your computer."

I did so, and asked, "Did you have an idea of how to spend the rest of the evening?"

"I thought we could go to bed."

"I'm not sleepy."

"I'm not either."

That was a good enough reason for me. After all, I reminded myself as we headed upstairs, we were on vacation.

Chapter 10

In deference to Vasti's deadline, we were up bright and early the next morning. Aunt Maggie was up and moving, too, and we went with her to get sausage biscuits at Hardee's before going our separate ways.

We got to the Marstons's house just before nine. There wasn't much money in Byerly, but what there was of it was in that neighborhood. Acyle Marston had been president of the Byerly Bank before he retired, and had done very well for himself. His wife Diamond had never had to work outside the home, other than charity work.

Even though Uncle John Ward had been an only child, the Marston house had five bedrooms and two and a half bathrooms. The Marstons had the carpet cleaned professionally twice a year, and replaced the curtains every time they got faded. The furniture was so fine that it required special polishes.

How did I know all of this? Because Vasti had told me all about it when we were growing up. Richard was right—I was jealous. My father's parents had died before I was born, and though Paw was always wonderful to me, he never had any money. The idea of rich grandparents to spoil me had sounded mighty attractive when I was younger. In fact, it still did.

Diamond Marston answered the front door almost before we rang it. She was a tiny thing, with snow-white hair and nearly translucent skin, but I could see a lot of Vasti's spirit in the way she moved.

"Well if it isn't Laurie Anne!" she said with a big smile. "You look wonderful. Vasti said she didn't think Boston was good for you, but I believe it is. And this must be Richard. I was *so* glad to hear that you found a job. Come on in."

"I see Vasti has been talking about us," I whispered as Richard and I followed her inside. Somehow Vasti had never understood that going to graduate school was at least as much work as a job, and that the teaching fellowships Richard had taken along the way *were* jobs. Well, I couldn't hold it against Mrs. Marston if she believed everything her granddaughter told her.

"I've got the envelopes and things set up in the kitchen," Diamond said. "I didn't have any idea it would take me this long to finish. It was awfully smart of Vasti to ask you to help."

I suppose I could have told her that Richard and I had volunteered, but all I said, was, "It sure was."

The kitchen was just as nice and shiny as Vasti had always said it was. Maybe the Marstons didn't really replace the appliances every other year, but everything was as neat as a pin. Acyle Marston, a plump man whose watery blue eyes seemed magnified by the thick lenses of his eyeglasses, was sitting at the head of the kitchen table, folding a flyer with infinite precision.

"Acyle, you remember Vasti's cousin Laurie Anne, don't you?" Diamond said. He kept on folding without looking up. "Acyle? Acyle! Turn your hearing aid back on!"

He looked up, and then stuck a finger in each ear and twisted. "That's better," he said in a surprisingly deep voice. "I turned them off when the dishwasher was going, and forgot to turn them back on."

"This is Vasti's cousin Laurie Anne Fleming," Diamond said, "and this is her husband Richard."

He stood and shook hands with us both. "Glad to hear about your job, young man," he said to Richard. "I know it's hard to get a start these days, even with a college degree."

"Times are tough, Mr. Marston," Richard said solemnly.

"Oh just call us Acyle and Diamond," Diamond said brightly. "We're all related to Vasti, so that makes us almost family, doesn't it? Now you two sit yourselves down. Can I get y'all some iced tea or a soft drink?" Richard and I accepted something to drink, and then we all settled around the table.

"Now this is what we have to do," Diamond began. "We fold these papers in three so they'll fit into an envelope. Then we seal them up, and address them. Acyle's been folding, and if Richard will put them in the envelope and seal them, Laurie Anne and I can address them." She patted a list beside her. "We're mailing one to every registered voter in Byerly, and that's quite a few."

We got started in silence. "Why don't you use a computer to generate mailing labels?" I said after a while of addressing envelopes by hand. "It would be a lot quicker."

"But that would be so impersonal," Diamond said. "Byerly folks wouldn't like that. The way I look at it, we're asking these people for their votes. That's an important thing to ask for, and they deserve a few minutes of personal attention at the very least."

My computer programmer's soul didn't like it, but it did make sense. I kept addressing envelopes, wondering how I could ask about what I wanted to know. "Aunt Daphine showed me some pictures of Uncle John Ward last night," I finally said. "He sure was a handsome fellow."

"Wasn't he though? Just like his father," Diamond said, looking at Acyle fondly.

I must admit I couldn't see much of a resemblance between this man and the boy in the photographs, but I nodded anyway.

"What a shame that he and Aunt Daphine didn't have any more time together than they did," I said. "His dying so soon after their wedding was so sad."

I was watching Diamond's face carefully, but I couldn't see any signs of guilty knowledge when she said, "It's a terrible thing losing a son so young, but at least we've had Daphine and Vasti to love all these years. Daphine was like the daughter we never had, even before John Ward died, and I can't tell you what a comfort she was to us afterward."

I looked at Richard, and he gave the tiniest of shrugs. Maybe Diamond was faking it, but her affection for Aunt Daphine sure sounded sincere to me.

She went on, "And of course Vasti has been our pride and joy. You two are too young to know what I mean, but when you've got children and grandchildren someday, you'll understand. Seeing her happy is so important to us. Isn't that right, Acyle?"

He nodded emphatically. "Vasti's the best little girl in

the world. She'd give us the shirt right off her back if we needed it."

Only if the shirt was borrowed, I thought meanly, but then I relented. Vasti probably was at her best around her grandparents, because she sure wasn't wasting it on me.

"I just hope Arthur wins this election," Diamond said. "Vasti is so ambitious for herself, just like John Ward was. Of course he never got a chance, but he had such plans." She shook her head sadly. "War is a terrible thing. We always lose the best and brightest."

"Byerly must have lost a lot of young men," I said.

"Too many," Acyle said. "We used to look at the paper every week and count up our dead. John Ward was the first. Then Small Bill Walters just a few months later. There was a real smart boy named Philip who used to run errands for us down at the bank. Philip . . . What was his last name, Diamond?"

Diamond thought for a minute. "I can't remember for the life of me. They say that the memory is the first to go." She shook her head ruefully. "So many lost. And some who did come back never were the same. Reggie Rogers had nightmares for years, and he never would talk about them. Larry Parker still has that limp. Ed McDonald lost two fingers on his left hand, but luckily he was right-handed. Did you hear that Ed died just recently, Laurie Anne?"

"I heard," I said. "What a shame."

"You know she and Ed never had any children," Diamond said, "so Clara doesn't have a soul to look after her now."

"I'm sure she'll be fine," I said. Clara was a grown woman, after all.

"I suppose so, but I can't help but think that I could

94

have ended up the same way, what with John Ward dying so young and if Acyle were to pass on before me. Of course, I've got Vasti."

Acyle rumbled, "Diamond, can't you find something more cheerful to talk about? These young folks don't want to hear about this."

Diamond smiled. "I'm sorry. When you get to be my age, you start thinking a lot about things like that. What were we talking about before?"

"About Aunt Daphine and John Ward," I prompted. "Only I guess I should call him Uncle John Ward, since he was Aunt Daphine's husband."

There was no reaction from the Marstons other than interested nods.

"I remember Vasti telling me about them when we were little," I went on. "Aunt Daphine driving all night to get to him, their eloping, the honeymoon. It was such a romantic story."

Diamond just smiled like she was remembering. If I hadn't known better, I would have thought that she had never known that Aunt Daphine hadn't married Uncle John Ward. Maybe the Marstons had been telling the story for so long that they had started to believe it themselves.

I gave up after that, and put my attention toward addressing envelopes. Richard did steer the conversation over toward finances, and from what they said, the Marstons were in good shape. Of course, like Paw used to say, you can't always believe people when they're talking about money, but what they said did fit in with what people in town had always said about them.

After that was settled, at least in my mind, we talked about all kinds of things: a trip they had once made to Boston, the way Byerly had changed, even a little about

Shakespeare. We got the envelopes finished by eleven–thirty, and Richard and I had to insist that we couldn't stay for lunch, explaining there wasn't time if we wanted to get the fliers in the mail. Then we hugged and shook hands goodbye.

I could see why Aunt Daphine couldn't believe that the Marstons were involved in blackmail. I envied Vasti her grandparents more than ever before, and it wasn't because of their money. They were nice people.

Chapter 11

Our next stop was Arthur's campaign headquarters, which was in the basement of his and Vasti's house. We had to ring the doorbell twice before we finally heard Vasti running up the stairs.

"It's about time," she said. "I thought you were going to be here by eleven-thirty."

"You said by noon," I reminded her.

"Did I? Well, come on in. You don't need any help carrying those, do you?" She was halfway down the stairs to the basement before we could answer, and Richard and I followed her.

There were four or five other people rushing around the basement with posters and boxes of buttons. "Not in there!" Vasti called out to a woman as we came in. "Put them over by the things for the garden party."

A harried-looking woman complied.

"There's the postage meter," Vasti said, pointing. "Run the envelopes through just as fast as you can, and you should have enough time to get them in the mail today." The telephone rang, and she ran to answer it.

"Quite an impressive setup," Richard said as we put

down our boxes and pulled off our jackets. "I didn't realize that Arthur has so many supporters."

"Well, not to put down Arthur, but I recognize most of these people as either working for him at the dealership or being married to someone who does. That might have something to do with it."

"A political machine in Byerly?"

"Something like that." We figured out how to use the postage meter and started running the envelopes through as people kept moving all around us. There was just a small stack left to go when Vasti came over holding two posters with "Bumgarner for Byerly" in different typefaces.

"Laurie Anne, which do you like better?" Vasti asked.

I pointed to the left one. "That one."

Vasti wrinkled her nose at it. "That one?" She shook her head. "I don't know. I think I like the other one better." She waved her choice at one of the workers and said, "Jane, order a batch of this one and tell them that we need them right away." She reached for the phone, which was ringing again.

"So touching that she trusts your opinion," Richard said with a trace of irritation. "Why did she ask if she wasn't going to listen?"

"She always does that," I answered. "That's why I picked the one I *didn't* like instead of the one that I did. It works every time."

"Of course," Richard said, shaking his head.

By then we had the envelopes finished, and Vasti was off of the phone for a minute. I asked, "Vasti, do you want us to take these down to the post office?"

"Would you? Is there time to get them in today's mail?" Then she looked at her watch, and answered her own question. "There is, thank goodness, if you hurry."

"Then we'll see you later," I said, and Richard and I picked up the boxes.

We were halfway up the stairs when Vasti said, "Wait! Did I invite y'all to my garden party? You're going to be in town through this weekend, aren't you?"

"We're planning to be," I answered. "What garden party?"

"It's for charity, one of Dorcas Walters's projects. She said something about it last week, and I knew she wanted me to volunteer to put it together, though how she thought I'd have the time, I'll never know. But of course I had to say I would so she'd see how civic–minded I am. It's bound to help get votes, and maybe Big Bill will finally make up his mind to endorse Arthur."

"What charity is it for?" I asked.

"Oh, widows or orphans or something like that. I've got some literature on it somewhere around here, if you're interested." She waved her hands around vaguely.

"That's all right," I said. "I'm sure it's a good cause. Richard?"

He nodded. "Sounds good to me. When is it?"

"Saturday. So y'all will come?"

"Count us in," I said.

"Good! Do you have enough cash now or do you want to write a check?"

"I beg your pardon?"

"I said it was for charity, didn't I? It's only forty dollars a couple, and I felt sure that Richard had been working long enough to be able to afford that."

I opened my mouth to tell her off for *something*, but honestly, I didn't know where to start. In the meantime,

Richard put down his box, pulled out his wallet, and extracted two twenties to hand to Vasti. "Here you go."

"Oh good!" she said and tucked the money into her pocket. "I hope you don't want a receipt for taxes, because I don't have any idea of where the pad is."

"That's all right," Richard said, retrieving his box.

We started back up the stairs when Vasti said, "Oh, I should warn you that Linwood and Sue are going to be at the garden party, too."

"I can handle Linwood," I said. I wasn't thrilled about it, but I wasn't about to spend the rest of my life avoiding him.

"I was kind of surprised he wanted to come, to tell you the truth," Vasti said, momentarily forgetting that she was supposed to be in a hurry. "I know he's out of work so I told him that I wouldn't think anything of it if he didn't have the money, but he pulled out a wad big enough to choke a horse and peeled off the money just as quick as anything. I wonder where he's getting it."

"Have you heard anything. . . ?" I started to ask, but Vasti looked at her watch again.

"Well what are y'all waiting for? You're going to miss the mail if you don't get a move on."

I bit my tongue and headed up the stairs. What with the campaign and all, I was willing to cut Vasti some slack this time. And she wasn't that much worse than usual.

"Did you hear what she said about Linwood?" I asked Richard as we were getting back into the car.

"How could I not hear something that Vasti says?"

"Her voice does carry, doesn't it? Anyway, what she said about Linwood means that he fits into one of our categories. Someone who has more money than he should."

"It's possible," Richard said mildly.

I nodded sadly. Goodness knows that Linwood and I had had our differences, but I really didn't want to believe that he could be a blackmailer.

"Do you think he'd blackmail his own aunt?" Richard asked.

I shrugged. "I don't think I should make that kind of prediction about my family anymore, not after last time."

Richard patted my hand comfortingly, but said, "It probably wouldn't hurt to check him out."

We dropped off the fliers at the post office, and then headed back for Aunt Maggie's house. After making and eating sandwiches for lunch, I hit the telephone. Since Linwood and I weren't on speaking terms, I thought it best to approach the subject of his income via the family grapevine.

Aunt Nora was generally a good source, but since she wasn't home, I called Aunt Ruby Lee instead. Of course, I couldn't jump right into the reason I was calling, so that meant a few minutes of talking about her kids. This gave me a more or less smooth opening to talk about other cousins, and then to work my way over toward Linwood.

"That new baby of Linwood's sure is a cutie," I said once I thought it wouldn't sound too much like it was out of the blue.

"Isn't she though?" Aunt Ruby Lee said. "She's a good baby, too. With Tiffany and Jason around, their house stays stirred up, but Sue says Crystal doesn't seem to mind, no matter how loud it gets."

Considering how noisy Tiffany and Jason were, I wondered if I should suggest a hearing test for the baby.

"Linwood and Sue must be having a tough time. I heard Linwood lost his job."

"I guess they're doing all right. He's got himself another job."

"Oh? What's he doing now?"

"I'm not sure. I haven't talked to him about it myself because Linwood's kind of hard to speak to these days. You understand."

I made an affirmative murmur.

"Anyway," Aunt Ruby Lee continued, "Ilene has a friend in Linwood's neighborhood, and she says that Linwood leaves every morning and doesn't get back until dinner time. So he must have some kind of a job. I just don't know what it is."

"Doesn't Aunt Edna know what he's doing?"

"Well, they aren't getting along too well these days. I know they'll work it out, but it's kind of awkward right now."

I could understand why, after what had happened with Paw and Aunt Edna's husband Loman. Aunt Edna's loyalties were with Paw, while Linwood was still mourning his father. It was a complicated situation by anyone's standards.

"Anyway," Aunt Ruby Lee went on, "after Linwood got fired, Edna asked if he needed any help, but he said no. We've all been kind of checking around to see, but nobody knows where he's working. Edna was afraid it might be something a little shady, but I feel sure that he wouldn't do anything like that."

I told her I agreed with her, which was partially true. We chatted a while longer, but that was all I really needed to know. As soon as I got off of the phone, I repeated the information to Richard.

"Do you want to try calling another aunt?"

"No need," I said. "If any of them knew, all of them would. I'm afraid that it does sound suspicious."

"I don't know," Richard said. "If Linwood were the blackmailer, he wouldn't have to leave the house every morning."

"Unless he was trying to cover up."

"Kind of elaborate for a coverup, don't you think? Is Linwood that thorough?"

"Linwood's not stupid," I said. "He's just ignorant in some ways." Richard didn't look convinced. "You have to admit that he knows more Yankee jokes than anyone else we've ever met."

"A sterling recommendation," he said dryly. "Does that mean he is or isn't a suspect?"

"Is. Since he goes somewhere during the day, maybe I'll go over to his house and see what I can find out from Sue."

"Shall I come with you?"

"I don't think so. Sue will probably be more talkative with just me. You know, woman-to-woman."

He nodded sagely. "Then I'll go visit the offices of the *Byerly Gazette*. From what Acyle said, the paper gave a lot of ink to the boys in Vietnam, so I'll look up some old issues and try for leads."

I dropped him off at the *Gazette* office with a promise to retrieve him later, and drove to Linwood's house.

Linwood and Sue didn't live in a bad neighborhood, but it wasn't a wonderful one either. What with marrying and starting a family so young, they probably wouldn't have been able to buy a house at all if it hadn't been for help from Aunt Edna and Paw. Still, most of the houses on the block were decently tended to, and there were lots of other families with children around.

After I drove by once to make sure Linwood's truck

was gone, I parked in the driveway behind Sue's station wagon. Then I went to ring the doorbell.

I heard Tiffany's and Jason's voices and somebody came to the door and opened it just a crack, not enough for me to see inside.

"Yes? What do you want?" someone said in a squeaky falsetto.

"Sue?" It sure didn't sound like her, but I said, "It's Laurie Anne. Can I come in?"

"Sue isn't here," the voice said, cracking a bit. "You can call her later."

Who was that in there? Certainly not Sue, and in fact, it didn't much sound like a woman at all. "Linwood, is that you?"

The door slammed shut.

I rang the bell again, and when no one answered, I rang it yet again. Then I pounded on the door. "Linwood! What are you doing?"

The door opened all the way this time, and I saw Linwood standing there with little Crystal in his arms. "Stop that before someone hears you." He looked up and down the street. "You may as well come inside," he said, and stepped back to let me in. Then he quickly closed the door.

He led me into the living room, which looked neater than I had ever seen it. Jason and Tiffany were arguing over a coloring book in one corner, and Linwood said, "You two stop that fussing and go outside."

"Do we have to?" Jason asked.

Then Tiffany said, "I get the good swing," and ran toward the back.

"No fair! It's my turn!" Jason yelled, and followed her. Two slams of the back door confirmed that they had gone outside.

Linwood sat down in the rocking chair, expertly jostled Crystal, and glared at me.

"I wasn't expecting to see you here," I said. I knew that if I waited for an invitation to sit down, I was going to be waiting for an awful long time, so I took a seat on the couch. "Where's Sue?"

"She had to run some errands, so I'm watching the kids for a little while."

"Oh," I said.

"What do you want, anyhow?"

"I wanted to come visit Sue and the children while I'm in town, and I thought it might be more polite to come when you weren't here."

He snorted at that, but didn't say anything else.

"I hear you have a new job."

"I took the day off."

"What are you doing now?"

"Why do you want to know?"

"Just curious."

"Just nosy is more like it."

Crystal picked that moment to assume a look of deep concentration, and I'd been around enough children to know what that meant. A second later, the scent of her accomplishment wafted through the air.

"I think Crystal needs to be changed," I said.

Linwood peeked inside Crystal's diaper, and wrinkled his nose. "I'll say she does."

Considering how I had seen Linwood react to dirty diapers in the past, I was about to offer to help, but before I could, Linwood said, "I better get her cleaned up."

He carried her into the back, and a minute later I followed him down the hall and into Crystal's room. I didn't say anything, and I guess he didn't realize I was there. He already had the offending diaper off and was efficiently wiping Crystal's behind with a baby wipe. Then he powdered her, pulled a fresh diaper from the stack on the changing table, and had her fixed up again as neatly as I've ever seen it done.

"Did Crystal make a mess?" he cooed. "Daddy's got her all cleaned up now, doesn't he? Crystal's all clean now." He tickled under her arms, grinned when she giggled, and then saw me standing there.

"What's the matter?" he said with a frown. "Haven't you ever seen anybody change a baby's diaper before?"

"I never saw *you* change a diaper before." As far as I could remember, I never even saw him hold Jason and Tiffany when they were babies.

"I do a lot of things you don't know about," he said, and brushed past me. Back in the living room, he put Crystal into a baby swing, wound it up, and started it swinging.

"You may as well leave," he said. "I don't know when Sue will be back."

I was starting to get suspicious. Linwood looked awfully darned comfortable taking care of Crystal for someone who was only babysitting for an hour or two. And with the kind of work Linwood typically did, I found it hard to believe that he could take a day off in the middle of the week for anything short of an emergency. I said, "Maybe you're right. Tell Sue I'll call her later. What time does she get home from work?"

"About five-thirty," he answered, and then his face turned dark red. "How did you know that? What are you snooping around in my business for?"

I held up one hand. "I haven't been snooping, Linwood, honest I haven't. It was just a lucky guess." I could tell that he wasn't sure whether to believe me or not, so I added, "If you don't want anybody to know that Sue is working, then I'm certainly not going to tell."

He looked a little happier. "It ain't nobody's business, anyway. This is just temporary until I get me another job."

"But Linwood, a friend of Ilene's says she sees you going to work every morning."

"Sue drives the pickup. And she wears my hat sometimes."

"And your jacket, too?" I guessed.

"If she wants to. I suppose my old jacket wouldn't be fancy enough for some people, but Sue don't put on airs."

"That's true," I said. Then I couldn't help it any longer. I started snickering.

"What's so damned funny?"

"I'm sorry, Linwood, but this really tickles my funny bone." He started to say something else, but I went on. "I really have to hand it to you. Paw always said that living in Byerly is like living in a fish bowl, and I never did figure out a way to keep my private business private. I just think it's hilarious that all of our aunts are going nuts trying to figure out where you're working, and you've got them all fooled. It's brilliant!"

I guess he started to see the humor of it, too, because he snickered and said, "They can keep on trying to figure it out, but they're never going to find Sue. She's working in a lady's lingerie store in Dudley Shoals, and I bet they won't be looking for me in there."

That did it. My snickers graduated to a full-blown belly laugh, and Linwood was right there with me. Even Crystal joined in with a few giggles.

We finally stopped to wipe our eyes, and Linwood remembered that he didn't trust me. He asked, "Did you really come over here to see the kids?"

"That wasn't the only reason," I admitted.

"That's what I thought. Does it have something to do with Aunt Daphine's troubles?"

"How did you hear about that?"

He snorted. "How do you think? Didn't you just say that Byerly is like a fish bowl? When Aunt Daphine asked you to come over last night, Aunt Nora knew that she must have told you what was wrong. Aunt Nora told Aunt Ruby Lee, Aunt Ruby Lee told my mama, and Mama told Sue."

People up North might need cellular telephones to keep up with everything, but not down here. "Aunt Daphine did talk to me," I said, "but she made me promise not to tell anyone what she said. I'm sure it's not because she didn't trust anybody else, but—"

"I imagine she's got her reasons," Linwood said. "I don't have to know everything about everybody else. Not like some people."

"Linwood," I started, but then stopped. It wasn't worth the effort. "I'm glad you understand."

"So why did you come over here? You don't think I'd do anything to hurt Aunt Daphine, do you?"

There wasn't a whole lot I could say to dodge that, because it was exactly what I had been thinking. "I didn't want to think you were involved, but I had to be sure."

"Why in the hell did you think I'd do something to harm someone in my own family?" Then he reddened, and I guessed he was thinking about his father. "Well, I guess you had your reasons. Let me set you straight, Laurie Anne. The only Burnette I've got anything against is right here in this room. I haven't forgotten about my daddy."

He glared at me, but I met his eyes and said, "I don't expect you to. I haven't forgotten about Paw, either." We stared each other down, and we'd probably still be at it if Crystal's swing hadn't picked that minute to stop, which made her start fussing. Linwood winding up the swing broke the tension.

I guessed that that was the closest either of us was ever going to come to apologizing, which was just as well. I'm not real sure who it was that should have apologized for what. Anyway, Linwood was downright cordial after that. Cordial for Linwood, that is. He offered me a beer, and only told a couple of Yankee jokes. I turned down the beer, laughed at the jokes, and promised once again to keep his secret before leaving.

Chapter 12

I wasn't sure if Richard would be finished at the *Gazette* office or not, but he came running out the door just as I drove up. He leapt into the car, flung a folder fat with papers into the back seat, and swept me into his arms.

After several minutes of passionate embrace, I got a chance to say, "Well! You're awfully cheerful this afternoon."

"And why not? To quote your once–and–future– Uncle Roger, 'I'm in love with the prettiest woman on this earth.' " He smooched me again.

"Does this mean that you found out something good at the *Gazette* office?" I asked hopefully.

"As regards Aunt Daphine, probably not. I did, however, make an instrumental breakthrough in the investigation of the death of the mysterious Leonard Cooper."

"Is that so?" I started driving toward home. "Tell me more."

"As an icebreaker, I started with a request for out–of– town subscription rates. The worthy Hank Parker was delighted to help. Since the amount was not high, I decided that two doses of Byerly news each week is just what we need to fulfill our lives. Hank accessed a program by which mailing labels are generated so he could enter our name."

"A database manager," I said impatiently. "Get on with it."

He cleared his voice indignantly before continuing. "It seems that Hank only rarely has occasion to enter new out–of–town subscribers, which comes as no great surprise. As a result, he is not familiar with the program and couldn't remember how to add a record. He eventually determined that he could modify an existing entry and then save it with a new name."

"Of course he could," I said. "Almost all database managers work that way."

"Interruptions merely slow the process of explication," Richard said with a lofty expression. "Since our name begins with 'F' he went to the closest entry in the list, which started with 'C.' Obviously, the number of out–of–town subscribers is small."

"Richard," I said seriously, "I am going to hit you upside the head if you don't get to the point."

"I have arrived at the point. The entry Hank happened to choose to modify was for Leonard Cooper, late of Richmond, Virginia."

I was impressed. "Really? Why would he want the Byerly newspaper? It never has anything in it but local stuff."

"Hank and I asked ourselves that same question. By looking at the records and consulting the *Gazette's* secretary, we found out that Cooper first subscribed over twenty years ago. Each year, he sent a typewritten note and a check asking for a renewal for the coming year. Interestingly enough, the papers were not sent to his home but to his office address."

"That *is* interesting," I admitted. "Did you call Junior and tell her?"

"Immediately. Hank let me do the honors, so he could then interview me about Junior's comments. Her response was, and I quote, 'I'll be damned. That's mighty interesting, Richard.' "

"Clearly a success like this deserves reward," I said. By now we had reached Aunt Maggie's driveway, so I stopped the car and kissed him.

"Is that it?" he asked. "It *was* a major breakthrough."

I kissed him several more times, until he agreed that he had been suitably rewarded.

As we went inside, I said, "Now, not to denigrate your achievement, did you find anything we can use to help Aunt Daphine?"

"I don't know yet. After our mutual adventure, Hank was more than happy to let me explore the old papers and I photocopied everything from that era which dealt with the soldiers from Byerly. Since the war was almost the only news topic for several years, it may take us some time to go through this information." He indicated the folder.

It was an imposing stack. "Let's get comfortable first." We got cold Cokes from the refrigerator, and arranged ourselves around the kitchen table. I took the top half of the stack of photocopies, and left him the rest. "We may as well get to it."

"What is it that we are looking for, exactly?" he asked.

"I don't know, exactly. Since Aunt Daphine didn't tell anybody about her nonmarriage, I guess what we're hoping to find out is whether or not Uncle John Ward could have told anybody. That means trying to track down anyone else from Byerly who went to Vietnam at around the same time as he did."

"I think that we can safely limit ourselves to the survivors," Richard pointed out.

"Agreed."

The next hours were long and tedious, punctuated only by Richard pointing out grammatical errors in the articles he was reading. We finally finished reading all of the papers late in the afternoon, and I handed Richard my notes so he could coordinate them with his.

"The way I see it is thus," he said after a few minutes. "There were at least twenty Byerly–bred soldiers in Vietnam. John Ward Marston was among the first to go, but seven others from his graduating class were drafted at or around the same time: Sid Honeywell, Philip Jones, Ed McDonald, Larry Parker, Reggie Rogers, Alex Stewart, and Small Bill Walters. There were others drafted a few months later, but Uncle John Ward was dead before they arrived in Vietnam. For now, I think we can ignore them."

"That sounds reasonable."

Richard went on, "Of that crew, Sid Honeywell survived, and was planning to work at the family filling station." He peered at me over his notes. "I assume that a filling station is similar to a gas station."

"Of course it is. He still runs it as far as I know."

"Philip Jones, the former gopher at the Byerly Bank, died in a bout of so–called friendly fire. Ed McDonald, despite the loss of two fingers, went to work at the mill. Larry Parker is the older brother of our own Hank Parker. He worked for the Army news corps, and went to work at the *Byerly Gazette.*"

"I remember hearing that Hank has a brother, but I don't think he lives in Byerly anymore."

"Reggie Rogers spent some time in an Army mental hospital, and didn't return home until long after the others. His plans were not known at the time the last article was written. Alex Stewart survived unscathed, and went to work at the mill. Small Bill Walters died in Vietnam several months after Uncle John Ward did. There you have the fruits of our labor."

"Not very fruitful," I said. "We don't know whether any of those fellows actually encountered Uncle John Ward over in Vietnam, and if they survived, where they are now. I think we need to see who we can track down."

"We could try to get more newspapers," Richard said, not very enthusiastically.

"I have a better idea. Two better ideas, in fact. First, one of us can consult the Burnette rumor mill in the form of Aunt Nora. She knows where most of the bodies are buried in Byerly."

"By one of us, I presume you mean yourself."

"That might be the better choice, considering my second idea."

"Which is?"

"To go visit Byerly's V.F.W. post. I think the veterans would be a lot more likely to talk to a man than to me."

"Good point."

I checked my watch. It was nearly five. "Why don't I call Aunt Nora and see if she's free this evening? If she's available, you can drop me over there and then go on to the V.F.W." I reached for the phone, but Richard put his hand over mine.

"Just out of curiosity, is the timing of this phone call in any way related to the time of day?"

"I'm sure I don't know what you mean," I said as innocently as I could manage, but I don't think he was fooled. He knew what time Aunt Nora fixed dinner as well as I did, and I noticed that he didn't argue with the idea.

Aunt Nora said she'd be glad to have some company that evening, and when I happened to mention that Richard and I had no plans for dinner, she assured me that they had plenty of chicken and dumplings. In fact, she implied that most of the food would have to be thrown out if we didn't rush right over there and help out. Of course I had seen Uncle Buddy, Thaddeous, and Willis eat, so I knew that they'd do just fine on their own, but I had also eaten Aunt Nora's chicken and dumplings. I told her we'd be glad to help, hung up, and we headed for the car.

Chapter 13

Dinner was wonderful, of course. If they gave out the Nobel Prize for light and fluffy dumplings, Aunt Nora would be a shoo–in. After we stuffed ourselves silly, Uncle Buddy went outside to rake leaves, Thaddeous went to call Joleen, Willis left for the night shift at the mill, and Aunt Nora cleaned up the kitchen. I took the opportunity to see Richard off.

"Where do Byerly soldiers go to fade away?" Richard asked as he got into the car.

"Downtown, across the street from the police department. There's a big flag pole in front, so you can't miss it." I thought for a moment. "Richard, I know you have somewhat mixed feelings about our role in Vietnam."

"Doesn't everyone?"

"Maybe veterans don't."

"I take it that you're suggesting that I not come on like a Massachusetts liberal, filled with indignation at the way American imperialism led to the loss of uncounted lives."

"Something like that," I admitted. "You'll be discreet, won't you?"

"I will be the soul of discretion, the best of good ole'

boys. I won't even think about mentioning Jane Fonda."

I wasn't completely reassured. "You do realize that the average good ole' boy doesn't quote Shakespeare with any regularity."

Richard raised his eyebrows in mock surprise. At least, I think it was mock. He said, "Actually many household words have their origin in the Bard's work, including 'household words,' which first appeared in *Henry V*, Act IV, Scene 2. The supposedly folksy expression 'dead a a doornail' comes from *Henry VI, Part 2*, Act IV, Scene 10. And—"

"However," I said, "when most people use these expressions, they don't follow up with the play, act, and scene from which the expression came."

"You have a point. I'll restrain myself."

He drove away, and I headed back inside and met Thaddeous in the hall.

"How's Joleen?" I asked.

"She wasn't home. I guess she's gone out with the girls." He joined Uncle Buddy outside.

Poor Thaddeous, I thought again as I went into the kitchen.

Aunt Nora was a fast worker. She already had the kitchen back in shape, and was stirring something in a bowl.

"What are you making?" I asked, and scooped up a taste with my finger.

"You're as bad as the boys," she said, swatting at my hand with her wooden spoon. "I'm just mixing up a batch of brownies. Buddy and Thaddeous like to have one with a glass of milk sometimes at night. If you want one, you're going to have to wait until they're baked."

"After all those dumplings?" I objected, but we both

knew that I'd talk myself into it when the brownies were ready.

"Where's Richard off to?"

"He had to go run an errand."

Aunt Nora gave me a look, so I amended, "To tell you the truth, he's off tracking down some information for Aunt Daphine's problems."

"That's what I thought. And what about you? Did you just come to visit, or is there something I can help you with?"

"A little of both. I want to pick your brain about some Byerly gossip."

"Is that so? Well, let me get these into the oven and we'll sit down and talk for a spell." She poured the batter into the waiting pan, pushed it into the oven, and switched on the timer. Then we settled down around the kitchen table.

I felt a little funny about quizzing her without an explanation, so I started with, "Aunt Daphine told me what's going on, but she made me promise not to tell anybody else. I'm sorry—"

"I know all about your promise," Aunt Nora said. "Linwood told Edna, and Edna told me, so don't you worry about hurting my feelings. You just do what you can for Daphine." Then she prompted me, "Now, what do you need to know?"

I was keeping in mind the categories Richard had laid out the night before. "First off, do you know anyone who's come into money unexpectedly or without an explanation?"

Aunt Nora thought about it for a minute, then said hesitantly, "Well, there is Linwood."

"No, somebody other than him," I said firmly, glad that I could be sure.

She thought for a little while longer. "I can't think of anybody else. The only one I know of to come into money all of a sudden is Faye Higgenbotham, and that's because her aunt died."

"Are you sure?" I said. It would be easy enough to invent a rich aunt.

"I'm pretty sure," Aunt Nora said. "I was at the funeral, and Faye's aunt had been saying for years that she wanted her insurance money to go to Faye."

"Okay," I said. That sounded pretty reasonable to me. "Next, do you know of anybody who doesn't like Aunt Daphine? I don't mean somebody with a little grudge; I mean somebody who really has it in for her."

"Daphine? Why would anybody not like Daphine?"

I shrugged. Maybe the blackmailer was just interested in money, but I didn't believe it. Those letters were too nasty. "What about in business? I know she doesn't have any competition in Byerly, but has she ever fired anybody?"

"Not for years. There was one girl she let go because she was stealing from the cash register, but then Daphine found out that she needed money for a sick child. So she lent her the money and gave her another chance. She still works there, as a matter of fact."

"Any feuds with neighbors?"

Aunt Nora shook her head.

"Old rivals from high school?" I said, knowing that I was grasping at straws.

Aunt Nora frowned. "Laurie Anne, if you want a blow-by-blow of the fight Daphine had with Junior Norton's mother when they both ran for president of the sophomore class, or the time she and Clara McDonald showed up at a school dance wearing the exact same dress, I'll be glad to tell you about it, but otherwise you're out of luck. Daphine isn't the kind of woman to make enemies."

"That's what I thought. One last question, and this goes back a ways, though not as far as Aunt Daphine's sophomore year in high school. I want to find out about some of the fellows from Byerly who went to Vietnam."

"All right. You know about John Ward already."

"Yes, ma'am."

"And Small Bill Walters was in the same platoon or company or whatever it was."

"Was he?" I hadn't known that. It was the first definite tie between Uncle John Ward's time in Vietnam and Byerly, and was especially interesting considering Uncle John Ward and Small Bill had been best friends. Of course, Aunt Nora's next words reminded me of the problem with that idea.

"Small Bill died a few months after John Ward. What a send-off Big Bill gave that boy. I've never known anybody to spend that much money on a funeral. They had to ship in flowers from florists all over the county because Byerly Blooms couldn't keep up. I hear Big Bill wanted to put in an eternal flame like they did for President Kennedy, but his wife talked him out of it."

"That would have been a bit much," I said. "Ed McDonald was in Vietnam, too, wasn't he?"

Aunt Nora nodded. "He was one of the lucky ones. He lost a couple of fingers, but it wasn't enough to keep him from making a living. Of course he's dead now. Heart attack, and I don't think they even knew he had heart problems. Ed was a pretty good fellow. He and Clara lived near Daphine, and he was always helping her out with yard work and such. Come to think of it, if you really want me to go back . . ."

"What?"

"Well, Ed used to be sweet on Daphine, but she never was interested in him."

"How come?"

"First off, as far as Daphine was concerned, there wasn't any boy in the world other than John Ward Marston. And second, Ed wasn't all that bright and he didn't have much of a personality. He faded right into the background, kind of a . . ." She searched for the right word.

"A wimp?"

She chuckled. "I shouldn't speak ill of the dead, but that's what he was. Needless to say, Ed was not Daphine's type. He was perfect for Clara, though, since she never would say boo to a mouse, either. They got married a little while before he went to Vietnam."

Ed could be a promising suspect, a spurned lover and all. I asked, "When did you say he died?"

"Back in the late spring, early summer. Not long after Paw."

That took him out of the running. Aunt Daphine received the first blackmail letter a good month after that.

I asked, "What about Alex Stewart? Is he related to May and Ralph Stewart?" I knew Ralph from the mill, and I went to school with his sister May.

"Alex is their uncle. I know you've seen him at church. Tall and skinny with dark hair. He's married to your old Sunday school teacher."

"That's right. I always called him Mr. Stewart, so I had forgotten his first name. He used to teach Sunday school, too, didn't he?"

"Still does."

That was certainly going to put him at the bottom of my list of suspects. Though I knew that I probably shouldn't eliminate him just because he was a church—

going man, he had always struck me as a sincerely devout Baptist.

"What about Larry Parker?" I asked.

"I'm surprised that you dug up all those names," Aunt Nora said. "He got injured, but not too badly."

"I heard that he limps now."

Aunt Nora nodded. "He got a Purple Heart, too, even though he wasn't in the fighting proper. He worked for the Army newspaper. He came back and worked at the *Byerly Gazette* for a year or so, but I guess it was too quiet for him after what he had seen over there. He used his G.I. benefits to go to journalism school in Chapel Hill, and went to work in Chicago."

"Is he still there?" I asked, because if he was, he would be in the clear. Aunt Daphine's blackmail letters had a Byerly postmark.

"No, he's working at the *Charlotte Observer* now."

That made it a bit more interesting. Charlotte was less than two hours away by car, so he could easily have driven down to mail the letters.

"Isn't he Hank Parker's brother?" I asked.

She nodded. "Larry helped get Hank into journalism school, and wanted him to go work in Chicago with him, but Hank never cared much for living in a big city. He came back to work on the *Gazette.*"

That gave me three possibilities. If Larry had found out, he could be the blackmailer, or if he had told Hank, it could be him. Or the two of them could be in it together. I mentally filed it away.

"Does Sid Honeywell still run the gas station on Main Street?" I said.

"He does, but I don't know for how much longer. Did you not hear about this? His son Tom was working there with him, but he took off about a year ago. With a fair amount of the profits, or so I hear. Apparently the boy had been stealing from his Daddy for years. It about broke Sid's heart, and nearly run him out of business. He pulled through, but he switched over to self–service a few months back so he can run the station by himself."

"What happened to the son? Did the police catch him?"

"Sid was too embarrassed to press charges. The terrible thing is that Tom is back in town, working up at the mill. I guess he used up all that money and didn't have anyplace else to go. He wanted to go back to work for Sid, if you can believe it, but Sid told Tom that he'd see him in Hell before he'd let him work for him again. Wrote him out of his will and everything."

This was promising, too. I didn't really think that the blackmailer was Sid, a cheerful man who always gave us kids lollipops when our parents got gas. But if Sid had known about Aunt Daphine and Uncle John Ward, and told Tom, Tom could be the one. I didn't think a man who'd steal from his own father would hesitate to blackmail Aunt Daphine.

"Anybody else?" Aunt Nora asked.

"Reggie Rogers."

Aunt Nora shook her head sadly. "Poor Reggie never was the same after the war. He didn't come home with the others because he had to stay in a mental hospital for a long time. I don't know but what they let him out too soon. When he did come home, he lived next door to Ruby Lee. That was when she was married to Alton. Anyway, Ruby Lee said that he used to wake the whole neighborhood, screaming from nightmares. They must have been terrible, but he never would tell anyone what they were about. He took to drinking. And other things." Aunt Nora said this last with that expression of righteous indignation she reserves for talking about drugs. "He never could hold a job, never got married, never did much of anything."

"What happened to him?"

"He was out drinking one night and fell asleep on the road. A truck ran right over him and killed him." Aunt Nora shook her head again. "Poor Reggie. He was such a nice boy. We went out a few times before the war. It was nothing serious, but he was so much fun and always a perfect gentleman. He wouldn't even touch a beer, then. Now I don't begrudge Larry Parker his medal, but I think Reggie deserved a Purple Heart just as much as Larry did."

The way Aunt Nora talked about Reggie, I was glad I didn't have to add him to my list of suspects.

The timer on the oven picked that minute to go off, and Aunt Nora went to pull out the pan of brownies.

I was just as glad for the interruption. I was tired of talking about death and pain. Most of the people I know have such knee–jerk reactions to Vietnam as a metaphor, that sometimes we forget about the people who really were there and what happened to them.

Aunt Nora said, "The brownies have to cool for a few minutes, so let's go see what Buddy and Thaddeous are up to."

It was wonderful outside, crisp but not cold. I held open the bags so Thaddeous could rake in the last of the leaves, relishing the crunch they made against the ground. Then we went back inside for brownies and milk.

After most of the brownies were gone, Uncle Buddy and Thaddeous retreated into the living room to watch television. Aunt Nora and I stayed in the kitchen to visit some more, but I guess she had had enough talk of Vietnam, too. Instead we started talking about Aunt Ruby Lee and Roger, and their impending return to the altar. We had worked our way through what we thought the wedding should be like, what Richard's and my wedding was like, and what a fair number of the Burnette weddings had been like, when the doorbell rang.

"Now who on earth can that be?" Aunt Nora said, starting to fuss with her hair.

"It's probably Richard," I said.

"What did he ring the bell for? Why didn't he just come on in?"

I shrugged. "He just can't get used to the idea of letting himself in."

Aunt Nora was shaking her head at the silliness of Richard's attitude when she went to get him, and was scolding him with, "Now next time, don't stand out there on the stoop like a stranger," as she brought him into the kitchen. "Just yell out when you come in the door, and that's enough for us."

"Yes, ma'am," he said sheepishly.

"You just sit yourself down and I'll get you a brownie."

While Aunt Nora fitted her deed to her words, Richard raised his eyebrows at me, which meant, "Did you find anything out?"

I nodded, and then raised my eyebrows back at him. He nodded, too.

When I was younger, I always wondered how my parents knew what the other one was thinking without saying anything, but now that I had been married a few years, I knew how it was done.

Aunt Nora handed Richard his brownie and a glass

of milk and said, "Did you get your *errand* taken care of?"

"All set."

We didn't stay too long after that. Aunt Nora and her crew tended to go to bed pretty early, and I wanted to hear what Richard had found out at the V.F.W.

Chapter 14

I managed to wait for Richard to close his car door, but even before turning the key in the ignition, I asked, "What happened?"

"It was quite interesting," Richard said. "They were much friendlier than you had led me to believe."

"Details. Give me details."

" 'How poor are they that have not patience!' *Othello*, Act II, Scene 3."

"I'm going to give you patience upside your head in a minute."

He grinned and said, "Well, if you put it that way, how can I refuse? Now I have to admit that when I arrived at the V.F.W. post, I didn't think I was going to uncover much. First off, it took me a good while to find a door that was unlocked. Then when I did and went inside, a surly gentleman snapped, 'Bingo is tomorrow night.' "

"What did you say?"

"I said I was looking for someone. When I started to describe an imaginary man, the fellow cut me off and directed me to the basement so I could look for myself."

"Then what?"

"I descended and found the bar, which is the post's second favorite attraction. After the bingo, that is. Not a bad place. The shag carpet was somewhat threadbare and the panelling hadn't been cleaned lately, but it wasn't bad. There were only a few people there: the bartender, a older man staring at a beer and humming, two younger men talking earnestly, and a woman reading a book."

"You went for the woman, of course."

"Of course."

I wasn't jealous because I knew that the woman could have been as plain as a mud fence as far as Richard was concerned. It was the book that had attracted his attention. "What was a woman doing in there? I thought only veterans were allowed."

"Your prejudices are showing. She *was* a veteran. An Army nurse, as a matter of fact, who served in Desert Storm."

"Oops," I said. Less than a week in Byerly, and I had already forgotten what decade I was in. "So what brilliant opening gambit did you use?"

"I asked her, 'What are you reading?' "

I snickered.

Richard looked injured. "I thought I should keep it simple."

"You're absolutely right, and that's about as simple as you can get."

"Anyway, she didn't seem to mind my asking. It was Jane Austen's *Pride and Prejudice,* by the way. Not my period, but a decent choice. We chatted for a while, she told me that her name was Vivian, I bought her a beer, and we ended up comparing the Laurence Olivier *Henry V* to the Kenneth Branagh *Henry V.*"

"I might have known that you'd find some way to get Shakespeare into the conversation."

"I've never found it difficult to introduce Shakespeare into an intelligent conversation. In this case, it was quite applicable. After all, the first movie bordered on propaganda while the second clearly illustrated post–Vietnam sensibilities."

"Richard, you know that I'd usually love a chance to discuss film versions of Shakespeare, but you did have another agenda. Did this lady give you anything we can use to find Aunt Daphine's blackmailer?"

"You *said* you wanted details."

He was right. That's what I had said. "Sorry, dear."

He nodded, mollified. "Once I had broken the ice, we moved onto other subjects. It turned out that Vivian has not been living here in Byerly very long."

"Rats! I don't suppose that she knew any of the fellows we're trying to track down."

"On the contrary. She was quite knowledgeable. You see, Vivian is a very energetic woman and she was appalled by the, and I quote, 'sloppy record–keeping and half–assed organization' at the V.F.W. post when she arrived. She appointed herself the task of bringing it all up to speed and even found the money for a computer to catalog data about local veterans."

"What kind did she get?"

"Please, we had only met. I didn't think I should get that personal."

I grinned, but didn't pursue the subject.

Richard went on. "Once I told her why I was there, she graciously opened up her office and we went through the files together."

"You told her why you were there?"

"Don't worry, I didn't tell her the true story. I told

129

her that my father was trying to track down an old Army buddy, but he couldn't remember his last name and the only first name he had was a nickname. All he remembered was that he was from Byerly. Therefore, if we could track down where the Byerly soldier served, my father would be able to figure out which one was his long–lost companion."

"That's pretty good," I said, "but Vivian must think that your father has a weird memory. I mean, remembering Byerly but not the man's name?"

Richard shrugged. "Vivian said that she had heard stranger stories. Once she was asked to help track down a man when the only clue was a tattoo of a clown."

We reached Aunt Maggie's house about then, so Richard held off on the rest of his story until we got inside. Aunt Maggie was sleeping in front of the television, but woke up when we came in.

"How's Daphine?" she asked. "Have you found her a way out of her troubles?"

Richard looked surprised, but I didn't even bother to ask how she knew.

"Not yet," I said, "but we're still trying."

Aunt Maggie nodded. "Well, I don't know what Daphine's got herself into, but you come to me if there's anything I can do. All right?"

"Yes ma'am," I said. "It's not that I don't trust you, but—"

"I know Daphine made you promise not to tell anyone." She shook her head. "That girl always has had a lot of pride, never did want anybody to know it if she was in trouble. One time she lost a library book and the librarian told her that she was going to have to pay for it. Well, Daphine knew that her daddy didn't have the money right then because times were hard, but she also knew that he'd try to scrape it up somehow if she told him. So she took it into her head that she wasn't going to tell him, that she was going to get the money all by her lonesome.

"She went down to the dime store and offered to sweep floors or unpack boxes or do anything she could to get the money. It took her two months of hard work to do it, but she did it. And all that time she wouldn't tell anybody what she was up to." Aunt Maggie shook her head again. "That was I don't know how many years ago, and she hasn't changed not one bit. I'm just glad that she's told *somebody* what's going on. The rest of us know that you'll do what you can."

"Thank you, Aunt Maggie." It made me a little nervous to know that the entire Burnette family was counting on Richard and me, but I comforted myself with the knowledge that any one of them would help if they could.

I don't know if Aunt Maggie guessed that Richard and I had more talking to do or if she was just ready for bed, but she went on upstairs after that. Richard and I poured ourselves some iced tea, and then sat in the swing on the back porch while Richard finished his story.

"As I was saying, Vivian fired up her computer and listed Byerly's fighting men according to the year in which they were drafted. Interestingly enough, there were names other than the ones we found in the newspaper."

"Really? I got the impression that at least at first, every soldier was a hero."

"Only the white ones. Vivian pointed out the fact that the names we didn't have were of black men."

"Oh," I said, feeling embarrassed on Byerly's behalf.

Which was silly when I didn't have anything to do with it, but liberal guilt knows no logic. "Sometimes I forget how much things have changed. Of course, none of those men would be suspects."

"Why not? Several of them survived."

"Because they were black." Now I really felt like a redneck. "I never knew Uncle John Ward, but I'll lay odds that he would never have told a black man something as personal as his making love to Aunt Daphine." I looked at Richard sideways. "I know that sounds awful, but it's true."

"Don't apologize," Richard said. "You didn't have anything to do with it. You're just being realistic, and as you said, times *have* changed."

I nodded, but like every liberal I know, Southerner or Northerner, I'm scared to death that somewhere deep inside, I'm harboring racist feelings.

Richard went on. "Anyway, as it happened, none of those black men were in the same part of Vietnam as Uncle John Ward. Therefore the chance of their meeting was fairly low."

"What about the fellows we read about in the paper?"

Richard pulled a sheet of paper out of his shirt pocket and unfolded it with a flourish. "Vivian's computer knew the assignments of each veteran, so she printed out the information for the pertinent people so we could see who was in Da Nang."

"Da Nang?"

He looked smug. "I stopped at a pay phone on the way over to call Aunt Daphine and found out where Uncle John Ward was stationed."

"You're so clever," I said.

"True."

"So who was at Da Nang?"

"All of them, at one time or another. Vivian tells me it was a major base. In fact, she seemed to think that anyone should know that. I felt quite ignorant."

"I'll bet she can't name all the major characters in Shakespeare's plays," I pointed out.

"Well put. The three men whose stays in Da Nang overlapped with Uncle John Ward's are Larry Parker, Reggie Rogers, and Small Bill Walters."

"Rats," I said. "I had high hopes for Sid Honeywell." I told Richard about Sid's larcenous son. "I can eliminate two of your guys from what Aunt Nora told me. Small Bill died in Vietnam, and Reggie Rogers died here a good while ago. All that leaves is Larry Parker."

"Vivian had an address for him in Charlotte."

"Aunt Nora says he works for the *Charlotte Observer*."

"Do you think a road trip is called for?"

"Not yet," I said. "Let's try talking to Hank here in town, first. After all, Larry could have told Hank and Hank could be the blackmailer.

"I hope not," Richard said. "I like Hank."

"I've known him for years, and he doesn't act much like a blackmailer. But then again, what does a blackmailer act like?"

Richard had no answer for that.

"I trust you expressed your appreciation to Vivian."

"She did mention that they were trying to raise money for some improvements to the bar, so I took the hint and made a donation. Unlike Vasti, however, she gave me a receipt so we can deduct it from our taxes."

"Poor Richard," I said sympathetically. "Here you are on vacation, and you're spending all of your money on bribes and garden parties." I batted my eyes at him. "Is there any way I can make it up to you?"

"Well," he said shyly, "there is something."

"Yes?"

"If we don't have anything else to do tonight, that is."

"Yes."

"Can I read my new book? The Epstein book on Shakespeare? I hear it's got some wonderful Bardic trivia in it."

"I really had something else in mind," I said, and then leaned over to kiss him for a long time.

When we finished, he said, "Oh, that's a much better idea." He hopped out of the porch swing, and took my hand as we headed inside and upstairs. "The book can wait."

Afterwards, when I started to happily drift off to sleep, Richard slid out of bed for a moment. Knowing my husband as well as I do, I wasn't a bit surprised to see him return with his new book in hand. I just curled up next to him, and went on to sleep while he read.

Chapter 15

The next day we decided that Richard would go back to the *Byerly Gazette* office to talk to Hank Parker and try to see whether either Hank or Larry were potential black-mailers. Since the latest edition of the paper had come out that morning, Hank would probably be at loose ends and willing to talk. The weather was bright and breezy, and Richard decided to walk so I could have the car in case I needed to pursue another line of investigation.

I considered pursuing another line of investigation, I really did, but I couldn't think of one. So I called various aunts and cousins to see if anyone felt like having company, but was just as glad when nobody was available. I had a hunch that I might not have another chance to loaf during this trip, and I thought I might as well enjoy it.

Except the doorbell rang just as I was sitting down to read. I was expecting a salesman when I opened the door, but what I got was Junior Norton.

"Hi Junior. What's up?"

Junior smiled her slow smile, the one that meant she wasn't telling the whole truth. "I was just passing by, and I thought I'd stop in to see how you and Richard are enjoying your vacation. Can I come in?"

"Of course. Would you like something to drink?" I got us both Cokes, and we sat down at the kitchen table.

"Where is Richard, anyway?"

"He's running some errands," I said with a certain amount of truth.

"You've been running a fair number of errands yourself, I hear."

"I suppose I have. How did you know?"

"You know how it is in Byerly, Laurie Anne. You can't hardly blow your nose without someone calling up to say, 'God bless.' So how's your aunt doing?"

"Which one?" I asked, but I knew who she was talking about."

"Daphine Marston. I hear she's been having some kind of trouble, but no one is quite sure what kind."

I didn't know what to say. "I'll tell Aunt Daphine you were asking after her. I'm sure she'll appreciate it."

"Actually," Junior said, "I have a hunch that she won't appreciate it at all."

I took an especially large swallow of Coke.

Junior asked, "Laurie Anne, how much goes on in this town that I don't find out about?"

"Not much."

"Now how much of what I find out gets beyond me?"

"I know you can keep things to yourself, Junior, if that's what you're getting at."

"Good. Now let me run a question past you. One of those that isn't real, but could be real."

"Junior, you know the word 'hypothetical' just as well as I do. I'm not some Yankee you have to act typical with."

Junior grinned. "All right then, let me ask you a hypothetical question. Suppose one of the most pleasant women in town suddenly turned moody, started acting like something was bad wrong. Then suppose some man suddenly showed up dead somewhere where he didn't have any business being. And suppose that dead man served in Vietnam with that woman's husband."

"Leonard Cooper was in Vietnam with Uncle John Ward?" That was news to me.

Junior nodded. "Now we've got the moody woman, and we've got a dead man. Then assume that the woman has a niece visiting, a niece who has been known to indulge in private investigations before. This niece just happens to be one of the folks who discovered the dead man's body, and this niece and her husband start running all over town, talking to people. Assuming all of this, would you think that this niece was trying to solve herself another murder?"

I almost laughed, I was so glad Junior was barking up the wrong tree. "Speaking hypothetically, I might, but let me try a hypothetical question on you. Suppose that the niece told the police chief that she knows what's bothering the aunt and that she's trying to do something about it. And suppose she said that her being at that murder site was just a coincidence. If you were the chief of police, would you believe her?"

Junior nodded. "I imagine I would." She finished her Coke. "These hypothetical questions are all well and good, but I best be getting back to work. Thanks for the co-cola."

"Any time, Junior," I said.

"Now since these were all hypothetical questions, I'm hoping that what we talked about won't get spread all around town."

"You've got it." Okay, I was going to tell Richard, but telling Richard wasn't like telling Vasti.

Junior was just about out the door when she turned and said, "Now Laurie Anne, I don't know what your

137

aunt's troubles are, but I'm trusting you to let me know if it's police business."

"I'll keep that in mind, Junior," I said, and closed the door behind her.

I was grinning when Junior left, glad to hear that she didn't know about the blackmail and kind of tickled that she thought I would want to track down a murderer on my vacation. Doing it once had been plenty enough for me.

I went back to the couch and opened up my book, meaning to finish it by the time Richard returned. Only I eventually realized that I had been staring at the same page for ten minutes. I just couldn't concentrate on it. Junior's hypothetical questions had started me thinking.

I *had* told Junior the truth, hadn't I? Unless . . . Suppose that Uncle John Ward had told Leonard Cooper about him and Aunt Daphine, thinking that it wouldn't hurt anything since Cooper had probably never even heard of Byerly. I could see it happening pretty easily. A bunch of guys sitting around, telling tales about who could drink the most and who had slept with the most women. It could have slipped out.

Then Cooper could have been Aunt Daphine's blackmailer. Of course Aunt Daphine had received the latest ransom demand on Monday, after he was killed, but it was probably mailed on Saturday.

No, that was silly. How could Cooper have learned that Daphine was pretending to be a widow? How could he have learned about Arthur's campaign? Then I remembered Cooper's subscription to the *Gazette*, and the prominent ads and articles that Vasti had arranged recently. At least one of the articles Aunt Nora had sent me cited Vasti's being the daughter of an old Byerly family, and mentioned Daphine by name. He could have figured it out.

But Cooper had been receiving the Byerly paper for years. Why did he care anything about Byerly? And surely there had been something about Aunt Daphine in the paper over the years, so he could have figured out that she was using Uncle John Ward's last name long ago. Why did he pick now to blackmail Aunt Daphine? And how could the blackmail letters have been mailed from Byerly? Could Cooper have had a local accomplice? Could he and the accomplice have had a falling out serious enough for the accomplice to shoot him?

No, this was ridiculous. Respectable architects from Virginia didn't blackmail strangers in small North Carolina towns. But then again, the average architect from Virginia didn't end up dead in a North Carolina cotton mill. Damn! Junior had planted the seed, and now I was starting to think that the blackmail *was* connected with the murder.

I didn't like that idea, not at all, because it made Aunt Daphine a prime suspect for the murder. Of course I knew that she wouldn't kill anybody, not even a blackmailer, but would Junior believe that? Even if she did, she'd still have to investigate. In a town like Byerly, how long would it take for the blackmailer to find out, and how long before he sent the newspaper a letter about Aunt Daphine? Even if Hank Parker didn't print the story, word would get out.

I needed to talk to talk to Aunt Daphine, to find out if she knew anything about Leonard Cooper. I checked the clock. She would be at the beauty parlor, which was not the place for a private phone conversation. I'd be better off going to see her in person, so I scribbled a note for Richard and headed for La Dauphin.

Chapter 16

I guessed that Dorinda was on coffee break again, because there was no one at the reception desk when I walked into La Dauphin, but Aunt Daphine herself came out in answer to the bell.

"Hey there," she said. "How are you doing?"

"Pretty good. Have you got time to talk?"

She nodded. "My ten–thirty appointment cancelled on me. Do you want to come into the back?"

"Actually, maybe we should take a walk or something."

"All right." She peered through the curtain into the main room and called out, "I'm going to walk over to Woolworth's for a minute. Does anybody want anything?" She took a few orders for soft drinks, got her purse, and said, "Let's go."

Aunt Daphine waited until we were a few feet away from the shop before she asked, "So what's going on, Laurie Anne? Have you found out anything yet?"

"I'm not sure. Junior Norton came to visit me a little while ago."

"What did she want?"

"Don't worry—she doesn't know anything about your

problem." It was probably silly, but I just couldn't say blackmail while walking outside on a pretty fall day. "She knows that Richard and I are up to something, but she thought that it was the murder at the mill."

"Why would you care about that? You didn't even know that man."

"I didn't," I said, "but Uncle John Ward did. Leonard Cooper was in Vietnam with him." I waited a minute for that to sink in. "Did Uncle John Ward mention him in any of his letters to you?"

"He might have, now that you mention it. I thought that his name sounded familiar, but Cooper is a pretty common name." She shook her head. "I'd have to check the letters to be certain."

"I told Junior that I don't have any interest in her murder investigation, but now I'm not so sure."

"I don't think I follow you."

"Suppose Uncle John Ward told Leonard Cooper about him and you. He wouldn't have known you were pregnant, of course, but he might have told Cooper about your . . ." I searched for a polite way to put it. "About your time together."

Aunt Daphine shook her head emphatically. "No, he wouldn't have, not in a million years. John Ward promised me that he'd never tell another living soul, and I promised him the same thing. I broke my word with Maw and Paw because of Vasti, and then with you because of those letters, but I know that nothing less than that would have made him break his."

"But he was young, and you know how young men are. What if he got drunk? Maybe bragging a little?"

She kept shaking her head. "I'm sorry, Laurie Anne, but I knew John Ward Marston and you didn't. He knew how to hold his liquor, and he didn't show off, and he wouldn't have broken his word come hell or high water. And besides, he could only have known this Cooper fellow a few weeks at the most. John Ward was a private man—he wouldn't have told something like that to a man he barely knew. No, if he was going to tell anyone, it would have been Small Bill Walters because they were such good friends. And Small Bill died not long after him."

We got to Woolworth's about then, so neither of us spoke about the matter at hand until we had received our order and were carrying it back to La Dauphin. That gave me time to come up with another idea.

"What about Small Bill?" I said. "What if John Ward told him, and then Small Bill told Cooper. Couldn't that be the answer?"

Aunt Daphine shook her head again. "I don't think so, Laurie Anne. I knew Small Bill pretty well. There were only a dozen in our class at school, you know, and he was John Ward's best friend. Now I can see where John Ward *might* have told Small Bill, or even that Small Bill could have figured it out for himself. Small Bill knew that I was there in Norfolk, and John Ward was gone from the barracks for two nights. It wouldn't take a whole lot of brains to guess the rest. But even if he knew, Small Bill would never have told anybody else about it.

"Small Bill would have done anything in the world for me because of John Ward. Once when John Ward was out of town, a boy made a pass at me at a football game and wouldn't take 'no' for an answer. Well, Small Bill grabbed that boy by the collar to pull him away and shoved him halfway down the bleachers. No, Small Bill wouldn't have told anybody something like that."

I tried to suggest that Small Bill would have been

painfully lonely once Uncle John Ward died, and might not have thought that it was important anymore, but I might as well have been talking to a brick wall. Aunt Daphine just kept telling me that I hadn't known Uncle John Ward or Small Bill, and that she had.

I finally gave up, left her at La Dauphin, and drove back to Aunt Maggie's.

Chapter 17

I saw Richard walking down the street as I was driving back to Aunt Maggie's, and I stopped to pick him up. While we drove, I told him about the suspicions that Junior had roused and that Aunt Daphine refused to believe. I finished by the time we got to the house.

"I feel funny about not talking to Junior about this," I concluded as we went inside. "She's going to be awfully mad if she finds out."

Richard nodded. " 'Though she be but little, she is fierce.' *A Midsummer Night's Dream*, Act III, Scene 2."

"Of course we don't know for sure that Cooper's death is connected to the blackmail." I looked at Richard and he looked at me. "Okay," I said, "they probably *are* connected. But what can I do? I promised Aunt Daphine that I wouldn't tell, and I know that if I do tell Junior, the blackmailer will find out and tell everybody about Aunt Daphine and Uncle John Ward, and Arthur will lose the election, and Vasti will blame me and never speak to me again."

"That last part didn't sound all that bad."

"Richard!" I said, and bopped him with a sofa pillow, but I had to grin. "All right, maybe I am taking on more responsibility that I need to. What did you find out from Hank? Maybe you've made my angst obsolete."

"Sorry, love, but no such luck. All I did was to clear the brothers Parker from suspicion."

"Not another dead end?" I said disgustedly.

He nodded.

"Go ahead and tell me about it."

"I found Hank inspecting the latest edition of the *Gazette* with some satisfaction. The poor fellow rarely gets to cover a murder, though I couldn't manufacture much sympathy for that particular problem. Anyway, he read most of the article about the murder out loud, and presented me with a copy of the paper, free of charge."

"And then what?"

"Well, I worked up to it gradually, saying that I had enjoyed reading the papers I photocopied and I wondered where those fellows ended up."

"What excuse did you give for making those copies, anyway? I forgot to ask about that the other day."

"I told him that a colleague of mine is working on a book about different perceptions of the Vietnam War, especially in the views of the local press across the country."

"That's not bad," I said.

"I was rather impressed myself. I'll have to mention it to some people back at the college and see if anyone wants to give it a try. But back to the tale I've been trying to tell . . ."

"Sorry," I said, and then realized that had been yet another interruption. "That's the last thing I'll say."

He didn't look convinced, but he went on. "I mentioned Larry Parker by name, and asked if he were related, and of course Hank said that he is. I thought that he displayed a certain lack of enthusiasm, and delicately asked if perhaps they weren't close. Hank admitted that their relationship has been strained ever since Hank left Chicago to return to Byerly, and that Larry had called Hank's work on the *Gazette* a waste of time. Only Larry wasn't that polite. Apparently they're civil when they meet at family gatherings, but that's as far as it goes."

I started to point out that this made the idea of their being in collusion pretty unlikely, but I remembered just in time that I had promised not to interrupt. Instead I just nodded.

Richard looked gratified at my self–restraint. "Next I asked about Small Bill Walters, and what kind of fellow he had been. Hank, still thinking of his older brother, chuckled because he remembered a time that Small Bill and Larry had been in a fight, and Larry came out the worse for the experience. They were still on unfriendly terms when Small Bill shipped out for Vietnam, and Hank says that Larry later regretted that Small Bill died before they had a chance to bury the hatchet."

So much for the idea of Small Bill telling Larry about Uncle John Ward and Aunt Daphine. He certainly wouldn't have told something like that to a man he was on the outs with.

"Then I asked about Uncle John Ward, using the fact that he had been Small Bill's best friend as a transition. I wondered if he was involved in the feud. The answer was a positive 'yes.' The reason Small Bill and Larry fought was that Larry had tried, as Hank put it, to 'make time' with Aunt Daphine while Uncle John Ward was away, and Small Bill stepped in to defend her honor."

I couldn't stand it anymore. "Aunt Daphine told me about that, but she didn't mention that it was Larry

Parker that Small Bill pushed down the bleachers." I realized that I had spoken, and contritely said, "Sorry."

"That's all right," Richard said magnanimously. "I had come pretty much to the end of my tale. The way I see it, Larry and Hank wouldn't have worked together because they weren't getting along. Moreover, neither Uncle John Ward nor Small Bill would have been likely to confide in Larry under the circumstances. That means Larry is eliminated, and so is Hank, since Larry couldn't have told Hank something he didn't know."

"Rats, I thought we were getting somewhere," I said. "Now we're back where we started, only with fewer people to suspect."

"One of my scientist friends once told me that negative data is at least as valuable as positive data."

I snapped, "Then maybe your scientist friend can find out who's blackmailing Aunt Daphine!"

Most people would have taken offense, but Richard just put an arm around me and squeezed gently. I squeezed back, and he added his other arm. We kissed a few times, and after that it didn't seem so bad.

Then I noticed something: it was after noon and my stomach was growling. Feeling that I needed something more substantial than a hamburger to cheer me up, I enticed Richard into going to the Fork-in-the-Road Barbeque Lodge, so named because it was located at a fork in the road to Hickory.

The pulled-pork barbeque and hush puppies I ate were wonderful, but I still wasn't very cheerful when we got back to the house. Richard, who knows my moods well, got a book to read while I pulled out my laptop computer and pushed buttons angrily, ostentatiously to record our latest negative findings but really so I could brood.

The phone rang after a while, and Richard answered it. "Hi, Aunt Daphine. Yes, she is. Really? She'll be glad to hear that." He held his hand over the mouthpiece of the phone. "It's Aunt Daphine. She says she has an idea for our investigation."

I winced, but then told myself that I wasn't being fair. Considering how well I had done with this mess so far, Aunt Daphine's suggestion would likely do as much good as anything I had come up with. I took the phone from Richard and said, "Hey Aunt Daphine. What's your idea?"

"I have to talk quietly because I'm at the shop," Aunt Daphine whispered. "Have you found anything out?"

"Not yet," I had to answer, "but we're still looking."

"I hear you were over at Nora's asking about Byerly gossip, and I got to thinking that the best place for gossip is right here at the shop."

"You've got a point there," I said. "The only thing is, what kind of excuse would I have for hanging around?"

"Well, I figured you'd want to get your hair fixed for Vasti's garden party," Aunt Daphine said. "You were planning to, weren't you?"

Actually the thought hadn't occurred to me, but I said, "That's right. I do have to get that taken care of."

"Why don't you come over tomorrow morning? If I act like I'm not expecting you and then squeeze you in between appointments and maybe pretend like your hair isn't drying right, we could stretch it out for a good part of the day."

It was worth a try. "All right, I'll be there in the morning."

Richard and I tried to come up with something to investigate for the rest of the afternoon and evening, but we couldn't. Instead we drove to Valley Hills Mall in Hickory to buy me a dress for Vasti's garden party.

I had tried to talk myself into wearing the same outfit that I had worn to the reunion. Who would notice, or even if they did, who would care? Of course I knew the answer to both of those questions. Vasti would, and I didn't want to hear about it from her for the next year. Or maybe I was just glad for an excuse to do anything other than think about blackmail.

Chapter 18

The next morning, Richard dropped me off at La Dauphin so I could spend the day absorbing Byerly atmosphere and gossip. I wasn't sure it would do any good, but I didn't have any better ideas. If nothing else, I'd get a haircut out of the deal.

"Well, good morning," Aunt Daphine said brightly when I came in. She was standing next to the reception desk with Dorinda, who grunted something or another.

"Good morning," I said back.

"What can I do for you on this pretty day?"

"I was hoping you could squeeze me in for a haircut," I said, as per our agreed–upon script. I hoped that it didn't sound as fake to everybody else as it did to me. "I don't want Vasti to throw me out of her party."

"Don't you worry about that," Aunt Daphine said. "Dorinda, do I have time to fix my niece's hair?"

Dorinda looked over the appointment book. "I suppose so. You've got your appointments spaced out way more than they need to be. If you'd let me schedule them closer together, you could get half again as many people in."

"Now Dorinda, you know I don't want to have to

rush through anyone's hair, and I don't want anyone to have to wait for their appointment," Aunt Daphine said firmly.

"But—"

"Besides, this way I'll be able to fit in Laurie Anne." She turned back to me. "Laurie Anne, why don't you sit here by the hair dryers until I'm ready for you."

I took the seat, picked up a magazine, and used the mirrors to check around the room. Apparently no one thought that it was odd for me to be here; everyone was minding her own business.

Now, I thought, bring on the gossip. The first half-hour's conversation consisted of speculation about someone who was never actually named and the men she was seeing. I was pretty sure that that they were talking about Joleen, because they changed the subject when Dorinda walked in.

From the number of men's names bandied about, I didn't think that Joleen had time for blackmail. Interestingly, while Thaddeous had said that he was trying to defend Joleen from Burt Walters, local gossip had it that Burt Walters and Joleen had been an item since day one. Of course, Byerly gossip isn't always right, so I wasn't taking it for gospel.

The next topic to keep the ladies busy was Vasti's garden party. It was apparently going to be quite a shindig, complete with a live band and tons of food and waiters and waitresses to serve hors d'oeuvres. I was glad I had bought that new dress. Mrs. Walters had volunteered her house, which was the closest thing to a mansion in Byerly, and a lot of folks were going more for the chance to see inside than to support the charity. Come to think of it, I was pretty curious about that house myself.

I thought I caught a reference or two to Vasti putting on airs and specifying just what people should wear, but of course people weren't going to be rude with Aunt Daphine standing right there.

I was still waiting for Aunt Daphine to squeeze me in when Gladys bustled in. "Hey Dorinda. I'm not late, am I?" she asked, looking around the waiting area.

"Late for what?" Dorinda asked.

"For my appointment with Mrs. Abbott," Gladys said as she stowed her purse in the back of the shop and reached into the closet for her smock.

"Is Mrs. Abbott coming in today?" Dorinda asked with malicious innocence, making a big show of flipping though the appointment book.

Gladys said, "Don't you remember, Dorinda? You took the call yourself. She called the day before yesterday and made an appointment for today at eleven–thirty."

Dorinda looked surprised. "Now I remember. She called back yesterday and cancelled. Did I not tell you?"

"No, you didn't tell me. Did she reschedule?"

Dorinda smiled. "I forgot to ask if she wanted to. Sorry. Excuse me for a minute." She clattered away to the back room before Gladys could say anything.

"Tarnation!" Gladys said. "I don't have another appointment until two, so I came all the way over here for nothing." She started to pull the smock off again.

"As long as you're here," I said hurriedly, "why don't you do my nails so they'll look good for Vasti's party."

Gladys smiled gratefully. "Are you sure?"

"Absolutely," I said, and added the lie, "My husband was real pleased with the way you did them last time." Actually Richard hadn't noticed my nails until I stuck them under his nose, but my getting a manicure would make Gladys feel better. Besides, if I sat in that chair any longer, I was going to take root.

I let Gladys lead me to her table and get to work. "I suppose you want them painted clear again," she said with a sigh, obviously remembering the last time I had been there.

"Actually," I said, "I'm feeling adventurous today. I got a teal blue dress for the party, so what color would you suggest?"

Gladys immediately pulled forth a carousel of nail polish and started explaining the enormous benefits of each and every one. I wasn't convinced that the color that I finally chose would make my eyes look like pools of mystery, but it didn't look half bad.

We were just getting started when Aunt Daphine came by to escort a customer to the door. "I don't know why we didn't try this hairstyle years ago, Mrs. Minton. It makes you look so much younger."

"Do you think so?" Mrs. Minton said, peering into the nearest mirror.

"Absolutely. That style is just perfect for you. Your husband's going to think that he's got a brand new wife, and I can just imagine how that's going to affect him." Aunt Daphine actually giggled.

Mrs. Minton's eyes got wide, and she took a better look at the mirror. "Do you think?"

Aunt Daphine nodded solemnly, and Mrs. Minton didn't waste a second in getting out the door, and presumably, to her husband.

"Your aunt has seemed a lot perkier the past couple of days," Gladys said in a low voice.

"She sure has," I said, but I wasn't entirely glad to see it. I mean, I was glad she was feeling better, but it made me nervous that she was so sure that Richard and I would be able to get her out of trouble.

Gladys was just about done with my nails when Dorinda walked over with a copy of the *Byerly Gazette*. "Do you mind if I read your newspaper, Gladys?" she asked.

"Go ahead," Gladys said. "I'm done with it."

Dorinda turned a page, and said, "I don't know why I bother to look at it. It never has anything in it worth reading." She stopped on a page, and said, "Well, look at that." Then she didn't say anything.

I knew that what she wanted was for either me or Gladys to ask her what it was she was looking at, but I couldn't resist. "Anything exciting?" I finally asked.

"Not much," she said nonchalantly. "I was just looking at this picture of Daphine and her daughter." She held it out where I could see it. It was one of Arthur's campaign advertisements, designed to emphasize that Vasti and Arthur were authentic members of the Byerly community. "How much older than you is Vasti, anyway?" Dorinda asked.

I tried not to grin, because I didn't want to encourage her, but after all the times Vasti had reminded me that I was older than she was, I couldn't help but be tickled. "Actually, Vasti is younger than I am."

"Is she? I guess it must be the dress she's wearing. It makes her look older."

That made me think for a minute. Was she saying that Vasti dressed too old, or that I dressed too young? Or some combination of the two? "I think it's a very nice dress," was all I said.

"Of course, if my husband looked that old, I'd try to dress differently too."

"Which one?" Gladys asked under her breath, and it

wasn't easy for me to keep from laughing. I could tell from the way Dorinda turned to the next page that she had heard the reference to her multiple spouses.

"Well, look at that," she said again.

I should have known better, but I rose to the bait again. "What's that?"

She didn't answer, and I realized she was really staring at the paper this time. "Dorinda?" I asked.

She jerked her head up. "What?"

Gladys asked, "What's so interesting?"

"Nothing," she said too quickly. "Nothing at all." She carefully folded the paper, and went back to her desk. I saw her stuff the paper into her pocketbook, and then she just sat there with the oddest expression on her face, like she was thinking real hard.

"What was that about?" I asked Gladys.

She shrugged and said, "With Dorinda, there's no telling." She finished painting the last nail, stuck my hands into the nail dryer, and went to clean her implements.

I was itching to get a copy of the *Gazette* and see just what it was it was that was so fascinating. I was pretty sure I knew what it was. Most of yesterday's paper had been devoted to Leonard Cooper's murder.

"Laurie Anne," Aunt Daphine called from the back of the shop. "I'm ready to fix your hair."

It was the first time that Aunt Daphine had cut my hair in years. She had done it when I was younger, but when I went away to school, I was convinced that any haircut I got in Boston had to be more sophisticated that what I could get in Byerly. Now I knew that I had misjudged Aunt Daphine, and I rather liked the result. It was still shoulder length with wisps of bangs, but the bangs looked styled now, rather than just pushed out of my face.

This isn't to say that I was paying such close attention to my hair that I neglected the gossip going past me. Now the ladies were speculating about Leonard Cooper's murder.

Most of them were betting that Cooper was an illegitimate son of Big Bill's, and that he had come to town to claim his birthright. No one had a clear idea of the details involved, like how Big Bill had gotten some woman from Tennessee pregnant and how Cooper had found his way to Byerly and into the mill.

As for the murderer, most folks were betting on Burt, out to protect his inheritance. Burt's wife Dorcas was also suggested, for the same reason. Big Bill got a few votes for wanting to protect his reputation, although I couldn't resist pointing out that he couldn't have picked a more conspicuous place to kill somebody. There were a few other contenders, mostly pretty unlikely, including a faithful family retainer protecting the Walters and a mob hit for unspecified reasons.

Hank's article said that Cooper had been in Vietnam, and Gladys speculated on the reaction of Small Bill Walters if he had met Cooper there. Nobody mentioned the fact that Cooper *had* been in Vietnam with Small Bill. Obviously Junior had been able to keep that quiet so far, and I saw no reason to disturb the status quo.

Still, it started me thinking about something I should have realized as soon as Junior talked to me. Admittedly, I had been concentrating on the idea of Uncle John Ward knowing Cooper, and not Small Bill, but now I realized what a strange coincidence it all was.

Both Small Bill and Leonard Cooper had looked a lot like Big Bill. Therefore, Cooper had probably looked a

156

lot like Small Bill when they served together in Vietnam. What were the chances of two men who looked *so* much alike being in the same outfit? If Cooper had been Small Bill's illegitimate half–brother, the coincidence was even more remarkable.

I just couldn't buy that big a coincidence. So what did that leave me? Some unknown enemy wanted the two men to meet and somehow arranged to have them assigned to the same company. And then killed Small Bill so that all these years later, Leonard Cooper would take his place and run the mill. Only somebody killed him first.

I snorted at the whole idea.

"I beg your pardon," Aunt Daphine said.

"Nothing," I said. 'Nothing' was right. The whole sequence of events was too foolish to even think about. I focused my attention on the conversations going on around me.

As it turned out, I could have kept on creating imaginary plots. The conversation had left Leonard Cooper, and was now about some people I wasn't interested in and their noisy marital problems.

Aunt Daphine finished with my hair, and asked me, "Is there anything else we can do for you today?"

I hesitated, not sure how to answer her. I hadn't learned a whole lot yet, but I wasn't ready to give up. What excuse could I use for sticking around?

Gladys saved us by asking, "Laura, have you ever had a facial? I just got this mix from England I've been itching to try."

"How long does it take?" I asked.

"About an hour. Are you in a hurry?"

Aunt Daphine and I smiled at one another. "No," I said. "I've got all day."

157

While Gladys wrapped a hot towel around my cheeks and went to mix up whatever it is one uses for a facial, I kept an eye on Dorinda, hoping that she would leave her newspaper unattended long enough for me to sneak a peak. Unfortunately, just as Gladys returned with a bowl of what looked like oatmeal, Dorinda grabbed her purse and the paper and announced, "I'm going to lunch now. Would you listen for the phone, Gladys?"

"Sure," Gladys said, but Dorinda was already gone.

So much for getting a look at Dorinda's paper, but maybe I could find out more about Dorinda herself. "Does Dorinda always act like that?" I asked as Gladys removed the towel.

"Pretty much," Gladys said, and started smearing the oatmeal on my face. "Not at first, or Daphine wouldn't have hired her, but as soon as she realized she could get away with it. Like I said the other day, I don't know why your aunt puts up with her."

Of course, now I knew why Aunt Daphine hadn't been concentrating on the shop, but I couldn't tell Gladys that. "Why did she move to Byerly? She's from South Carolina, isn't she?"

Gladys nodded. "From some town near Columbia. She just divorced her third husband, and he's got a lot of friends and family around there, and they were just making her life miserable. Taking his side and all. So she said it was time to make a new start, and since she had a boyfriend in Byerly, this is where she came. Only when she got here, she found out that he's married and hasn't got any intention of leaving his wife. I was kind of surprised to hear that she cared whether or not he was married, to tell you the truth, but she says she did. Anyway, she decided that since both she and her daughter had found jobs, they might as well stick around."

I must have looked surprised at how much she knew, because Gladys grinned and said, "It sounds like I've been studying up on her, doesn't it? She told me all of this the first week she was here. That woman could talk the hind leg off of a mule, and she'd much rather talk than work. You would think that a woman wouldn't want to tell the whole world about her marital problems."

"Oh?" I tried to look interested, which I was, just not for the reason Gladys thought I was.

"Don't move your eyebrows so much," Gladys said. "You've got to let this stuff set."

That made it sound suspiciously like concrete, but I tried not to move my lips as I asked, "Anything juicy?"

Gladys set a white plastic timer for fifteen minutes, and said, "Would you believe that she started seeing her second husband while her first husband was in Vietnam? She said that he was fooling around on her over there, so she didn't see any reason why she couldn't do the same."

"How did she know?"

"No more talking until the fifteen minutes are up."

I nodded.

"She said he got drunk when he was home on leave, and confessed the whole thing. Now I'd be mad, too, and maybe I'd leave him, but I wouldn't run out and have an affair." Gladys lowered her voice to a whisper. "She's not even sure which man was Joleen's father."

I wanted to ask more about the man in Vietnam, get his name or something, but there were two reasons I couldn't. For one, Gladys had asked me not to. For another, the facial had stiffened to the point where I wasn't sure if I could. Gladys proceeded to tell me a whole lot more about Dorinda that I really wanted to know.

Dorinda wasn't the only one who could talk the hind leg off of a mule.

Finally the fifteen minutes were up, and Gladys started to peel the stuff from my face. "Doesn't that feel wonderful?" she asked.

"Absolutely," I said. It certainly was a relief, because I had started to worry about it not coming off, meaning that I would probably make the wrong impression at Vasti's garden party.

"Now I'll go mix up the next part," Gladys said. "You stay right here."

The phone rang while she was gone, and Clara McDonald came hurrying up to answer it. Her hair was still brown, but I thought she had added some highlights. After she had taken down an appointment and hung up the phone, she saw me and said, "Hey there, Laurie Anne. I didn't realize that you were still here."

"Just trying out Gladys's new facial." I wanted to express my sympathy for the loss of her husband, but I wasn't sure how to word it. Instead I just said, "I meant to tell you the other day. That really is a beautiful ring."

She looked down at her diamond for a second, then said, "It means a lot to me. Ed gave it to me, you know." Then her eyes teared up, and she mumbled, "Excuse me. I've got to—" She walked quickly away without finishing the sentence.

Rats, rats, rats! I had managed to say the exact wrong thing.

"What's the matter?" Gladys said, as she returned with a bottle of bright blue liquid.

"Just sticking my foot in my mouth." I explained as Gladys used cotton balls to apply the blue stuff.

"Don't worry about it," she said. "When a woman is in mourning, there's no telling what will set her off."

That made me feel a little better, and we talked about other things while Gladys finished up with the facial.

By the time I had attained a peaches–and–cream complexion, I was starved. I had hoped to talk to Aunt Daphine over lunch, but Gladys asked if she could come along and another one of the beauticians joined us. I didn't even get to hear any more gossip, because we mostly talked about politics. The irony of it wasn't lost on me. When I still lived in Byerly, I always fussed that no one wanted to talk about serious issues. Now that I wanted to hear gossip, I got commentary on the deficit.

I looked for Dorinda when we got back, but Clara told Aunt Daphine that she had left for the day. "Female problems," Clara said, with no expression on her face. That led Gladys to remark that Dorinda must have twice as many periods as anybody else, because she went home early because of cramps every two weeks.

Her being gone killed my chance to look at her newspaper and confirm that she had been reading about Cooper, so I thought I might as well head back to Aunt Maggie's. That is, until Gladys suggested a pedicure. I decided another hour or so wouldn't hurt, but this time I insisted on clear polish.

After that, I called Richard to come pick me up.

Chapter 19

Once I climbed into the car beside Richard and gave him a kiss, and he complimented me on my hairstyle, he asked, "What insights did the ladies of Byerly share with you today?"

"I'll tell you as soon as I get to a newspaper. You've still got that copy of yesterday's *Gazette*, don't you?"

"Not with me, but it's at the house."

"Good. When we look at it, we should be able to confirm my theory."

"And that theory is?"

"That Dorinda is the blackmailer, just like I thought all along." I told him how Dorinda had acted when looking at the newspaper, and concluded with, "She must be involved."

"I don't quite see the connection," he said mildly. "Dorinda looking at the paper proves that she's a blackmailer?"

"Well . . ." It did sound foolish when he put it that way. "That's not all. Gladys told me that one of Dorinda's ex–husbands served in Vietnam, so that could tie him in with Uncle John Ward and Leonard Cooper."

He nodded amiably. "Do you know for sure that he

was in Vietnam at the same time as Uncle John Ward, and that they were in the same area?"

"No," I said reluctantly.

"Did you find out his name?"

"Gladys didn't know. But don't you think it fits? If Uncle John Ward told the ex–husband and Cooper, and the ex–husband told Dorinda, then Cooper and Dorinda could have been in on it together. Hey! Maybe Cooper was Dorinda's ex–husband." Then reality stepped in. "No, Junior would have picked up on that. Still . . ."

Richard wasn't saying anything.

"Just you wait until we get a look at the newspaper," I said. "That will prove it."

He nodded again.

"There's something else I figured out." I explained that Cooper and Small Bill must have looked alike. "Doesn't *that* seem odd to you?"

"That is definitely odd," he admitted. "If this were one of Shakespeare's plays, we could do a lot with mistaken identities, but I don't know how it fits in here. What do you think it means?"

"I don't know." My fanciful ideas about hidden enemies and arranged meetings were far too silly to talk about. Instead I changed the subject. "So what have you been doing?"

"I accompanied Aunt Maggie on her rounds for most of the day."

"Really?" I had never thought of Richard as the type to enjoy scrounging around thrift stores. "Did you find anything interesting?"

"I picked up a few books and such," he said vaguely. "Mostly I just carried things for her. She's still at it, but

I figured you might be ready to come back, so I had her drop me off."

We got to Aunt Maggie's then, and as I opened the car door, I had an awful thought. "Richard, you didn't go back to that store where Aunt Maggie got her sneakers, did you?"

"Well . . ."

I ran around to the other side of the car, and my fears were confirmed. Richard was wearing hot pink high tops with purple tiger stripes, just like the pair Aunt Maggie had worn to the reunion.

"Richard."

"They had been reduced to three dollars," he said defensively, "and they're very comfortable. They've even got arch supports."

I sighed. "You're not going to wear them to work, are you?"

"No," he said in shocked tones. "They'd get ruined in no time."

I thanked the Lord for small favors.

I let Richard hunt up the newspaper while I got us bottles of Coke. He brought it over to the kitchen table and spread it out, and we went through it page by page. Other than the article about Cooper, the stories were pretty tame, nothing that would have caught Dorinda's attention like that. Now I was convinced that Dorinda had been interested in Cooper.

"See?" I said. "That proves it."

"What exactly does it prove again?"

"That Dorinda is involved. Somehow," I said. "Look, I know it's pretty shaky, but we don't have anything else to go on."

"Okay," Richard said. "How do we go about proving Dorinda's guilt?"

I thought about it. "We need to get into her house. If she's been cutting up newspapers to put together blackmail letters, maybe she left the scraps laying around. And the letters said that she had proof that Aunt Daphine and Uncle John Ward weren't married. I bet I can find it if I get in there."

"No offense, but I do draw the line at breaking and entering. Being arrested would probably keep me from getting tenure."

"Maybe we could go visit her," I said, not very convincingly.

"Some sort of pretext would be required, don't you think?"

"You're probably right." I thought about it for a few minutes. "I've got it. Let's call in the cavalry."

"I assume you're speaking figuratively, and not literally."

"Actually, it is fairly literal. Having Aunt Nellie and Uncle Ruben try to sell you something is a lot like being trampled by a herd of horses." I reached for the telephone to call them.

Chapter 20

Aunt Nellie answered the phone on the first ring. "Hello?"

"Aunt Nellie? This is Laura."

"Hey there, Laurie Anne. How are y'all enjoying your visit?"

"We're having a good time," I said, which was partially true. We talked family for a few minutes and then I said, "Aunt Nellie, I need a favor."

"What's that?"

"Have you and Uncle Ruben tried to sell Dorinda Thompson one of your water filters?"

"Well, I asked her if we could come show her one, but she said she wasn't interested. She was pretty ugly about it, too, when a simple 'no' would have sufficed. Why do you ask?"

"I need to get into Dorinda's house."

"You do?"

"I was hoping that my going with you while you show her a water filter would do the trick, but if she's not interested . . ." I saw that Richard was waving a twenty–dollar bill at me and mouthing the word, "bribe." "Aunt Nellie, could you talk to Dorinda again? Tell her you'll give her twenty dollars if she'll let you demonstrate the filter."

"Laurie Anne, does this have something to do with Daphine's troubles?"

"Yes ma'am, it does." Sometimes I wonder why they even bother to print a newspaper in Byerly. News spreads faster than the ink can dry.

"Then I won't ask any more questions, but you can count on me and Ruben. Hang up, and I'll get Ruben to call Dorinda. I've got an idea that she'll be nicer to a man than she would be to a woman."

"Thanks, Aunt Nellie."

I told Richard what was going on, and a few minutes later, Aunt Nellie called back.

"Either Ruben's flirting or the twenty dollars did the trick," she said. "Dorinda said we could come over this evening. Is that all right?"

"Perfect."

"Good. We'll pick you up after dinner. Who knows? Maybe we'll sell her one of our filters while we're at it."

"Could be," I said, and we hung up again. Of course, I didn't give a darn about water filters, but I couldn't wait to get inside Dorinda's house so I could look around.

Aunt Nellie and Uncle Ruben picked me up at six that evening, and we talked out our plans on the way over. Richard wasn't too thrilled about being left behind, but like I told him, three of us showing up could be explained, not four. I did let him supply the bribe money so he wouldn't feel left out.

If Dorinda was Aunt Daphine's blackmailer, she certainly wasn't spending her ill-gotten gains on her house. I'd guess that it hadn't been painted since I was in junior high school, and the grass hadn't been mowed or the leaves raked in nearly that long. The door looked like a pack of wild dogs had been scratching to get in, and when we knocked, Dorinda took her own sweet time in answering it.

"Oh, it's you," she said with a complete lack of enthusiasm.

I wanted to remind her that we had an appointment, but we had already decided that Uncle Ruben would be our point man.

"Good evening, Mrs. Thompson," he said. "My, aren't you looking lovely this evening. May we come in?"

She opened the door, and moved out of the way for us to step inside.

"What a nice home you have," Uncle Ruben said, and I was awfully impressed by how sincere he sounded. Dorinda's furniture was like her clothing, gaudy and cheap, and her housekeeping was nearly as thorough as her yard work.

Dorinda took the one chair, a recliner that had seen better days, and waved us in the direction of the sagging, green couch.

"You've met our niece Laurie Anne, haven't you?" Uncle Ruben asked. "She's interested in marketing our product in the Boston area, and she wanted to sit in on the demonstration. I hope you don't mind."

"I guess it's all right. I heard that her husband was out of work for a good while."

I forced myself to smile and nod, and reminded myself again to explain to Vasti that a graduate fellowship *is* a job.

"How long is this going to take?" Dorinda wanted to know. "I've got things to do tonight."

Uncle Ruben said, "Oh, it doesn't take long to show you the benefits of What–a–Filter."

"When do I get the money?"

"After the demonstration," I said firmly. I wasn't about to pay her until I got my chance to look around.

Uncle Ruben opened a leather–look briefcase and pulled out a set of charts and close–up photos of water organisms. "Before we begin, are there any other family members at home? We think that clean water is something the whole family should be involved in."

Dorinda shook her head. "Joleen's out. You didn't tell me that she was supposed to be here. I still get the money, don't I?"

"Of course," Uncle Ruben assured her. The real reason he had asked was to make sure that I wouldn't run into anybody if I got a chance to search. "Now let me explain why *you* need a What–a–Filter."

I couldn't really blame Dorinda for being bored at the lecture that followed. I didn't find Uncle Ruben's recitation of the dangers of fluoridated water and foreign germs very compelling either, but I did try to look interested. Not Dorinda. She spent the whole time tapping her feet, drumming her fingers, inspecting her nails, and yawning.

Still, Uncle Ruben went steadfastly forward, with Aunt Nellie making the right noises in all the right places. They were a good team, and I decided that if they ever did latch onto a legitimate product, they would be able to make some real money.

After at least twenty minutes of spiel, Uncle Ruben concluded with, "Now, if you'll allow me, I'll attach one of our travel units to your kitchen faucet so you can taste the difference What–a–Filter makes."

Dorinda sighed loudly, but got up from her chair.

"All right, but I didn't know that you were going to want to go in there. I didn't straighten up."

"I'm sure it's fine," Uncle Ruben said, and I couldn't imagine that it could be any worse than the living room. "Nellie, why don't you and Laurie Anne wait in here?"

"Well, if you think that will be better," Aunt Nellie said doubtfully, with just a slight quaver of the lower lip. If I hadn't heard them plan that maneuver in the car, I would have been convinced that Uncle Ruben wanted some time alone with Dorinda for a quick squeeze.

Certainly Dorinda was fooled. She smirked, and allowed Uncle Ruben to take her elbow as they went into the kitchen. Aunt Nellie winked at me as soon as they were gone.

Now was my chance. There wasn't much furniture in the living room, and I looked inside the drawers of the end tables while keeping up a meaningless dialog with Aunt Nellie. Actually, Aunt Nellie did most of the talking while I added yes's and no's as appropriate.

There was nothing incriminating in the living room, and only a coat rack in the front hall. I nodded at Aunt Nellie, who obligingly dropped her pocketbook to mask any noise as I opened the hall closet. There were only a few coats in there, no boxes or papers.

Aunt Nellie continued to talk to herself as I stepped quietly toward the back of the house. I wasn't sure which to be more grateful for: that I had thought to wear sneakers or that the house only had one story.

The first door I came to was another closet, this one half filled with linens. Unless Dorinda had folded something into a towel or sheet, I figured the closet was clean. Not literally, of course. I ran my hands along the undersides of the shelves in case she had taped something there, and confirmed that Dorinda didn't waste her time dusting.

The next door was the bathroom. There was nothing of interest in the medicine chest, and the true confession magazines stacked on the back of the toilet had all of their pages intact, meaning that they hadn't provided raw material for blackmail letters.

I could have quit right there for all the good searching the rest of the house did. I learned that both Dorinda and Joleen had lots of clothes and very few books, the exact opposite of Richard's and my apartment; found more eyeshadow and lipstick than I expected to need for the rest of my life; and quickly lost count of the bottles of perfume.

I never did find any of those drawers of insurance policies and tax records that most people keep, and decided that Dorinda either kept them in the kitchen or threw them out.

I was to the point of starting to search Dorinda's trash can when I heard Aunt Nellie call out, "Mrs. Thompson? Somebody's pulling into your driveway. Are you expecting company?"

I turned out the light in Dorinda's bedroom, decided I didn't have time to make it back to the living room, and ducked into the bathroom instead. As the front door opened, I flushed the toilet and walked out the bathroom door.

Joleen had just come in, looking a little worse for the wear. Her coat wasn't buttoned at all, and her blouse only had half the buttons fastened. I think I saw her bra hanging out of her coat pocket.

"Mama!" she yelled, and then caught sight of me. "What are you doing here?"

I smiled sweetly. "Hi Joleen. Didn't your mother tell

you that we were going to be demonstrating a water filter tonight?"

"Back there?" she asked suspiciously.

"Of course not," I said, squeezing by her to get back into the living room. "I had to use the bathroom." She watched me the whole time as I went to sit back down by Aunt Nellie.

Dorinda and Uncle Ruben emerged from the kitchen, with his arm firmly tucked into hers. Dorinda made a big show of disengaging, implying all kinds of things about what had been going on in the kitchen. "Hey Joleen," Dorinda said. "I wasn't expecting you back so early."

"That's what my date said about his wife," Joleen said, but I guess she realized that that hadn't been the right thing to say in front of Thaddeous's aunt, uncle, and cousin. "I mean, her husband. We were going to go shopping, but he got out of work early and she had to fix him dinner."

It wasn't even a good lie. Poor Thaddeous.

"Well Mrs. Thompson, what did you think about the What–a–Filter?" Aunt Nellie asked.

"I just can't decide," Dorinda said. "Why don't you let me think about it for a while?" She looked directly at Uncle Ruben. "I might need Ruben to come demonstrate some more."

"That would be fine," Uncle Ruben said as he packed up his charts and the filter. "We do appreciate your time, and here's the gift we promised you." He pulled Richard's money out of his wallet and presented it to her.

She took it from him, making sure to stroke his hand in the process.

"You be sure and call if there's any other questions I can answer, Mrs. Thompson," Uncle Ruben said.

"I'll just do that," Dorinda said with a knowing look. "And why don't you call me Dorinda?"

"We need to be getting to our next appointment now," Aunt Nellie said frostily. She tugged at Uncle Ruben's elbow, and said, "Come on Ruben."

Uncle Ruben smiled once more at Dorinda, and then we let ourselves out.

Aunt Nellie's indignation was so realistic that I halfway expected her to start snarling at Uncle Ruben on the way home. Instead the two of them burst out laughing as soon as we were out of Dorinda's driveway.

"Did you ever in your whole life see anybody so obvious?" Aunt Nellie said.

" 'Why don't you call me Dorinda?' " Uncle Ruben said in a fair imitation of Dorinda. "I swear that woman must believe what happens in soap operas. As soon as we got into the kitchen, she was hanging onto me so bad I couldn't hardly get the filter installed."

"She was even worse than Mrs. Shannon. At least Mrs. Shannon wasn't making cow eyes at you with me right there in the room."

"You mean this kind of thing has happened before?" I asked.

"All the time," Aunt Nellie said.

"Usually not this bad," Uncle Ruben said, "but a lot of women are more likely to buy something if you flirt with them. No harm in a little flirting, is there? The woman feels good, and we sell a filter." He shrugged.

Aunt Nellie patted his knee and said, "My Ruben just doesn't know his own charm. But enough of that. Did you find what you were looking for, Laurie Anne?"

"Not really," I had to admit. "Of course I couldn't

173

search the whole house, but I didn't find what I wanted to find." That was as specific as I could get, but they didn't seem to mind.

As they were dropping me back at Aunt Maggie's, Aunt Nellie said, "Now if you need any more help, you be sure and call. You hear?"

"I will. Thank you."

Richard had a book open when I found him in the bedroom, but he was clearly waiting for me. "Well?"

I shrugged. "I'm just not sure. I didn't find anything, but there were plenty of places I didn't get a chance to look." I gave a quick rundown of the evening's visit, and concluded with, "Dorinda could still be the one."

Richard raised one eyebrow. "Are you sure you're not just focusing on her because you don't like her?"

"Do you expect me to pick on somebody I do like?"

"No, but you can't let your dislike blind you to other possibilities. Face it: we didn't really have a good reason to suspect Dorinda in the first place."

I thought about it, and had to admit that he was right. There was nothing to connect Dorinda with Uncle John Ward other than an ex–husband who may or may not have known him. She wasn't showing any signs of spending inordinate amounts of money, and she had no particular reason to dislike Aunt Daphine. "There's still the funny way she acted when she saw the newspaper today."

He didn't say anything.

"All right, I concede," I said. "Dorinda is hereby removed as a suspect, unless we learn something new. So what do you suggest as our next move?"

He put down his book, closed the bedroom door, and grinned. After all, I told myself once again, we were still on vacation.

Chapter 21

I'm afraid the next couple of days were a bust as far as detective work went. Richard and I were barely through breakfast on Friday when Vasti called, even more frantic than usual. Somebody or another was sick, and somebody else had a death in the family, and Vasti recited the excuses of several other somebodies so quickly that I never did get them straight. The upshot of it was that she needed me and Richard to help her put together her garden party.

Since we really didn't have any specific plans, I just couldn't refuse her in her hour of need. I regretted it later on, of course, after hours of running around to the caterer, the florist, and several rental places to pick up stuff for the party. Vasti stayed busy, too, coming up with more stuff for us to do. Every time we got somewhere to pick something up, there was a message waiting with another chore.

By the end of the day, we were tired of doing things for my family, so we went to a movie to hide. Unfortunately, that only saved us for the evening. By the time we got back to Aunt Maggie's, there was a note waiting with more jobs to do the next morning. So most of Saturday was shot, too.

Still, despite all of the work we did for Vasti, the hardest thing I had to do that weekend was to talk Richard into putting on his suit for a second time on his vacation. He finally acceded, but kept mumbling about the "cunning livery of hell."

He did cheer up when he saw me in my new dress, with my hair all fixed and my nails painted. For once, I didn't mind him quoting Shakespeare to me. Though I wasn't sure that I was likely to be mistaken for the sun or if the moon would be envious of my beauty, I was certainly willing to let him think so.

One of the myriad tasks Vasti had asked me to perform was to check and see what Aunt Maggie was going to be wearing to the party. She was afraid that Aunt Maggie would show up in those tiger–striped sneakers, of course. Unfortunately, when I asked Aunt Maggie, she just grinned and told me to tell Vasti not to worry. For some reason, this did not reassure Vasti. I was hoping that Aunt Maggie would be ready before Richard and I left, but she was still getting dressed and yelled through the closed door that we should go ahead and she'd catch up later. So we drove ourselves to the party.

As we drove down the curving driveway to the Walters's house, I couldn't help but admire the place. Though it was actually built considerably after the Civil War, to look at the columns and the veranda, you'd have thought that General Lee himself used to come calling.

After Big Bill's wife died, Burt and his wife Dorcas had moved in with him, and Dorcas did love being the lady of the manor. She was standing at the front door to receive her guests, dressed in a royal blue silk dress and a simple string of pearls that was obviously real. Dorcas was letting her hair go gracefully grey but kept her figure intact, either by diet or by exercise or by main force of will.

When I expressed my admiration for the house, Dorcas had a maid give us a brief tour before firmly escorting us out onto the grounds. It wasn't the Biltmore House, but it was pretty darned impressive.

So was the garden party. After all was said and done, Vasti had done a wonderful job. She had scattered tables of food and drinks all over the lawn so that there was never a wait for anything. Roger Bailey and his band were playing by the lily pond, with Aunt Ruby Lee watching proudly, but there were plenty of quieter places for people to go and talk. I wasn't convinced that it was what the English would call a garden party, but it was perfect for a fall evening in Byerly.

Most of the Burnettes were there. I saw Thaddeous go by with Joleen, who was dressed a little more appropriately this time, and chatted with them for a few minutes. Joleen glared at me the whole time, as if daring me to mention her date on Thursday evening, but I didn't say a word. Thaddeous was a grown man, and he could sort out his own love life.

The triplets were there, wearing matching dresses as usual and eyeing the available men speculatively. Someday the three of them were going to stage themselves a triple wedding, and it was going to be a sight to behold. The problem wasn't going to be finding men, because they dated a fair amount. The problem was finding three at the same time.

Richard and I went our separate ways soon after we arrived. Though he enjoys parties once in a while, this one was a little large for his taste, and he didn't know everybody the way I did. After a while, he got tired of being introduced, explaining what he did for a living, and learning how it was that I knew the person to whom he was being introduced. I suspected that he was going to find a quiet corner and pull out the paperback copy of *The Tempest* I had seen him tuck into his suit pocket, but I didn't mind. I'd wait until a little later before getting him to dance with me.

The food was wonderful, which didn't surprise me. I had sampled quite a bit when picking it up. Still, I had somehow missed some of the best stuff and I was munching happily on a miniature country ham biscuit when Vasti appeared at my elbow. "Great party, Vasti," I said.

"Have you seen Aunt Maggie?"

"Not yet."

"Go find her for me."

"Why?"

"I have to find out what she's wearing. If she's got those horrible sneakers on, I've got to make sure that Dorcas Walters doesn't see her. Dorcas will pitch a fortified fit if she sees her in those shoes."

I turned and looked around. "Isn't that Aunt Maggie heading for Mrs. Walters right now? And isn't that Big Bill Walters standing there with Mrs. Walters?"

"Oh Lord! Come on!"

Since she yanked my arm nearly out of its socket, making me drop the country ham out of my biscuit, I had no choice but to follow. Vasti was aiming at the area between Aunt Maggie and Mrs. Walters, presumably intending to use her own body as a shield to keep them separated. If she hadn't been so intent, she might have noticed what Aunt Maggie was wearing.

Vasti reached her vantage point, turned her back toward Aunt Maggie, and pulled me beside her. I guessed I was part of the shield.

"Mrs. Walters," Vasti gushed. "Didn't I see your husband looking for you over by the band?"

"Oh, he'll find me if he wants me," Mrs. Walters said carelessly. "Big Bill and I were just saying how nice you've arranged everything."

"Mighty nice," Big Bill said, peering over our two heads, despite Vasti's attempt to stand taller. "Isn't that Maggie Burnette?"

"Where?" Vasti asked, but she was fighting a losing battle. Aunt Maggie was coming right toward us.

"Good evening, Miss Burnette," Big Bill said, and he even bowed and took off his hat to sweep the air. "You're looking particularly fetching this evening."

Vasti stiffened, and I knew she was wondering which sarcastic comment Aunt Maggie would spout.

Instead Aunt Maggie smiled widely, and said "Mr. Walters why don't all men talk like you do?"

"Perhaps they just don't know how to treat a lady like you."

"I bet they don't. Excuse me, Vasti, Laurie Anne." She stepped between us and said, "I had to come tell Dorcas what a lovely party this is."

"Thank you, Miss Burnette, but actually your niece Vasti did most of the work," Mrs. Walters said.

"Is that right?" Aunt Maggie said, as if she hadn't known. "Vasti, where do you find the time?"

Vasti didn't answer. She was looking at Aunt Maggie, having finally noticed she wasn't wearing jeans or a T-shirt. Instead, she had on a very nice blue gingham dress with a white lace collar and a flared skirt. Her shoes were light blue flats, not the hot pink and purple sneakers that had been giving Vasti nightmares.

Oddly enough, Big Bill seemed to be staring at Aunt Maggie's outfit, too.

"Excuse me, Miss Burnette. That dress of yours—"

"Do you like it?" Aunt Maggie asked, twirling a bit and sounding more like a Southern belle than I had ever heard her sound. "I've had it for years."

"The fabric . . ." He reached out, and it was clear that he wanted to touch the cloth. He was too polite to actually do it, but he did bend over to get a closer look. "It is! It's Walters gingham!"

Aunt Maggie nodded with a smile. "It certainly is."

How he knew, I will never figure out. Once I thought about it, I could tell that it matched that bolt of gingham locked up in a glass case at the mill, but it still just looked like plain old gingham to me. The mill only made socks and towels these days, nothing as fine as gingham.

"Where on earth did you find it?" Mr. Walters asked.

"It was my mother's. You Walters may have the first bolt of cloth from the mill, but we Burnettes had a good piece of the second. Mama made this dress herself, and of course I kept it."

"Remarkable," he said.

"I don't wear it often," Aunt Maggie confided. "But I thought that today warranted it. What with Arthur planning to speak and all. I think that he'll make a fine city councilor, don't you? Just what Byerly needs."

"I must say that I admire his taste in supporters. May I get you something to drink, Miss Burnette?" He offered her his arm, and Aunt Maggie delicately took it.

"I'd be honored," she said. "You know, you really

should call me by my first name. We're not on opposite sides of a picket line anymore."

"Maggie, then. And I hope you'll call me Bill. Excuse us, ladies." They ambled away, but Aunt Maggie managed to catch my eye long enough to wink.

Dorcas said something polite and went away, too. I don't think Vasti even saw her go.

"I don't believe it," Vasti said. "I just don't believe it." She repeated it a few more times, and might have still been at it if Hank Parker hadn't shown up right then, camera in hand. Some sixth sense prompted Vasti to transform her expression of disbelief into a gracious smile before Hank snapped the picture, and I heard Hank mutter something unhappy under his breath.

"Well, Hank Parker," Vasti said in honeyed tones. "I'm so glad you made it. Are you having a good time?"

Aunt Nora always said that it was a good thing that Byerly had a newspaper for Hank Parker to work at, because otherwise he'd have no way to support himself by being nosy. He wore that same straw hat all year long because it gave him a place to put his press pass.

Hank smiled genially, and said, "A very nice spread, Mrs. Bumgarner, very nice indeed." Then he jerked his head around in that dramatic way that warned that a searching question was coming, and barked, "Can you tell me how your husband's campaign can afford this kind of luxury?"

Of course Vasti had seen him jerk his head, so she was ready for him. "Hank, you know that this party isn't a political event. It's for charity, to help poor little orphans." Vasti must have finally found out what cause she was raising funds for.

"But isn't it true that your husband is going to give a speech in a few minutes?"

"Oh, it's not really a speech. He just wants to recognize Dorcas Walters and the other ladies on her committee for their dedication."

He nodded amiably again, which meant he was working on another question. He turned his gaze toward me. "Mrs. Fleming, how nice to see you back in town. I've enjoyed the opportunities to speak with your husband. Are y'all having a nice visit?"

"Very nice, thank you."

I never did find out what he was planning to ask me about, because he was only halfway through the head jerk when Burt Walters strolled by. "Mr. Walters," Hank called out, "would you join us for a moment?"

Burt Walters always tried to be as dapper as his father, but he just didn't have the style to carry it off. Somehow he always looked overdressed, and his hair dye, though impeccably applied, just didn't convince anybody.

"Hello there, Hank," he said. "Vasti, Laurie Anne. Don't y'all look pretty this evening. Vasti, you've done a wonderful job putting this party together. Dorcas has just been raving about it." Vasti tried to look modest, and Walters winked at Hank. "Feel free to quote me on that."

"Could I get a shot of you with the ladies, Mr. Walters?" Hank asked.

"Certainly, if the ladies don't mind."

Vasti managed to look both surprised and delighted at the request, which she had no doubt been hoping for. Mr. Walters stood between us with his arm around our shoulders, and we all smiled for Hank to take a picture.

"Just another couple of shots, if you don't mind," Hank said, and we kept smiling. Then I caught the hint of a head jerk from behind the camera, and Hank said,

"Mr. Walters, can you explain how Leonard Cooper looked so much like your father?"

I could only guess at the expression on Walters's face when Hank quickly snapped several pictures.

Walters let his arms drop from Vasti's and my shoulders. "I told you before, Parker, I didn't know that man and I don't know why he was at the mill. I hardly think that now is the time to be asking about such a thing."

"But isn't it true that you were expected at the mill that day?"

"That's enough!" Walters said. "I've said all that I'm going to say." He stomped off.

Hank grinned, tipped his hat to us, and said, "Ladies. Thank you for your time."

As soon as he was gone, Vasti fumed, "Of all the nerve, asking questions like that at a party."

"He is a reporter. He's supposed to ask questions," I reminded her. "Besides, you know he's not going to print the picture of Mr. Walters looking furious. He never does. He only takes that kind of picture because he can."

Vasti made a few more indignant noises, then spotted someone she thought might be important to talk to and headed away again.

I decided that it had been too long since I had seen my husband, and tracked him down sitting in a corner of the veranda. He shoved his book back into his pocket as soon as he saw me and tried to look innocent.

"Having a good time?" he asked.

"Pretty good. Something interesting just happened." I told him about the encounter with Hank Parker and Burt Walters.

"That was a dirty trick," Richard said.

I shrugged it off. "Hank always pulls that. Aunt Nora

183

thinks he must have seen it in a movie or something. I'm just surprised that Burt got so angry."

"You think he doth protest too much?"

"Something like that. Hank did remind me of something. Do you remember what Ralph said about Burt Walters calling to say he was coming over? It's a funny coincidence that he planned to come to the mill on the very day a man got murdered there, and a man who probably knew his brother at that. I don't know that Burt has ever come to the mill on a Sunday before."

"But Walters never made it to the mill. Or rather, he made it, but only after Junior called him."

"True," I acknowledged, "but it still sounds suspicious to me. Byerly gossip considers him a strong possibility."

"What about motive?"

"Suppose Cooper killed Small Bill so Burt could get his share of the mill, and was now blackmailing Burt as well as Aunt Daphine. Then Burt killed him to keep from having to pay more."

"It sounds a little farfetched," Richard said, which was putting it pretty mildly.

"It sounds pretty farfetched to me, too, but I swear Burt is lying about *something.*"

"I think you just don't like him."

"I guess it's reflex. No one is supposed to like the mill owners."

"Is that why you couldn't wait for a chance to come to their house?"

"Call it a love–hate relationship. So much of the town is dependent on the mill, and we're grateful for the work, but then we resent that we are so dependent. Kind of a Shakespearean irony, don't you think?"

He looked doubtful, but nodded anyway.

I said, "I think I'll go mingle some more. Want to come?"

"No thanks. I think I'll just enjoy the ambiance from here."

I gave him a quick kiss, started to go, then turned and said, "Enjoy your book."

Richard only grinned in response.

I chatted with more friends and family members, even to Linwood when I ran into him by the drink table. He was as polite as he ever was, probably because he must have realized that I hadn't told anyone about Sue working. It would have been all over Byerly by then if I had.

I was about ready for a rest when I came across Aunt Daphine alone at a table. She looked very nice, much better than she had at the family reunion, and I told her so.

"Thank you," she said. "How are you doing?"

"Pretty good. Vasti throws a nice party."

Aunt Daphine nodded, looked around to see if anybody else was within earshot, and then said, "How are *things* going?"

I had been afraid that she would ask that. "I wish I could tell you something more, but so far Richard and I haven't found out much." My ideas about Dorinda and Cooper and Burt Walters were way too tenuous to mention to her.

"That's all right," she said, patting my leg. "I know y'all are going to come through for me."

I just smiled, hoping that she was right.

Mrs. Walters's maid Charlene came over to us about then. "Mrs. Marston? You've got a telephone call," Charlene said.

"Here?" Aunt Daphine said. "Did they say who it is?"

"Yes, ma'am. It's Chief Norton."

Aunt Daphine went pale.

"Thank you, Charlene," I said. "We'll be right there."

"Junior's found out," Aunt Daphine said in a harsh whisper, her earlier confidence gone. "It's going to come out, Laurie Anne, and Vasti is never going to forgive me."

"Stop that!" I snapped. "It might be nothing at all." I started pulling her toward the house. "The only way to find out is to ask."

"You talk to her, Laurie Anne. I just can't think right now."

Charlene led us into a room I think was the parlor, and I picked up the phone. "Junior? This is Laura Fleming. Aunt Daphine can't talk at the moment. Is there anything I can do?"

"Is Mrs. Marston there at the party?" Junior asked, sounding oddly formal.

"Yes, she is."

"How long has she been there?"

"I believe she got here early this morning to help Vasti out," I said, and Aunt Daphine nodded in confirmation.

"And she hasn't left there since that time?"

"No, she's been here all day," I said. Aunt Daphine nodded again, looking confused. "Junior, what's all this about?"

"Well, we've got us a situation down at your aunt's beauty parlor."

"What kind of situation? Did someone break in? There hasn't been a fire, has there?"

"No, nothing like that. We got a report that some-body heard a gunshot in this area a little while ago, and saw the lights on in your aunt's place. When we went inside, we found Dorinda Thompson laying on the floor."

"Is she all right?"

"She's dead, Laurie Anne. I'm sorry to interrupt the party, but I need Mrs. Marston down here right away."

"We're on our way," I said, and hung up the phone.

Chapter 22

We left as soon as I told Aunt Daphine what was going on. Richard wasn't on the veranda anymore and I didn't have any idea of where he was, so I gave Charlene a note to pass on to him. In it, I told Richard what had happened, and deputized him to come up with an excuse for Aunt Daphine's and my disappearance that wouldn't worry anybody.

An ambulance was just pulling away from the curb when we got to La Dauphin, which was fine with me. After finding Cooper at the mill, I had had my fill of dead bodies for a while. I guessed that the town's best gossips were still at Vasti's party, because only a couple of people were hanging around and trying to get a look inside. Junior's deputy Mark Pope was standing outside the door to keep them out, but he let Aunt Daphine and me into the shop.

Junior or one of the other police officers milling around had drawn the customary outline around where Dorinda's body had been found, in the main room out of sight of the door. The floor of La Dauphin was often covered in hair clippings and rolling papers, but this was the first time that I had seen blood staining the linoleum.

Junior was looking through a drawer of hair pins and brushes, but when she saw us, she stopped and led us to the back room where Aunt Daphine stores supplies and keeps her desk.

I kept a firm hand on Aunt Daphine's elbow. She hadn't regained any of her color, and I was afraid she was going to faint. Junior pulled over a stool, and waved Aunt Daphine to the desk chair. "I appreciate your bringing Mrs. Marston over, Laurie Anne," she said. "You can wait out front. Just stay out of the other officers' way."

"I'll stay with Aunt Daphine, if you don't mind."

"Actually, I do mind. I'd like to talk to Mrs. Marston alone."

Normally I would have done as Junior asked, but not today. Aunt Daphine needed me. I asked, "Is she under arrest?"

"No."

"Then I'm staying here. Unless Aunt Daphine wants me to go, that is."

"I'd like Laurie Anne to stay," Aunt Daphine said.

That settled it as far as I was concerned, and I pulled over a stool for myself. Junior looked grim, but she didn't argue the point any further, just pulled out a notebook and a ballpoint pen.

"Mrs. Marston," Junior began, "I imagine that Laurie Anne has already told you that we found Dorinda Thompson here. She had been shot." She consulted her watch. "We found her just over an hour ago, and she hadn't been dead for long. Can you tell me what Ms. Thompson might have been doing here this evening?"

"I don't know," Aunt Daphine said. "The shop closed at five."

"Are you sure? I thought that you weren't here today."

"I wasn't, because I was helping Vasti get her party together, but I did call just before closing time to make sure that everything was all right."

"Did you speak to Ms. Thompson then?"

"No, Gladys said she had left a little early. Dorinda's bad about that. I mean, she was bad . . . I mean . . . I guess it doesn't make any difference now."

I handed Aunt Daphine a tissue from my pocketbook so she could wipe her eyes, and willed Junior to get this over with.

"Do you suppose it might have been robbery?" Aunt Daphine asked, almost hopefully. "Maybe Dorinda came to get something she forgot and caught a burglar in the act and he shot her."

"We thought of that, but your cash register hasn't been disturbed. In fact, as far as we can tell, nothing at all has been disturbed. Did Ms. Thompson have a key to the shop?"

Aunt Daphine nodded. "All of the women who work here have keys, because we take turns opening up in the morning."

"So Ms. Thompson could have let herself in, and then let her killer in."

"She must have," Aunt Daphine said. "Unless . . ." I wouldn't have thought it possible, but she went even more pale. "You don't think that it was one of us that shot her, do you?"

Junior said calmly, "I'm just trying to work out the circumstances." She asked Aunt Daphine a lot more questions, mostly about what kind of person Dorinda had been and whether anyone had disliked her. I could tell from the way Aunt Daphine answered that she felt uncomfortable speaking ill of the dead, but I could also tell from the questions that Junior already knew quite a bit about Dorinda.

Finally Junior said, "I think that's all I need for now, but I may need you to sign a statement later on." She looked at me. "Now I'd like to talk to Laurie Anne for a few minutes. Alone, if that's possible this time."

"You go on, Aunt Daphine," I said. "I'll be along in a minute."

As soon as Aunt Daphine was gone, Junior took her place in the chair and leaned back. "Laurie Anne, if somebody had asked me yesterday whether or not I could trust you, I would have told him that you were as truthful as they come."

I squirmed a little but didn't say anything.

Junior went on. "What was it, Wednesday when we had our talk? You said that you were checking into something or another, but swore up and down that it didn't have anything to do with Leonard Cooper's murder, that you were just trying to help your aunt with a problem. Now a woman has been shot in that aunt's shop, and I just have a hunch that she was shot with the same gun. Now I'm asking you again. Do you know anything about Leonard Cooper's murder?"

I thought for a minute. Was there *anything* I tell Junior without betraying Aunt Daphine? "Junior, when I spoke to you before," I said slowly, "I honestly did not think that what I was doing had anything to do with Leonard Cooper. Now I just don't know. I did think for a while that Dorinda Thompson might have something to do with Aunt Daphine's problem, but it doesn't look like she did now." I wondered if Junior had found out about my visit to Dorinda's house, and decided that if she didn't know yet, she would soon. "I even went over to her house Thursday evening with Aunt Nellie and Uncle Ruben, and while they were showing her their water filter, I looked around."

"Not strictly breaking and entering," Junior said. "Should I alert our people that you might have left fingerprints?"

I nodded unhappily.

"And did you find anything to connect Mrs. Thompson with your aunt's problem?"

I shook my head. "Not a thing."

"I'll be looking over there myself later on, but did you see anything to connect Mrs. Thompson with Leonard Cooper?"

"Junior you know darned well that I would have told you if I had."

"That's what I would have thought before Mrs. Thompson was killed."

"Junior . . ." I started, but then stopped. What was the use? She wouldn't believe me now, and I couldn't blame her. "I'm sure you'll figure it all out."

"I appreciate your confidence," she said dryly. "I guess that's all I need for now. You and your husband will be in Byerly for a few more days, won't you?"

"We won't leave town without letting you know," I said.

She nodded and I went back into the main room. Aunt Daphine looked concerned when she saw me, but I just said, "Shall we go back to the party?"

During the drive back to the Walters's house, I was trying so hard to figure out why someone had killed Dorinda that I didn't hear what Aunt Daphine said the first go round. "I'm sorry," I said. "What did you say?"

"I said that maybe I ought to tell Junior what's going on after all."

"Not now!" I said. A few days ago I would have been tickled to death if Aunt Daphine had offered to go to Junior, but not anymore.

"But I have to tell Junior now that Dorinda is dead," she insisted. "There must be some connection."

"That's why we can't tell her. Don't you see? Leonard Cooper knew Uncle John Ward and he might have known that you and he weren't married, which means that he could have been your blackmailer. That makes *you* a prime suspect in his murder."

"Laurie Anne, you know that I didn't kill anybody."

"Of course I know that, but it would look awfully suspicious."

"But I got that note telling me to bring more money after Cooper died."

"He could have been working with Dorinda, and maybe they had a falling out. Maybe she wanted to ask for more money, and that's just what she did once he was out of the way."

"Then who killed her?"

"Junior would think that it was you."

"How could I have? I was at the Walters's house all day."

"Could you have snuck out during the party?"

"I suppose I could have, but Junior knows me too well to think that I would kill somebody."

"Are you willing to stake your secret on that? If she takes you in for questioning, the blackmailer will almost certainly find out and then talk to the newspaper. That would kill Arthur's chances of being elected, if your being questioned didn't do it first."

She looked doubtful.

"Look, Aunt Daphine, it's Friday. The election is the Tuesday after next. If we don't find out something by then, we can go to Junior and tell her without it affecting the election."

"All right," she said, but she didn't look happy. I wasn't real happy about the situation, either, but I just didn't know what else to do.

Chapter 23

The party was still going strong when we got back to the Walters's house, but neither Aunt Daphine nor I were in any mood to enjoy it. I left her in the car and went to find Richard. He was back in his corner on the veranda.

I tapped him on the shoulder. "Hey there."

He stood to give me a quick hug, and said, "Are you all right?"

I nodded. "I take it you got my note."

"Vasti saw me receive it, and it took no small effort to convince her that it was from you and not from an admirer."

"Aren't I an admirer?"

"I stand corrected." He lowered his voice. "Is Dorinda really dead?"

I nodded. "Someone shot her at La Dauphin. You didn't tell Vasti why we left, did you?"

"I thought it best not to. I just told her that Aunt Daphine wasn't feeling well."

"That's true enough. She's pretty upset, and I think we ought to take her home."

"Shall I make our regrets to our hostess?"

I looked around but didn't see Vasti. "We probably should, but I don't want to bother her. Let's just go. Vasti will hear the news soon enough."

We were on our way back to the car when Richard said, "Are you sure Aunt Daphine should be alone tonight?"

"I didn't even think of that. The phone is going to be ringing off the hook as soon as people find out what happened, and she doesn't need that. Maybe we can talk her into staying at Aunt Maggie's."

When we got back to the car, Aunt Daphine's eyes were red and I knew that she had been crying, but I didn't want to embarrass her by mentioning it. Instead I said, "As late as it is, why don't you just come back with us to Aunt Maggie's? She won't mind, and it's closer than your place."

It wasn't really that late, and it was maybe five minutes further to Aunt Daphine's place, so I imagine she knew what my real reasons were, but all she said was, "That would be nice. I am tired."

As if by unspoken agreement, we avoided talking about Dorinda or blackmail or anything like it on the way to Aunt Maggie's. Instead we talked about Vasti's party, agreeing that it had been a success.

"We better keep it quiet when we get to Aunt Maggie's," I said as we approached the house. "With the flea market tomorrow, she's probably already gone to bed."

That showed how much I knew. Not only was Aunt Maggie not asleep, she wasn't even home yet. She didn't make it in until long after Richard and I had installed Aunt Daphine in a spare bedroom, and had gone to bed ourselves.

Richard fell asleep right away, but I was trying to stay

awake long enough to warn Aunt Maggie about Aunt Daphine being in the house. Despite my good intentions, I had dozed off half a dozen times when I heard voices from downstairs, and crawled out of bed to peer out the door. Aunt Maggie was tip–toeing up the stairs with the cutest grin on her face.

"Did I wake you?" she asked when she saw me.

"Not exactly. Did you hear about Dorinda Thompson?"

She nodded. "Some folks were talking about it down at The Mustang Club."

"The Mustang Club? I thought you were at Vasti's party."

"That broke up hours ago, but Big Bill and I weren't ready to call it a night yet. That man sure can dance."

I was distracted for a moment by the idea of Aunt Maggie and Big Bill cutting a rug together, but then remembered why I had stayed awake. "Aunt Daphine was pretty worked up about Dorinda, so we brought her back here. I hope you don't mind."

"Of course not," she assured me. "It must have been terrible for her." She looked at me sharply. "Laurie Anne, don't you forget what I said. If you need my help, you just holler. Otherwise, I'll just mind my own business." She looked at her watch. "Good Lord, it's after two. I better get some sleep or I'm never going to make it to the flea market."

"You're not still going, are you?"

"Of course I am. My regular customers will be looking for me. Besides," she added with that same cute grin, "Big Bill is going to come by and let me show him around. Would you believe that he has never been to the flea market?" She was shaking her head in amazement as she went to her room.

I was pretty amazed myself, but for different reasons. I was trying to decide whether or not I would like having Big Bill Walters as a great–uncle when I slipped back into bed beside Richard.

I never knew whether or not Aunt Maggie made it to the flea market on time the next morning, because Richard and I slept later than we had intended. I'd have slept even longer if I hadn't heard the phone ring. I stubbed my toe twice on the way to the kitchen, and was not feeling happy when I answered it.

"Hello?"

"Laurie Anne?" I heard Vasti's unmistakable voice say. "Is Mama there?"

"Yes, she is. Is something wrong?"

"Something wrong? A woman dies in my own mother's place of business, and I have to hear it from the neighbors. Then when I want to talk to her, I can't find hide nor hair of her? Does that sound like there's something wrong?"

"Good Lord, Vasti, I'm sorry. We didn't tell you last night because we didn't want to spoil your party, and we brought Aunt Daphine over here because we didn't want to leave her alone. I should have called to let you know, but I just didn't think of it."

"Well," she said, sounding somewhat mollified. "As long as she's all right."

"She's still asleep as far as I know," I said, but then I saw Aunt Daphine behind me, wrapped in one of Aunt Maggie's bathrobes. I mouthed, "Vasti," and she reached for the phone. "Here she is now, Vasti."

I left her talking, and went to check on Richard. He looked cuddly as all get out, and it wasn't easy to resist the temptation to climb back into bed with him, but I knew that once Vasti knew where Aunt Daphine was, the other Burnettes would soon find out and the rest of Byerly wouldn't be far behind.

"Richard?" I said. "Time to get up."

He mumbled something Shakespearean.

"Come on."

More mumbles.

"Tell you what. I'll go shower, but you have to be up by the time I get up."

I think that the next mumble was affirmative.

Aunt Daphine was still talking to, or rather listening to, Vasti when I went into the bathroom, and I wouldn't have been surprised if she had still been on the phone when I got out of the shower. Instead, I found her and Richard in the kitchen scrambling in the refrigerator.

"What are you two doing?"

"Looking for something for breakfast," Aunt Daphine asked. "I know Aunt Maggie doesn't like to cook, but I thought she'd at least have a carton of eggs."

"I can run up to Hardee's and get us some biscuits," I offered.

"I don't know about you," Aunt Daphine said, "but I'm in the mood for a real breakfast, and a little old biscuit just isn't going to do it. Why don't you go to the store and get some eggs and bacon for me to fix?"

I started to suggest going out for breakfast, but then I realized that the last thing Aunt Daphine needed was to be around people who had heard about Dorinda. And besides, it might be better for her to keep busy. "You make a list," I said, "and I'll go get my pocket-book."

Forty-five minutes later, Aunt Daphine was happily frying bacon while Richard whipped eggs and I grated cheese for omelettes. When Aunt Daphine got an urge to cook breakfast, she did it right.

Like last night, I think we were all reluctant to discuss what was really on our minds. Murder and blackmail just didn't seem like appropriate topics for Sunday breakfast. Only after the last slice of bacon had been split three ways and eaten, did Aunt Daphine say, "I've been thinking about what I should do today."

"Do about what?" I asked, thinking that she meant to go see Junior.

"I'm supposed to deliver the money to the graveyard this afternoon," she said.

"That's right," I said. In the midst of everything else, I had forgotten. "You're not still planning to take it, are you?"

"I don't know," she said. "What do y'all think?"

"I don't think you should," I said. "If Dorinda was the blackmailer, then you're off the hook now."

"But how could she have been?" Aunt Daphine asked. "How could she have known?"

"I'm not sure," I said, more than a little ashamed at how little I had found out. "I feel sure that she was up to something, and she was married to a man who went to Vietnam."

"I'm sure that John Ward never told anybody," Aunt Daphine said. "And we don't know that Dorinda's ex–husband even knew John Ward."

I nodded, knowing she was right.

"Besides," Aunt Daphine persisted, "what if Dorinda wasn't the blackmailer? Can I risk not paying now? The election's only a little over a week away."

"There's another consideration," Richard said. "Junior Norton. From what Laura said last night, Junior thinks that we know more than we're telling. That means she's going to be watching us. Especially you, Aunt Daphine."

"Come to think of it, I saw Mark Pope in the parking lot when I left the grocery store," I said. "I didn't think anything of it at the time, but I suppose he could have been watching me."

"Junior should know better than to think I had anything to do with Dorinda's death," Aunt Daphine said indignantly. "I've known that girl since she was a baby."

Richard shrugged. "She's a police officer, and she's suspicious. She'll be keeping an eye on you, or having someone else do it. If she sees you putting something on Uncle John Ward's grave, she's going to want to know what it is, and if Junior gets to it before the blackmailer, she'll be asking questions. If the blackmailer gets to it first and Junior sees him, that could lead to the whole story coming out. I don't think you should risk it."

"Richard's right," I said. "Junior was furious last night. She's going to be watching us like a hawk. Besides, you don't have the money. Do you?"

Aunt Daphine shrugged sadly. "I've scraped together what I could, but I'm still two hundred dollars short. If it was for anything else, I'd go to one of my sisters, but I just can't this time."

"Then it's settled," I said. "We'll lay low today, and let Junior get bored with watching us. Who knows? Maybe she'll find out who killed Dorinda and that it had nothing to do with the blackmail." I didn't really believe that, of course, but I was hoping.

We spent most of the day on the telephone. As I expected, once Vasti knew where Aunt Daphine was, the rest of the Burnettes found out in short order. Aunt Nora, Aunt Edna, Aunt Nellie, and Aunt Ruby Lee were of course concerned about their sister, and we let Aunt Daphine talk to them. Hank Parker called half a dozen times and sounded personally insulted that Richard hadn't called him right away, after their earlier experience together. We told him and all the other non–Burnettes who called as little as possible.

I must admit that it felt like we were under siege. I found myself looking out the window every few minutes to see if somebody was watching the house. I don't think there was anybody stationed outside the house constantly, but I saw the Byerly police cruisers going by a lot more often than usual.

At around four, we heard on the radio that it had been determined that the bullet that killed Dorinda had come from the gun that killed Leonard Cooper. Somehow or another, the two murders were connected.

I tried to convince Richard and Aunt Daphine that it didn't necessarily mean that the murders were connected to the blackmail, but I couldn't even convince myself. The fact that Cooper was in the Army with Uncle John Ward couldn't be a coincidence. Despite what I had told Junior, it looked like we were going after a murderer.

Chapter 24

"We've got a little time before Aunt Maggie gets back from the flea market," I said after hearing the news. "We better make our plans now. Any ideas?"

Aunt Daphine shook her head. "I feel like I've caused so much harm. Two people are dead."

"It's not your fault," I said firmly. "Would it have been better if you had aborted Vasti?"

She looked shocked. "Of course not."

"Then stop blaming yourself. All you did was to raise your daughter the best way you could, and I think Uncle John Ward would be damned proud of you. You didn't ask to be blackmailed, and you didn't kill anybody. So stop talking like that, and let's figure out how we can get out of this mess."

"You're right," she said, and took a good, long breath. "What do y'all think we should do next?"

Richard said, "Now that we know that Cooper was involved, shouldn't we see what we can find out about him?"

"Junior already tried that," I said.

"But she didn't know about the blackmail. Besides

which, she's not likely to share what she knows with us now."

"True. Do you think we should go to Virginia and check him out?"

"Maybe not so far as that. Didn't Junior say Cooper's son was a student at NC State in Raleigh?"

"So she did. Raleigh's just a few hours' drive from here. We could drive down and talk to him tomorrow. What was his name?"

Richard located Wednesday's *Gazette* and found out that Cooper's son Michael was an engineering major. "A friend of mine teaches at NC State," Richard said. "She might help us locate him."

"An old girlfriend?" Aunt Daphine asked with a little of her usual twinkle in her eye.

"Hardly," Richard said dryly. "She's never read anything earlier than the Romantic poets."

I'm fairly sure that Aunt Daphine didn't understand why this was such a damning indictment, but she nodded as if she did.

Richard called his friend and she promised to try and track down Michael Cooper by the time we arrived in Raleigh the next day.

"What about Junior?" Aunt Daphine wanted to know. "She's bound to find out. Won't she guess why you're going to Raleigh?"

"She'll know, all right, because I'm going to call and tell her," I said. Before Aunt Daphine could object, I added, "She told me yesterday not to leave town without letting her know, so I have to. Anyway, it doesn't matter if she knows because she thinks that we've been investigating Cooper's murder all along. Our going to Raleigh will only confirm it for her." Luckily for me, it was Mark Pope who answered the phone, and he took my message without comment.

Aunt Daphine said, "I wish I could go with you, but I can't. Some of my regulars are coming in tomorrow, and I know we'll have lots of drop-ins after what happened to Dorinda."

"Don't you think there having been a murder there will scare customers off?" I asked.

"Probably not. Curiosity is a lot stronger than fear, at least in the daylight."

Aunt Maggie arrived right after that, and we decided to go out to Fork-in-the-Road for barbeque. Obviously the news about Dorinda had spread because there was a lot of staring, but Aunt Daphine was feeling strong enough by then to ignore it. Plus Aunt Maggie stared right back until folks got the idea and left us alone. After dinner, Aunt Daphine insisted on going back to her own house, and Richard and I planned our trip to Raleigh.

Chapter 25

Despite our reason for going, I enjoyed the next day's drive to Raleigh. I love driving in North Carolina. The drivers are so polite that I hardly ever need to use any of the nasty driving tricks I've learned in Boston.

We got to Raleigh a little before noon, found a place for lunch, and then drove to NC State. Richard's friend Leslie had not only tracked down Michael Cooper, but had set up an appointment for us and was loaning us her office for the occasion.

"What did you tell her to get her to be so cooperative?" I asked Richard while we were waiting for Cooper.

"I just mentioned that my office is next to the one occupied by Elisabeth Hubert, the leading light on poets of the Romantic era these days, and asked if there were any papers Leslie wanted me to pass on to her. This was more than enough inducement for her to perform these small services."

"The world of literature is pretty cutthroat, isn't it?"

"It's not for the weak of heart," he agreed solemnly.

A young man tapped on the office door at one–thirty on the dot. "Dr. Warren?" he asked, looking at me.

I'm afraid that I just stared at him.

"Michael Cooper?" Richard asked in response, and when he nodded, said, "Come on in, and shut the door behind you."

He did so and sat down opposite us.

Richard and I had decided that I was going to ask the questions and he was clearly waiting for me to get started, but I was still staring. I knew it was rude, but I couldn't help it. I guess it had taken me a while to spot Leonard Cooper's resemblance to Big Bill Walters because of the circumstances, but I knew as soon as I saw Michael Cooper, that no matter what his last name was, that boy was a Walters.

His hair was dark and curly, like Big Bill's used to be, and he had that strong Walters chin. Even his uncertain grin when I didn't speak right away reminded me of Burt Walters. And the only way that Michael Cooper could be a Walters was if his father was a Walters.

I finally gathered my wits enough to say, "Excuse me, Mr. Cooper. I was just trying to decide how I could explain this all to you. I should start by telling you that I'm not Dr. Warren. My name is Laura Fleming, and this is my husband Richard. Dr. Warren is a friend of my husband's and she set up this meeting at his request."

Somebody had taught that boy his manners. He shook our hands without even asking why we had wanted to see him.

"Mr. Cooper, I was born and raised in Byerly, North Carolina."

"That's the town where my father died," he said, looking confused.

"That's part of the reason we're here. We want to try to find out who killed him, and why."

"I'm sorry, I don't understand. Are you police officers?"

I shook my head. "No, we're not." This was the tricky part. "The day before yesterday, a woman who worked at my aunt's beauty parlor was shot and killed. My aunt is quite upset about it, and that's how my husband and I got involved." That was close enough to the truth that I didn't feel too guilty. "The woman was shot with the gun that was used to kill your father, so it looks like they were killed by the same person. That's why we're here. Do you mind answering some questions for us?"

I wasn't going to push him if he didn't want to answer, but again his upbringing showed and he nodded politely. Most of the young people from the South that I know have been raised not to question adults. It can be charming and it can be dangerous, but today it was darned convenient.

I went on. "The woman who died was Dorinda Thompson. Does that name mean anything to you?"

He shook his head.

"Your father never mentioned her?"

"No, ma'am. He never talked about anyone from Byerly that I can remember. I told the police chief that I didn't know why my father would even have gone to Byerly."

"You're from Richmond, aren't you?"

He nodded. "I've lived there my whole life, until I came here to school. Dad had been there since he got out of college."

"What about before then?"

"He was born in Tennessee, but after he got home from Vietnam, he decided to go to school up North. He

208

got a job in Richmond right out of college, and met my mother a couple of months later."

"I understand that your mother passed away a while back."

"About three years ago. She never mentioned Byerly to me, either."

"What about your father's family in Tennessee? Did you ever visit them, or did they visit you?"

"Dad was an orphan, no living family at all."

"Then you're alone now," Richard said, and I felt awful for asking Michael questions when he had just lost his father.

Michael smiled a little, and said, "Mom had a large family. They've been a big help these past few days."

Richard leaned back, satisfied.

I made myself go on. "Did your father have any family photos or scrapbooks, anything like that?"

Michael shook his head. "His parents died in a fire, and everything was destroyed. Even his birth certificate." He hesitated. "At least that's what he said."

"You don't think that's true?"

He shook his head. "I'm not sure what to think. I mean, I always considered my father an honest man, but the way he died has me pretty confused. That police chief asked me about the people who run the mill, some family named Walton."

"Walters," I corrected.

"Walters. She said there was a pretty strong resemblance between that family and my father, and she wanted to know if Dad had ever said anything about them to me."

"Had he?"

"No, ma'am."

"What about John Ward Marston?"

"That name sounds familiar," Michael said, and he looked like he was trying to remember. "I think he was in Vietnam with Dad."

"That's right," I said. "John Ward was in the same outfit as your father. He was my uncle, as a matter of fact. Did your father say much about him?"

"I think they were pretty good friends, but he said that Marston died soon after they got to Vietnam. He showed me a picture of him once, taken a couple of days before he died."

"Anything else?" I prompted.

"I don't think so. Dad was really upset when Marston died, and he didn't talk about him because of that."

"What about Daphine Burnette?" I asked. When he shook his head, I said, "Then you don't know any of these people from Adam's house cat?"

He grinned suddenly. "Dad used to say that. I used to laugh at him, because he sounded so country." Then his grin faded and he looked down at his hands. I think I knew how he felt. When my parents died, I felt like I was supposed to be polite and not show my grief in public, but sometimes it came out despite everything I could do.

"Are you all right?" I asked as gently as I could.

He took a deep breath and nodded. Then he looked up at me again. "Mrs. Fleming, do you know why somebody killed my father?"

"No, I don't, but we're sure going to try to find out." He looked so forlorn, and I wished there was some way I could comfort him, to tell him that the pain would eventually ease, but it wouldn't have been right coming from a stranger. Instead I said, "I think that's all I wanted to ask you." I looked at Richard and he nodded. "We do appreciate your talking to us."

He shook our hands again and left.

"Not terribly enlightening," Richard said.

"Are you kidding?" I asked, surprised that he hadn't seen what I had. "Meeting Michael Cooper has broken things wide open as far as I'm concerned."

"He didn't tell us anything."

"I'm not talking about what he said—I'm talking about who he is. That boy is a Walters. I don't have any way to prove it, but I can tell that he's a Walters just by looking at him."

Richard raised an eyebrow at me.

"Look, when I was younger I got into all kinds of trouble by telling things to the wrong people. Once I heard Aunt Nora tell my mama that Mrs. Mayhew was running around on Mr. Mayhew, and I told Wanda Tyler."

"I can see how that would convince you that Michael Cooper is a Walters," Richard said dryly.

"I'm not finished yet. What I didn't know is that Wanda's mother is Mr. Mayhew's sister. So Wanda told her mother, and Wanda's mother told Mr. Mayhew, and Mr. Mayhew confronted Mrs. Mayhew."

"Then what?" he asked, interested in spite of himself.

"Mrs. Mayhew told him it was a lie. So Mr. Mayhew got mad at Wanda's mother, and Wanda's mother found out from Wanda that I was the one who had told her, and she called my mother and fussed about me spreading lies."

"So it wasn't true."

"Oh it was true, all right. That's not the point."

"What is the point? I seem to have lost it."

"The point is that I learned to tell who was related to who by family resemblance, and not just by names. If I had had one lick of sense, I would have been able to see that Wanda had the Mayhew nose."

"The Mayhew nose?"

"It was obvious that she had to be related to the Mayhews."

"Laura, I wouldn't dream of arguing with you about the Mayhew nose, but if Leonard Cooper looked like a member of the Walters family, isn't it reasonable that his son also looks like a Walters?"

I shook my head emphatically. "Maybe a passing resemblance I could accept, but not his looking *that* much like the rest of the family. He's related by blood all right."

"So you think that Cooper was a result of Big Bill's wild oats?"

I thought about it, but the theories about Leonard being Big Bill's illegitimate son still seemed silly, especially when coupled with the coincidence of Cooper being stationed with Small Bill. The answer had to be more reasonable than that. "I think he was Big Bill's son all right, but I don't think he was illegitimate," I said slowly.

"I don't understand."

"Richard, I think that Leonard Cooper *was* Small Bill Walters." Before he could say anything, I went on. "That's the only answer that makes sense. There had to have been a real Leonard Cooper or Junior would have found out about it. So somewhere along the line, Small Bill traded places with Cooper. Probably after Cooper died. So they buried Cooper and Small Bill became Cooper and . . ." That's where I stopped. I didn't have any idea of what came next. "Am I talking crazy?"

Richard shook his head slowly. "No, I don't think you are. I just don't understand how it could have happened, or why."

212

I didn't understand it all either, but I was sure that I was right. It certainly explained why Cooper had subscribed to the Byerly paper all those years, and how he had known how to sneak into the mill.

Leslie returned then, and politely let us know that she wanted her office back. After we thanked her for her help, we headed back to Byerly. The answers about Small Bill Walters had to be there somewhere.

Chapter 26

I asked Richard to drive back to Byerly, and I have to admit that I wasn't much company for him. I was too preoccupied with trying to figure out why Small Bill had exchanged identities with Leonard Cooper. From what Aunt Daphine had said, Small Bill had had everything going for him. After the war, he would have come back to run the mill and a good piece of Byerly. Why would he have thrown all of that away?

Why did Small Bill go to Vietnam in the first place? I hadn't thought about it before, but surely Big Bill could have kept him out of it, fixed his draft status somehow. Could Small Bill have done something to be ashamed of, something to run from? Everybody I had spoken to about him had said that he was a pretty nice fellow, but people have a way of only remembering the good things about a man who dies young. Still, Big Bill could have taken care of almost anything short of murder.

What about in Vietnam? I'd heard stories of otherwise normal men who did monstrous things during the war. Could Small Bill have committed some atrocity? Then why hadn't we heard about it from the Byerly men who came back from Vietnam? I didn't think that Small Bill would have been desperate enough to abandon his whole life unless he was sure he would have been punished. Or could the crime, whatever it had been, have been covered up because he was believed dead?

It was after five when we got back, and Aunt Maggie was on the telephone when we came in.

"Hold on Daphine," she said when she saw us. "They just this minute walked in the door." She handed me the phone. "Daphine's all upset about something."

"Aunt Daphine?" I said. "What's the matter?"

"Laurie Anne, I got another letter. He wants even more money now, three times as much as what he asked for before because I didn't pay yesterday like I was supposed to. I just don't know what to do. The only way I could raise that kind of money would be to sell the shop and I can't get anybody to buy the shop in less than a week."

"Aunt Daphine, calm down. You are *not* going to sell the shop!" I realized that Aunt Maggie was looking awfully interested, despite herself. "Look, why don't Richard and I come over there?"

"I wish you would. I'm so upset I just don't know what to do."

"We're heading out the door as soon as I get off the phone. Don't do anything until we get there."

"All right. Bye."

Aunt Maggie was shaking her head as I hung up the phone, but all she said was, "I'll see y'all later."

It didn't take us but a few minutes to get to Aunt Daphine's house, and she opened her door almost before we could knock.

"I knew I should have paid that money yesterday, I

just knew it," she said before we were all the way inside. "What am I going to do?"

"The first thing you're going to do is calm down," I said firmly. "Where's the letter?"

"Here." She picked it up from the coffee table and handed it to me.

As with the previous messages, the words were put together with pasted letters from magazines and newspapers. Richard and I read it together, him looking over my shoulder.

Miss Burnette,

You don't think you have to take me seriously, but you do! You didn't bring the money Sunday, and now you have to pay triple. Bring it to the old graveyard on Sunday, or I'll tell. There will be plenty of time to get the truth out *before* the election.

Tell your nosy niece to stop asking questions, or I won't wait for Sunday. Tell her to stop, or she'll be sorry.

Don't you think I won't do it, because I will. This is your last chance.

"This came in the mail today?" Richard said.

"It was in the mailbox, but there wasn't any stamp. Whoever it was just put it in the box." She handed me a plain, white envelope, without any name or address.

"Do you suppose that any of your neighbors might have seen who left it?" I asked.

She shook her head. "Most of them work, same as me. He could have waited until there was no one around before he left it."

I folded up the letter, and put it back in the envelope.

"Aunt Daphine, do you want me and Richard to stop asking questions? I don't really think that the blackmailer will go to the newspaper, because if he does, he'll lose his meal ticket, but we'll stop if you want us to."

Aunt Daphine took a couple of long breaths, and then shook her head. "Whoever it is isn't going to stop until he's bled me dry, I know that now. I want to find out who it is that's doing this. It's just that . . ."

"What?"

"Well, now I'm afraid of what he might do to you. What if he is the one who killed Dorinda and that man at the mill? How do we know that he won't try to hurt you or Richard?"

"We don't," I had to say, and I didn't much care for the feeling.

"Maybe we should just go to Junior after all," Aunt Daphine said dejectedly.

I tried to think about it objectively, and I just wasn't ready to give up. "Not yet," I said. "I feel like if he was really going to do something to me and Richard, he wouldn't have warned us. He'd have just gone ahead and done it."

"Besides," Richard said. "I don't intend to let him get away with what he's done to you, threat or no threat. Laura and I can take care of ourselves."

"All right," Aunt Daphine said, "but I want you to promise me something. If *anything* dangerous happens, we'll go to Junior right away."

"It's a deal," I said.

After that, Aunt Daphine remembered our trip to Raleigh and we told her what we had learned from Michael Cooper. Or rather, what I thought we had learned. I halfway expected her to laugh at the idea, but

217

instead she was quiet for a long time, and I could tell that she was considering it seriously.

I asked, "What do you think, Aunt Daphine? Could the man we found at the mill have been Small Bill?"

"I just don't know, Laurie Anne. That picture of Cooper that Hank Parker printed in the paper sure looked like Big Bill a few years ago, just like Small Bill would have if he had lived. You saw the dead man and you saw those pictures I have of Small Bill. What do *you* think?"

"The pictures you showed me were over twenty years old," I pointed out.

"But if that man was Small Bill, who did we bury?" she wanted to know.

"I'd guess that it's Leonard Cooper in that grave, but I don't know if it can be proved now. Somewhere along the line, he and Small Bill switched places. The question is why."

Aunt Daphine shook her head. "I can't for the life of me figure out why Small Bill would have gone off like that. He had money and a good job waiting for him, and just about any girl in Byerly would have been proud to marry him."

"That's what I thought," I said. "Are you sure that he hadn't done anything he wanted to hide from? Not necessarily a crime, but maybe something scandalous." I was going to suggest that he could have gotten some girl pregnant, but caught myself in time.

Aunt Daphine thought about it. "I'm pretty sure he didn't. You know how Byerly is. There would have been a rumor at least."

"You kept your secret all these years," Richard pointed out.

"That's different," Aunt Daphine said. "I was just one

of the Burnette girls. Small Bill was a Walters, and that means a lot around here. He'd have had a much harder time hiding anything, at least anything big enough to make him go away like that. I just don't know, Laurie Anne."

I said, "Maybe the reason he left isn't all that important anyway. What I'd really like to know is why he came back to Byerly after all this time."

Aunt Daphine shrugged.

"Aunt Daphine," I said slowly, "you did admit that Small Bill might have figured out about you and Uncle John Ward."

She nodded.

"Could he have been the blackmailer?"

"I don't think so. I told you how much I thought of Small Bill."

"He could have changed a lot since you knew him. How much can you trust a man who had been living a lie?"

"Maybe," she said, "but whoever that man was, he's been dead for over a week now. I just got this letter today."

That stopped me. For a while I had thought that Dorinda might be involved, but she was dead, too. Somebody else had put that letter into Aunt Daphine's mailbox.

"You're sure that it was put into the box today?"

She nodded. "I didn't check Saturday's mail because of Vasti's party and all the confusion afterwards, so I got out everything that was in the mailbox this morning. The letter was in with today's mail when I checked this evening."

That meant somebody else was involved. Who? Joleen? Even if I could believe that she would shoot her

219

own mother, I had been with her when Small Bill was killed and she was at Vasti's party when Dorinda died.

We had gone back over the facts several more times without getting anywhere when I noticed Richard looking at his watch in rapid succession. That's when I remembered that we hadn't had any dinner. Aunt Daphine hadn't eaten either, so Richard volunteered to go and bring back hamburgers and fries from Hardee's while Aunt Daphine made a pitcher of iced tea. I didn't know if eating would help our thought processes, but I was pretty sure that it wouldn't hurt them any.

Chapter 27

"Well one thing is pretty sure," I affirmed as we nibbled on the last of the french fries. "Since that letter was left in the mailbox today, neither Small Bill nor Dorinda could have been the blackmailer."

"Granted," Richard said. "However, if we have to wait for a person to die to eliminate him as a suspect, we're not going to solve this before this Sunday."

I ignored his remark. "It seems that Leonard Cooper's, or rather Small Bill Walters's, arrival precipitated all of this."

"But the blackmail began months ago," Aunt Daphine said.

"Not the murders," I said. "Why did Cooper come back now, particularly? Why not years ago, and why not never? If Uncle John Ward were still around, we could ask him."

"If Uncle John Ward were still around, we wouldn't have the problem," Richard said.

"True." Still, that thought had led to another idea. "What about letters?" I asked. "Did Uncle John Ward talk about Small Bill in any of his letters?"

"I guess he did, but those aren't the parts I was paying the most attention to." She smiled, and I got a glimpse of how she must have looked as a young girl in love. "John Ward wrote such sweet letters."

"I hate to ask this, Aunt Daphine," I said, "but can Richard and I read those letters? There might be something you missed."

Aunt Daphine thought about it, and then nodded decisively. "Of course you can read them, if you think it might help." She went to the shelf where she kept her photo albums, and pulled out an old candy box.

"There's only a few of them," Aunt Daphine said, handing us a small bundle tied up with a baby blue ribbon. "On account of him dying not long after he got there."

"Are you sure you don't mind?" I asked Aunt Daphine as I picked up the first envelope.

She shook her head emphatically. "Of course not. I've read them so often I should know them by heart, but there might be something I didn't notice. John Ward would understand."

"All right," I said, and opened the envelope. The first two letters were written from boot camp, and didn't mention Small Bill at all. Instead they talked about how much he missed Aunt Daphine, and how everything reminded him of her. I was more than a little embarrassed to read them, but I kept going.

The third letter had obviously been written after Aunt Daphine went to Norfolk to see him.

Dear Daphine,

It seems like it's been years since I left you, instead of only days. I cannot tell you how much I miss you, but if I had a dollar for every time I've thought of you, I'd buy the mill from Big Bill Walters.

I had some real good luck when I got here. Small Bill and I got assigned to the same outfit. Having him with me is like having a little bit of Byerly with me. The other guys kid us some about how we talk, but we just kid them right back. They're good guys, really.

Small Bill and I have made lots of friends already. Only I guess I shouldn't call him "Small Bill" anymore. When we met the other fellows, he said for them to call him Bill. I went along with it, of course, but it sure sounds funny to me. Bill said he didn't want to be small anything anymore, and I couldn't argue with that.

Bill and I had a layover in Tokyo on our way here. We didn't have but a few hours there, but we saw what we could. Daphine, that city is like no place I have ever seen before. Cars and bicycles and rickshaws (that's a cart pulled by a man on foot) all going every which way. It reminds me of when we used to stir up ant hills with a stick.

Bill said he thought the women there were the prettiest he had ever seen, but I told him that the prettiest woman on earth was back home in Byerly, North Carolina. That's when I decided I wanted to get you something, and I did. I won't tell you what it is, because I want it to be a surprise. Bill helped me pick it out, and I think you'll like it. I was going to mail it, but the other fellows told me that the mail can't be trusted. Besides, I want to give it to you myself.

We're in Vietnam now, and it's not what I expected. Not very pretty, I have to say, and it smells funny. I guess I'll get used to it. It sure is hot, and it rains a lot. When I get back home and hear someone talking about the heat and humidity in Byerly, I'm going to laugh.

I've got to go now. We're going into the jungle tomorrow. Only the guys don't call it that, they call it something kind of ugly. I guess it can get pretty bad out there, so I can't blame them for it. I'll write you again when I can.

Love,
John Ward

"What was the present?" Richard asked as I folded up the letter and put it back into the envelope.

"I never got it," Aunt Daphine said. "It wasn't with his things when they sent them back, so I guess it got lost somewhere along the line. Probably a geisha doll or something like that."

"That's a shame," I said sympathetically. "It would have been his last gift to you."

"Next to the last," Aunt Daphine said with a smile. "I got Vasti a few months after that."

The next letter was dated a week later.

Dear Daphine,

Now I know why the other guys call going into the jungle "being in the shit." It's hot and wet all of the time, and the bugs are just about big enough to carry you off. I'm not ashamed to tell you that I was afraid for my life for most of the mission. I thought I'd see who it was shooting at me, but that's not how it is at all. There's just gunfire coming out of nowhere, and booby traps that will take your leg off if you're not extra careful.

That's enough of that. I don't want you to be worrying about me, and I've got some real good fellows watching after me. Bill for one, and a fellow named Leonard Cooper from Tennessee. We all got here at the same time, so the other guys called us three virgins until we made it through that first mission. I had to laugh when they said that, and Bill wanted to know why, but of course I wouldn't tell him.

I've been thinking about that, our weekend together. Some days, it's the only nice thing I can come up with to think about. I don't know if I should be ashamed that we didn't wait or not, but I'm not. I only wish it had been a month instead of just the two nights. As soon as I get home, we're going to have the biggest wedding Byerly has ever seen. You wait and see. I'm counting the days until I come home to you.

Love,
John Ward

The next envelope was a telegram, and I didn't have to open it to know what it was. "The Marstons let me have that after he died," Aunt Daphine said quietly. She sat watching as I carefully replaced the ribbon around the letters and put the packet into the candy box. Then Aunt Daphine put the box back on the shelf, and said, "Excuse me for a minute. I need to go to the bathroom."

The walls were thick enough that I couldn't hear Aunt Daphine crying, but I knew that's what she was doing. I was pretty close to it myself. It wasn't just sadness, it was anger. How dare somebody take advantage of Aunt Daphine's tragedy? How dare somebody use her love against her like that?

After a few minutes, Aunt Daphine came back, trying to smile. "Do you think there was anything in the letters that will help?"

I had to shake my head. "I'm sorry, Aunt Daphine. Dredging all that up for nothing."

She patted my hand. "Don't you worry about it. You're just trying to do what you can. Now, Dorinda's funeral is tomorrow. Are y'all two going?"

"I hadn't even thought about it," I said honestly. I felt a little guilty about it, too. I hadn't really liked Dorinda, but the poor woman had been murdered. Besides, her daughter was kind of dating my cousin.

Aunt Daphine said, "I'm closing down the shop, and all of us are going together."

"Maybe we'll go with you," I said, and Richard nodded.

We made plans to meet at the funeral parlor, and then Richard and I headed back for Aunt Maggie's. I hated leaving Aunt Daphine like that. Although she had lived by herself ever since Vasti got married, this was the first time I had ever thought of her as living alone.

Chapter 28

Aunt Maggie was gone somewhere by the time we got back. I asked Richard, "Where's that stack of photocopies from the *Cazette?* I want more details about Small Bill's 'death.'"

"I'll go get them," Richard said, and I cleaned off the table so we could spread them out.

Not surprisingly, there were a lot of articles about Small Bill. There was a piece about his leaving and how proud Big Bill was of him. Then there were stories about how well he was doing at boot camp, and a copy of his boot camp graduation photo that filled the entire front page. Big Bill graciously allowed the paper to print excerpts from several of Small Bill's letters home, and a number of snap shots of him in uniform.

When word came of his death, the front page was ringed in black, and his funeral also filled the front page. No wonder Aunt Daphine didn't think he could have committed any misdeeds without rumors spreading. The poor fellow probably couldn't have picked his nose without the whole town knowing.

"According to this," I told Richard, "Small Bill's body was pretty torn up. 'For reasons of delicacy, the coffin

227

remained sealed. William Walters, Sr., though confessing his dismay, said that perhaps it was best that people remember his boy as he had been when alive, not after the ravages of war.' So it could have been Leonard Cooper and no one would have known."

"If the body was that torn up, how did he ever come to be identified as Small Bill in the first place?"

"Dog tags," I said, reading further. "Those would be easy enough to switch."

We kept on reading. "Richard, are you finding any reason for Small Bill to leave?"

"Not a one. What about amnesia brought on by a head injury? When he came to in the hospital, they told him he was Cooper."

"How did the dog tags get switched?"

"So I don't have all of the answers yet," Richard said huffily.

The fact was that we didn't have any answers, just more questions. Richard, who can read me like one of Shakespeare's plays, saw that I was getting disgusted and plucked the photocopy I was glaring at from my hand.

"Quitting time," he said firmly.

"But—"

I had expected one of his reasoned arguments about why it would be best to rest, but instead Richard pulled the sneaker and sock off of my right foot so he could tickle me. I tried to retaliate, but I was laughing too hard. Papers flew everywhere, of course. I got my right foot away from him, but then he got to the left.

The battle raged for a while, and by the time we called a truce, I couldn't even consider doing anything serious. Instead I raced Richard up the stairs to bed, and I won, too.

Chapter 29

The way things turned out, I was glad that Richard and I went to Dorinda's funeral. Admittedly Dorinda had been new in town and apparently hadn't gone out of her way to make friends, but I would have thought that more people would turn out. There's something terribly depressing about a poorly attended funeral.

Joleen was there, of course. Thaddeous came, and so did Aunt Nora, mostly for his sake. Then there were Aunt Daphine, Gladys, Clara, and the other ladies from the beauty parlor. And Richard and me. That was it.

Oh, Junior and Mark Pope came, but they were in uniform, which meant that this was part of their investigation, and Hank Parker was there to cover the funeral for the *Gazette*, but they didn't really count. Richard was drafted at the last minute to be a pall bearer, along with Thaddeous. They had to use Mark, the funeral director, his assistant, and the limousine driver for the other pall bearers. I couldn't help but think of all the people we had to choose from at Paw's funeral.

I could tell that Joleen felt the slight from the way she looked around when it was time to go into the funeral parlor. The funeral director must have asked if she wanted to wait for a few more minutes, because I heard her say, "No, this is all that's coming. To hell with anybody else."

Aunt Daphine whispered to me, "That's how grief affects people. Some cry and carry on, and some just get angry." Obviously Joleen was one of the angry ones.

In keeping with the number of mourners, the funeral service was brief. It was the only funeral I had ever attended where no one gave a eulogy. Richard and I hadn't really planned to go to the graveside service, but under the circumstances, we decided we should. I don't know if our being there comforted Joleen or not, but I felt like the proprieties should be observed.

The graveside service was also quite short, and Joleen didn't even wait to receive the usual polite words of sympathy afterwards. After tossing a handful of dirt onto her mother's coffin, she stalked off alone to the limousine. Thaddeous tried to escort her, but she just shook him off and had the driver take her away. While part of me registered her rudeness, mostly I just felt sorry for her.

Junior came over to us after Joleen left, and asked, "How was your trip to Raleigh?"

"Very nice," I said blandly. "The leaves are lovely this time of year, aren't they?"

Junior was not amused. "If you find out something about Dorinda Thompson's murder, I expect you to report it."

"If I do," I said, "you'll be the first to know."

She nodded, then moved away.

Since Dorinda had been buried in the same cemetery as my parents and grandparents, I had planned to visit their graves while we were there. Now, after feeling so uncomfortable at the funeral and the encounter with Junior, I just wanted to get out of there.

"I hate being on the outs with Junior," I said to Richard as we drove away from the cemetery. "I know she thinks I'm up to something."

"You are up to something," Richard said.

"True," I admitted. "I'd trust her, if it was me, but I can't get Aunt Daphine to. Once this is all over, I'll try to explain it to her."

As we headed back to Aunt Maggie's, I realized what was really bothering me. What if we didn't find the blackmailer? What if we never solved the murders? Would Junior ever forgive me then?

Chapter 30

"Richard," I said after we got back to Aunt Maggie's and changed our clothes. "I've been thinking. Burt Walters has been particularly vehement in denying any knowledge of Leonard Cooper."

"Wouldn't you be? Maybe he really doesn't know anything."

"But he has to see the resemblance to his father. Like Thaddeous said, that man was a dead ringer for Big Bill."

"People don't always want to face facts."

"But still."

"Laura, would you rather I keep poking holes in your thoughts or should I just let you lay it all out?"

I couldn't help but grin. "All right, this is what I'm thinking. Small Bill came back to Byerly for a reason, and he went to Walters Mill. Doesn't it seem reasonable that the person he was going to meet was either Big Bill or Burt?"

"Are you thinking that one of them killed him? I thought that Junior checked both of them out, and that they both have alibis for the time of the murder."

"Actually, I don't suspect either of them of the murder. I just suspect them of planning to go see him. Or rather, one of them. Ralph Stewart told us that Burt was supposed to come by that afternoon."

"I'm sure that Junior followed up on that."

"Probably, but I can't exactly ask her now. I don't think I'd have much luck asking Burt either."

"We did pretty well with him before," Richard said, reminding me of an occasion when we convinced Burt to do something he didn't want to do.

"Yes, but we had to threaten him with a lawsuit that time. This time, we've got nothing to hold over him. He's got no reason to talk to us, and possibly lots of them not to."

Richard leaned over and pulled up the hem of my blue jeans.

"Richard, what are you doing?"

"But has the reputation of having an eye for the ladies, and I was wondering if the flash of a well–turned ankle would befuddle him enough to answer our questions. 'Beauty provoketh thieves sooner than gold.' *As You Like It*, Act I, Scene 3."

I regarded my ankle. "And what was your verdict?"

He tugged my pants leg back into place. "I'm afraid that he would be *too* strongly affected. He'd likely be struck speechless at your wondrous charms, and then what would we do?"

I pulled him over for several kisses. "Your appreciation of my ankle is appreciated, but I don't really think I'm Burt's type. I have a hunch he goes for a flashier brand of female, women with more up here." I demonstrated what I meant with my hands. "Don't forget that Thaddeous told us that Burt was interested in Joleen."

"Do you think his feelings were reciprocated?"

"I'm not sure. The gossip at the beauty parlor took it

233

as a given that Joleen was sleeping with Burt, but I didn't hear any specifics. Is this idle speculation, or do you have a reason for wondering?"

"You said we didn't have anything to hold over Burt. What about Joleen? If there is anything going on, he wouldn't want his wife finding out."

"That's ugly," I said wrinkling my nose.

Richard shrugged. " 'To do a great right, do a little wrong.' *The Merchant of Venice*, Act IV, Scene 1." When I still looked uneasy, he added, "We wouldn't really go to his wife. We'd just use it to nudge him."

"Maybe," I said, still not convinced. "I don't think we've got enough to use, anyway. Just rumors."

"What if Joleen confirmed it for us?"

"Richard! Are you planning to go ask Joleen if she's been sleeping with Burt Walters?"

"Not me," he said. "You." Before I could respond, he explained what he had in mind, and it wasn't as outrageous as I had originally thought.

"Do you really think that I should go see her today?" I asked doubtfully. "Her mother was just buried this morning."

Richard shrugged. "It won't hurt to try. After all, we are trying to catch her mother's murderer."

A few minutes later, I was on my way to see Joleen.

The house looked even more forlorn than it had before, but there was a car in the driveway so I figured Joleen would be home. She didn't answer the door right away, but she did answer.

I felt so sorry for her when I saw her. Her eyes were red, her hair wasn't brushed, and she had changed out of the black dress from the funeral and was wearing a sloppy sweatshirt over faded blue jeans. Dorinda hadn't

234

struck me as an ideal mother, but obviously Joleen was hurting.

"If you've brought me something to eat, you can take it back home with you," she said tonelessly. "I don't need any more casseroles."

To tell the truth, I felt a little ashamed that I hadn't brought something. Food is a traditional expression of sympathy. Of course, my guilt was pretty silly considering that she had just said that she didn't want anything.

I said, "I just came by to talk, if that's all right."

"I suppose so. Come on inside." She lead me into the living room. "Sorry it's a mess in here. I haven't been thinking about cleaning."

"I understand," I said. Actually, it looked no worse than it had before her mother's death.

"What can I do for you?" Joleen asked.

I took a deep breath and said, "Joleen, I hate to bother you at a time like this, but I've got some questions I need to ask."

"About what?"

I suppose I could have worked my way up to it, done something a little more subtle, but instead I blurted, "Are you sleeping with Burt Walters?"

She didn't answer for a long time, and I spent that whole time trying to decide whether she was going to yell at me or throw me right out the door. Finally she said, "I don't think that that's any of your business. Now let me ask you something. Was it Thaddeous's mother who put you up to this, or was it Thaddeous himself?"

"Thaddeous?" I realized what she was getting at. "Joleen, this doesn't have anything to do with Thaddeous."

"I went out with him a few times, that's it. He doesn't

own me, and I don't owe him a thing. If he thinks anything different, then he's got another think coming."

"I swear, neither Thaddeous nor Aunt Nora know anything about this. I've got my own reasons for asking."

"Like what?"

"Like trying to find out who killed your mother."

Her eyes narrowed. "Are you saying that Burt Walters shot Mama?"

"No, but he might know something about who it was." She started to ask another question, but I held up my hand to stop her. "Let me explain. It looks like the person who killed your mother was the same as the one who killed that man at the mill."

"Junior Norton told me it was the same gun, but I told her and I'm telling you: I don't know anything about that man. My asking you to come to the mill and help out with my computer that day was just a coincidence."

I nodded. "That's what I thought. Still, that man Cooper must have had some reason for going over to the mill. Maybe it was to see Burt Walters."

"Maybe," Joleen said doubtfully. "Why don't you ask Walters about it?"

"Because I don't think he'll tell me anything."

"You want me to ask him?"

"Not exactly. I want you to help get him to talk to me."

"How am I supposed to do that? Look, Laurie Anne, I know what people are saying, but I'm not sleeping with Burt Walters. Oh he's made a couple of passes, but nothing I can't handle. He's not my type, for one, and for another, I'm not about to tangle with Dorcas Walters."

"That's perfect," I said. The bait would be a lot more tempting if it were something Burt wanted but hadn't had. "All you have to do is call him and ask him to meet you. You won't actually have to see him—I'll take care of the rest."

She looked at me speculatively. "You really think this is going to help you find out who killed my mother?"

"I won't lie to you Joleen. The fact is that I don't know for sure that Burt knows anything. Still, I think it's worth a shot. Now if you're afraid that this might affect your job—"

"To hell with my job! I want this son of a bitch who killed Mama!" She took a couple of ragged breaths. "Look Laurie Anne, I know what my mama was. She liked men, and she drank too much, and she could be a real bitch. None of that bothers me one bit. The fact is that when I was growing up, she made sure that I had a bed to sleep in and food to eat and clothes on my back. I don't know that I liked her, but I loved her and I owe her. If I can help find the bastard that killed her, I don't care about that lousy job at the mill or anything else. You just tell me what you want me to say, and I'll call Walters right now."

I wanted to hug her or show my sympathy somehow, but her anger and pain were so raw that I didn't think that she would accept it. Instead I just explained Richard's idea, and what she should tell Burt Walters.

She grinned, nodded, and picked up the phone to call him.

Chapter 31

Joleen didn't need any coaching; she knew just how to handle Burt Walters. All it took was a couple of hints that it was a bad time for her to be alone, and Burt fell all over himself in offering her a shoulder to cry on.

Joleen said she'd rather not have him at her house, so she arranged for him to come to the Bide–a–Wee Motel in Hickory, Room 332. Which is where Richard and I were waiting for him at six o'clock that evening. Burt showed up right on time.

I opened the door to his knock, and said, "Hello Mr. Walters."

He looked at me, lowered the nosegay of flowers he was carrying, and went white. "Laurie Anne? What are you doing here? Where's, um, I mean, what's going on?" When he saw Richard sitting on a chair behind me, he turned even paler.

"We wanted to have a talk with you, and we thought that this might be the best way for us to speak privately. Why don't you come in and sit down?"

He stepped inside the door and kind of fell into the chair I had ready for him. He kept looking back and forth between Richard and me, blinking rapidly. I felt like a rat, and I could tell from Richard's expression that he wasn't pleased with himself either.

I had planned to start with a veiled threat to tell Dorcas Walters what Burt had hoped to be up to, but I just couldn't do it. Instead I said, "Look, Mr. Walters, I just want to get the answers to some questions. It's not for publication, but I do need to know."

He didn't look any less nervous. "Just what do you want to know?"

"It's about Leonard Cooper." Being blunt had worked with Joleen, so I thought I might as well try it with Burt, too. "Was Cooper really your brother Small Bill?"

He didn't say anything, not even to deny it, which was almost an answer in itself.

"He was Small Bill, wasn't he?" I prompted.

"I suppose you're going to talk to my wife about Joleen if I don't tell you," he said bitterly. That pompous mill owner tone that irritated people so much was gone from his voice.

"No, sir, I'm not," I said. "If you want to walk out of here right now, you go ahead. Nothing more will ever be said about this." I meant it, too. Walters was considering his options when I added, "Part of the reason I want to know is to find out who killed that man. If he was Small Bill, I'd think you'd want to help."

He let out a deep breath. "All right, ask your questions."

"Then Leonard Cooper was Small Bill Walters?"

Burt nodded.

"Did you know he was still alive?"

"Not all along," he said. "Not until years after I thought he was killed in Vietnam."

"How did you find out?"

239

"It was when our mother passed away. After Mother's funeral, I wanted to spend a few minutes alone with her. I rode back over to the cemetery, and Small Bill was there, crying over her grave. I guess he didn't hear me coming, because he didn't look up until I was right there. When he saw me, he started to back away, but I knew him right off, and he knew I knew."

"When did your mother die?" I asked.

"Fifteen years ago."

"You've known for that long? And you never told anybody?"

He shook his head. "Small Bill asked me not to, and I promised him that I wouldn't."

"Why did he go away like that?"

"That's what I asked him. We drove to a bar in Hickory where no one knew us so he could tell me the whole story. Now you're too young to know how Daddy treated Small Bill."

"From what I hear, he was the apple of your father's eye."

Walters nodded. "That's how everybody saw it, all right. Daddy bragged on Small Bill all the time, and told everybody what a good job he was going to do with the mill, and how he was going to step right into Daddy's shoes. The only thing was, Small Bill didn't want to step into Daddy's shoes. He wasn't even sure he wanted to stay in Byerly." He looked at me. "I guess you know how that feels."

I nodded.

"Anyway," Burt went on, "even though everybody thought Small Bill had the world by its tail, he really felt trapped here. Even his name bothered him. He didn't want to be Small Bill. Just Bill or Billy or Will or anything else would have pleased him more."

I remembered Uncle John Ward's letter, when he told how Small Bill had taken the first opportunity to change the name he went by. Just like I preferred Laura to Laurie Anne.

Walters continued, "When Small Bill got drafted, Daddy could have got him out of it, but Small Bill wanted to go. He thought it might be his only chance to get away, at least for a few years. He said it was funny, but he loved being in Vietnam. Not the fighting, of course, and he hated it when John Ward was killed, but he loved being away from Byerly and seeing a little of the world. He loved not being Small Bill anymore. He made new friends who didn't know that his Daddy owned the mill, and they liked him anyway. The one he got to be closest with was Leonard Cooper."

"So there was a real Leonard Cooper."

Walters nodded. "They traded life stories, the way young men will, and they were just about opposites. There was Small Bill, nearly smothered by his family and Byerly, and there was Leonard from Tennessee, who didn't have any family at all. Small Bill said Leonard didn't mind fighting and there wasn't a braver man over there, but Leonard hated the idea that if he died, there'd be no one to mourn for him. He kept thinking that his grave would probably be in a potters' field somewhere, and even if it wasn't, it would be neglected and he'd be forgotten."

"Then what?" I asked, though I was pretty sure I knew where this was leading.

"They were in a battle together, and they both got hit. Cooper kept on breathing, but half his head was blown off and Small Bill could tell that he wasn't going to make it. Small Bill was hurt, too, but not nearly so bad. He was waiting for the medics, feeling bad about Cooper, when he got the idea."

"He traded dog tags with Leonard Cooper, didn't he?"

"That's just what he did. By the time a medic showed up, he had traded tags and switched all their papers and such around. He'd have switched back if Cooper had lived, but he just barely lived long enough to make it to the hospital. So they shipped the body here, and we buried him in as fancy a ceremony as anybody could have ever hoped for. His grave gets fresh flowers every week."

"What about Small Bill?"

"He was hurt badly enough to get discharged. They sent him back to Tennessee, but he didn't stay there long. He used his G.I. benefits to go to school up North, and he became an architect, just like he always wanted to."

These days I couldn't imagine abandoning everything like that, but there had been times when it would have been awfully tempting. "Didn't he ever want to come back?"

Walters shrugged. "He said not, other than when he heard about our mother. He did regret not having a chance to say goodbye to her, and he wanted to apologize to me, too."

"What for?"

"He said that he had always felt a little guilty for leaving me in the hot seat. With him gone, he figured Daddy would treat me just like he had him, and I'd be stuck with the mill. The only thing was, that's just what I had always wanted. I was always jealous of Small Bill. With him gone, Daddy finally spent some time with me.

Maybe what Small Bill did wasn't right, but it seemed to work out the best for everybody."

"So now that he's really dead, why don't you tell your father the truth?"

Walters looked me right in the eye. "You think that I'm afraid to, don't you?"

I had to nod.

"Well, maybe I am afraid to tell an old man with a bad heart that his oldest son would rather live under another name than to come back to him."

I looked down at my feet. "I'm sorry. I've got no right to judge you."

He nodded. "When I was your age, things seemed a lot simpler to me, too. Right now, I think that the best thing to do is to let Leonard Cooper and Small Bill Walters lie just where they are."

" 'He that dies, pays all debts,' " Richard said softly. "*The Tempest*, Act III, Scene 2."

"What about Michael Cooper?" I asked. "He is your nephew, and by rights, some of the Walters money ought to come to him."

"I asked Bill about that when I found out he had a son, and he said that he'd left all the Walters money behind him and that was the way it was going to stay. He said he'd provide for his family without any help from us. I checked into his financial situation as best I could, and he had enough money put away to get the boy through school. I'll keep an eye on him to make sure he's got what he needs, and after my father is gone, maybe I'll go talk to him and see what he thinks."

That seemed fair enough to me. Unfortunately, though Walters's story had been fascinating, I still didn't know what I wanted to know. "Mr. Walters, do you know why your brother came back to Byerly?"

He shook his head. "That was the first time since Mother's funeral. He called me that Friday night and said that he was on his way here, and that he wanted to ask me about something. I couldn't get away the next day, but I told him that I'd meet him at the mill Sunday evening."

"Is that why you put the fear of God into Ralph Stewart? To keep him busy so your brother could sneak in?"

"Yes," he admitted, looking a little embarrassed. "I told Small Bill I'd be there when I could, but my wife had plans for me that afternoon."

"I'm guessing that he met somebody else while he was waiting for you. Do you have any idea of who it might have been?"

"If I did, don't you think I would have told Junior Norton?"

He was right, of course. "Mr. Walters, I'm afraid I owe you an apology. It sure doesn't sound like your brother was involved with. . . . With what I thought he was involved with."

He cocked his head. "Just what did you think?"

"I can't tell you." When he looked like he was going to object, I added, "I promised somebody I wouldn't."

Walters smiled a little. "I guess I can understand that." He pulled himself up a little, and I noticed that when he spoke again, his usual pompous tone was back. "I hope I can rely on your discretion in this matter, too."

"I'll keep it secret if I possibly can," I said.

"Obviously, if letting it out is necessary for finding my brother's killer, I will understand. If that does happen, however, please let me know first so I can be the one to tell my father. I wouldn't want him to hear it from the newspaper."

"Of course," I said.

"Now, is there anything else you need from me?"

I wanted to ask if he knew anything about what had happened between Aunt Daphine and Uncle John Ward before he left, but I couldn't think of a way to do it without compromising Aunt Daphine's secret. So I shook my head.

"Then I guess I better be getting back home before my wife decides I've gone and done something I shouldn't have." He looked at the nosegay he was still holding. "Maybe I'll take her these flowers. I don't suppose that Joleen wants them."

I must have looked disapproving because he added, "Remember what I said about life not being so simple at my age, Laurie Anne."

"Yes, sir."

He looked at me and shook his head a few times. "Now I know how you managed to find out who it was that killed your grandfather. If there is anything I can do to help you find out about my brother, you just call me."

"Yes sir, I will."

He had his hand on the doorknob when Richard said, "Actually, Mr. Walters, there is something you can do. Did you get many letters from your brother when he was in Vietnam?"

"A few."

"Do you still have them?"

"Of course."

"Could Laura and I borrow them?"

Burt looked curious, but said, "I don't see why not. You're staying with Maggie Burnette, aren't you?"

245

"Yes, sir."

"I'll have someone bring them over there in the morning. Will that be all right?"

"That will be fine," I said. "We'll get them back to you right away."

This time he did leave.

"Why do we want to see those letters?" I asked Richard.

He shrugged. "Nothing definite, just another straw to grasp at. We've heard so much about Small Bill that I'd like to hear what he had to say for himself."

I looked at him curiously. "You like him, don't you? Small Bill, I mean."

"I guess I do. He's a romantic figure, don't you think? Leaving all he knew to try to create a life of his own, never looking back."

"I guess," I said. "I just keep thinking of the folks who mourned for him. Like his parents. Wouldn't it have been better if he had confronted his father? Maybe he'd have helped him, and if not, the worst thing Big Bill could have done would have been to kick him out. Which Small Bill did for himself."

"But where's the poetry in that?" Richard objected. "What kind of play would it have been if Hamlet had just confronted his uncle, or if Juliet had told her father she was already married, or if Cordelia had told Lear what wretches her sisters were? That would have taken all the fun out of it."

"I seem to recall that Hamlet, Juliet, and Cordelia all ended up dead. Tragedies are fine in the theater, but they aren't much fun in real life."

"Maybe not," Richard said, "but I still think I would have liked the younger Bill Walters."

"Me, too," I admitted. I was starting to want to solve

his murder, not just for Aunt Daphine's sake, but for Small Bill's as well. I peered out the hotel window. Burt was long gone. "We can leave now."

Richard patted the bed. "You know," he said with a grin, "we've paid for this room for all night."

"We've got a perfectly nice room waiting for us at Aunt Maggie's."

"No offense to your aunt, but I find her presence a little inhibiting."

"Well . . ." I was tempted.

"We don't have to stay all night, just long enough to get our money's worth."

He reached for me, and I let myself be convinced. Like he said, we had already paid for the room, and it would have been a shame to let it go to waste.

Chapter 32

We made it back to Aunt Maggie's by around nine, and went to bed a few hours later. Or rather, back to bed.

Burt Walters kept his promise promptly the next morning. Ralph Stewart drove over with the packet of letters before Richard and I finished breakfast, making it easy for us to plan the first part of the day.

There were about a dozen letters, neatly stacked in chronological order. There were a couple from boot camp and one that described Small Bill's and Uncle John Ward's short stay in Tokyo, but it was the fourth that really caught my interest. It described how my uncle died.

Dear Burt,

I hope all is well in Byerly, but I'm not feeling too good myself. I guess you will have heard about John Ward Marston by the time you receive this letter. I was with him when he died, and little brother, I hope you never have to watch a friend die like that.

I don't know what the Army has told his parents

and Daphine Burnette, but it wasn't an easy death for him. A shell fragment hit him in the stomach when we were pinned down by the Viet Cong, and the medics couldn't get to us. I stayed right there with him, but there wasn't anything I could do but to give him some water and keep telling him that he was going to be all right. But John Ward knew all along that he wasn't going to make it.

I don't know if it will make his folks feel any better, but his last thoughts were about them. Well, about them and Daphine Burnette, but I'm sure they'd understand that. John Ward gave me something he bought for Daphine in Tokyo, and made me promise to make sure it got to her, and I held the paper for him to write her a final letter, too. We can't trust the mail from here, and sometimes bodies get robbed before they get sent back, so I'll be bringing it home for John Ward. It's the least I can do for the best friend I ever had.

Having John Ward die like that doesn't seem right, somehow. It's made me think a lot about where I'm going and what I want out of life. Knowing that you could die all of a sudden makes you sit up and take notice.

Burt, I don't know if I ever told you how much you mean to me. You've been a good brother. I know it's been hard not to hold it against me when Daddy talks about me the way he does, and I want you to know I appreciate it. I love you, little brother.

I guess that's all I wanted to say. You be sure and hug Mama for me, and tell the Marstons and Daphine Burnette what I said.

Your brother,
Bill

I carefully folded the letter, and put it back into the envelope. "Nothing there," I said, embarrassed when my voice came out funny. I was on the verge of crying for an uncle I never even knew and for a man I had only seen after he was dead.

Richard handed me his handkerchief, and I wiped my eyes.

"There was one thing," Richard said. "That's the second mention we've found of a gift Uncle John Ward was sending to Aunt Daphine, and Bill mentioned a letter, too. What ever happened to them?"

"I guess Small Bill put them with all of his other effects, the stuff that came back with Leonard Cooper."

"But surely the Walters would have passed them on to Aunt Daphine."

I shrugged. "Like the letter said, Cooper's body was probably robbed before it got back to the States."

"Maybe," he said. "It's just hard for me to imagine that Small Bill would have left anything like that on Cooper's body."

"What do you think happened to it?" I asked.

"I don't know. I just think that if a buddy's last act was to give me something to bring home to his girlfriend, I'd have made sure it got to her no matter what. 'The tongues of dying men enforce attention like deep harmony.' *King Richard II,* Act II, Scene 1."

"Of course, Small Bill was willing to abandon his family and his friends to start a new life. Would a souvenir from Japan have been that important to him?"

"Maybe not. We could ask Small Bill's son if there was anything among his father's effects that could have been Uncle John Ward's present."

I looked at him for a minute, and then leaned over to give him a quick smooch. "You're a hopeless romantic, my love. You just want Aunt Daphine to get her present."

He smiled sheepishly. "I guess you're right. But I think I'll call Michael Cooper and check with him anyway."

Richard caught Michael in his dorm room, but he didn't know anything about a souvenir from Japan. "I guess it's lost forever," Richard said in resignation. "Let's tackle the rest of the letters."

We did, but didn't find anything important in them. We learned that the real Leonard Cooper had been a pretty nice guy, and knowing what we did, we could trace Small Bill's growing reluctance to come back to Byerly, but that was about it. Finally we gave up and packed them up so we could return them to Burt Walters.

"So what do we do now?" Richard asked.

"I don't know," I said gloomily. "I'm stuck."

"Do you want me to get you your computer?"

"It wouldn't help. Garbage in, garbage out."

"Cut that out!" Richard said sharply. "We've found out a lot."

"Like what? That somebody is blackmailing Aunt Daphine? We found that out ages ago. We still don't know who, and we don't know how whoever it is found out."

"At least we've got a motive," Richard said helpfully. "Money."

"Money may be the motive," I agreed, "but it seems like there must be more than money involved. So that's all we've got on the blackmail. Then we've got Small Bill's murder. Nothing about who, nothing about why."

"Not completely true. The who must have been

someone who knew he was really Small Bill. That limits our possibilities."

"True." I thought about it for a moment, but didn't come to any grand conclusions. "Then Dorinda is murdered. I must admit that I hadn't given her murder that much thought before, other than how it affects Aunt Daphine." The idea made me feel a little guilty, but I reminded myself that murder was Junior Norton's job, not mine. "The who is probably the same as before, but why?"

"I've forgotten. Do we think Dorinda was blackmailing Aunt Daphine?"

I shook my head. "I guess not. You were right—the only real reason I suspected her was that I didn't like her."

"So why was she killed, if she wasn't already involved in the blackmail?"

"Maybe she was knew something about the murder. Bill Walters's murder, that is. Could she have seen something incriminating?" Then I shook my head in answer to my own question. "That doesn't make sense. Obviously Bill Walters snuck into the mill and I can accept that the murderer could have, but I can't picture Dorinda following along behind."

"Her daughter was at the mill," Richard reminded me. "Could Joleen have seen something and told her mother?"

"I've got two objections to that. One, Joleen was with us the whole time and I don't think she could have seen anything we didn't. Two, I think that if Joleen had seen something she didn't tell Junior about, and then told her mother, she'd tell Junior about it now. Joleen wants her mother's murderer caught."

"Still, if Dorinda's death isn't because of the blackmail, then it must have something to do with the murder. Right?"

"I guess so."

"So Dorinda found out something other than through Joleen."

I considered the notion for a moment. "Remember how I told you about her finding something in the paper and acting funny?"

"We looked at every page of the paper, and didn't see anything."

"I know, but then we were looking at it from the blackmail point of view, not the murder. Let's look at it again."

Not surprisingly, the newspaper hadn't changed. But now the fact that the biggest story was about Leonard Cooper's murder seemed even more meaningful. Especially the large photo of Cooper.

I said, "You know, Dorinda hadn't lived in Byerly very long, so she certainly never knew Small Bill, and may not even have known Big Bill or Burt. If she had seen Small Bill that Saturday or Sunday he was in town, she wouldn't have connected him to the Walters. Or to the murder, until she saw this picture."

"Interesting," Richard said. "You're guessing that she did see him."

"That's what I'm guessing."

"But she didn't go to the police."

"Nope. Now I'm willing to admit that Dorinda wasn't Aunt Daphine's blackmailer."

"Big of you," Richard said dryly.

I ignored him. "But I think that my view of her character was right on the money. What if she saw Small Bill with someone, and once she realized who it was that she saw, she thought she could blackmail that person." I looked at Richard. "You don't think I'm just dumping on Dorinda again, do you?"

He shook his head. "No, you might have something here. It sounds like our next step is to trace Dorinda's steps that day."

"Right." I looked at the packet of Small Bill's letters to Burt. "Why don't we go over to the mill for the official reason of returning these letters, and for the unofficial reason of talking to Joleen."

Chapter 33

Ralph Stewart was in the guard house when we got there, but I guess he was getting used to Richard and me coming around. He just waved us on through when we told him we wanted to take something to Mr. Walters.

Joleen wasn't at her desk when we came in, so we took the elevator on up to Burt Walters's office. Everybody in Byerly thought that Dorcas Walters had chosen her husband's secretary for the woman's complete lack of attraction to men, and the chilly expression with which she favored us when we got off the elevator did nothing to dispel that legend.

I smiled at her anyway. "We'd like to see Mr. Walters for a moment and return these." I held up the packet.

She stretched out a hand. "I'll see that he gets them."

"I'd rather put them in his hand personally." For one, I thought that Walters would prefer that no one else have a chance to see what he had loaned us, because that would only cause speculation as to why. For another, I just didn't like that secretary.

"I don't know when he'll be free," she said. "There are others waiting to see him." Sure enough, three men were lined up on a couch, briefcases perched on their knees.

"Just tell him that Laura and Richard Fleming are here. I expect he'll find a few minutes."

I'd say she frowned, except that she was already frowning, but certainly her frown deepened as she picked up her phone and murmured something. Then the frown became a straight line, which was probably as close to a smile as she ever got. "He says come right in." She even opened the door for us.

I suppose that I should have felt guilty about throwing our weight around that way, but I didn't. I simply said, "Thank you," and swept in.

I couldn't help but look down at the place where I had found Leonard Cooper's, or rather Small Bill Walters's, body. There were no stains because the carpet had been replaced. I didn't blame Walters for that—I'd have done the same thing.

Burt stood to shake Richard's and my hands as we came in. He moved like he was more sure of himself than he had been the night before, much more like his old self. Both he and we remained standing.

"We dropped by to return these," I said, and handed him the packet of letters.

"Did you find anything useful in them?" he asked.

"Not really. If your brother knew anything about the problem we're investigating, he didn't say so in those letters."

"There was one thing," Richard said. "In the letter describing John Ward Marston's death, your brother referred to a gift and a final letter he was to deliver to Daphine Marston. Do you know anything about them?"

Mr. Walters shook his head. "I was there when my father and mother examined my late brother's effects, and there was nothing like that among them. I assumed that my brother sent them along to Daphine at some point."

"No, she never received them," Richard said.

"A pity." Walters glanced at his watch. "I don't like to rush you, but I have an appointment waiting."

"I did want to ask if I could borrow Joleen Dodd for a few minutes," I said.

"Certainly, if she's still on the grounds. Miss Dodd has given her notice, and I told her that she could leave right away if she wished to."

"Joleen's leaving?" I said.

He held up his hands in an air of dismissal. "It was her idea, I assure you. A letter of resignation was waiting when I arrived this morning. As far as I'm concerned, she has nothing to worry about because of what happened last night."

Or what didn't happen, I thought to myself. "We'll see if we can catch her. Thank you again."

"Certainly. And as I said before, please let me know if there's anything I can do to help you with your investigation."

We shook hands again, and he called for his secretary to send in his next appointment. While we were in the elevator, I asked Richard, "Are you still hoping to find that present for Aunt Daphine?"

"Partially," he said, "but as you were returning Burt's letters, it also occurred to me that if that note still existed, it might somehow indicate that your aunt and uncle weren't married."

"You're right!" I said. "That makes all kinds of sense. I can't believe that I missed that."

He looked smug. "I would think that a reward would be appropriate."

I kissed him quickly. "Here's the down payment," I

said as the door opened. "I'll pay the balance after we talk to Joleen."

Our timing was perfect. Joleen was walking toward the front door carrying a box.

"Here, let me get that for you," Richard said, and took the box from her.

"Thanks," she said. She turned and waved half-heartedly at a couple of other women, and then we went out the door.

"Mr. Walters told us you resigned," I said once we were outside. "It wasn't because of what I asked you to do, was it?"

Joleen shook her head. "No, it's just that talking to you yesterday kind of reminded me that I don't much like this job, and that I don't much like Byerly either. So I figured, to hell with it. I'm packing up and moving on."

By now we were at her car, and she unlocked the trunk for Richard to put in her box.

"How did things go with Mr. Walters last night?" Joleen asked. "Did you get what you were after?"

"I think so," I said. "Have you got a minute for us to ask you a few questions?"

"Go ahead."

I knew I'd have to word my questions pretty carefully or it would sound like I was bad-mouthing Dorinda. "We think that the reason your mother was killed was because she knew something about the murder of that man at the mill."

Joleen nodded.

I continued, "We're guessing that she saw Leonard Cooper when he was in town, probably that Saturday or Sunday. Maybe she even saw the killer with Cooper, not realizing it at the time, of course. The murderer knew she could place him with Cooper, and shot your mother to protect himself."

There were a lot of holes in what I was saying, like why Dorinda hadn't gone to the police and how the murderer had found out that Dorinda knew, but I couldn't very well accuse Joleen's dead mother of attempted blackmail. Still, something in the way Joleen cocked her head while she was listening made me think that she knew just what my story implied.

"Anyway," I said, "we want to find out where your mother was on that Saturday and Sunday."

Joleen said, "Well, she would have been at work on Saturday, but I think she left early because it wasn't her turn to lock up." Then she shook her head. "No, she meant to leave early but she forgot her coat and had to run back and get it. Saturday night she went out with me and a couple of friends of ours." She paused significantly. "Men friends. I'd just as soon not kiss and tell, if you don't mind."

Meaning that the men were probably married, I concluded, but I just said, "Then if she had seen anything, you'd have seen it, too."

Joleen nodded. "I'm fairly sure that we didn't see that Cooper fellow anywhere, because he would have stuck out like a sore thumb in the places we went."

"How about Sunday?"

"Well, we stayed out pretty late on Saturday night, so I just barely got up in time for Thaddeous to pick me up for the reunion. Mama was still snoring when I left, and I don't think she left the house all day. She didn't mention it to me if she did."

I asked, "What about the last few days before she was killed? Did she talk about the murder to you?"

Again she gave me that look, the one that said she

259

knew exactly what I was getting at. "We talked about it some, because of my finding the body."

"She didn't say anything about maybe seeing Cooper? I was there at the beauty parlor when she looked at the *Byerly Gazette* on Thursday, and it seemed to me that she was awfully interested in his picture."

"I didn't see Mama for very long Thursday night. I went out straight from work, and you were there when I got back. She was pretty full of herself that night and had one beer too many after y'all left. She always got ornery when she drank, and she started picking on me for something or another, so we didn't talk a whole lot that night."

It seemed a shame that Joleen's last conversation with her mother had been an argument, but she seemed to be taking it in stride. I asked, "What about Friday?"

"Me and the fellow from Thursday night tried again." She winked at me. "This time his wife was out of town, so we made hay while the sun was shining. We spent the night over at his place, and I was with him all day Saturday. I just barely got home in time to get ready to go to that party with Thaddeous, and Mama wasn't home. The next thing I knew, Junior Norton had sent her deputy to come tell me that Mama was dead."

I looked at Richard and he shrugged. "I guess that's all we wanted to know. Thanks, Joleen."

"No problem."

"So where are you moving to?" I asked.

"I haven't decided yet. Maybe Raleigh, or Charlotte. There's a lot going on around Charlotte, not like this hick town."

I felt kind of awkward, because I thought I was probably the closest thing she had to a friend in Byerly. "Do you need any help packing or anything?"

260

"That's all right. I'm only taking my clothes and stuff. The furniture is all junk, and the landlord's welcome to it."

I hesitated a moment, but I had to ask the next question. "I know you two weren't going steady or anything, but did you tell Thaddeous?"

"I'll call him tonight. Don't worry. I'll let him down easy."

"I'd appreciate it if you did."

"Well, I better get going. It was nice knowing you, Laurie Anne. I'll be leaving my address with Chief Norton, so you be sure and call if you find out anything about what happened to Mama."

"I will," I said. Then I gave her a quick hug. "Take care of yourself, Joleen. Look us up if you ever get to Boston."

She looked surprised at the hug, but said, "I just might do that. Bye." She climbed into her car and drove away.

"Poor Joleen," I said as we went back to our own car. "I hate to see her leaving alone like that."

"She's not quite alone," Richard said.

"Oh?"

"That box I was carrying was filled with socks, towels, a stapler, yellow-sticky pads, and I don't know what else. She's taking a little bit of Byerly with her."

I probably should have been indignant that she was pilfering from the mill, but I wasn't. Joleen was going to take care of herself just fine.

Chapter 34

"So?" Richard asked as we drove away. "What next?"

"Why do you keep asking me that?" I said with some irritation. "Why don't you come up with a plan for a change?"

"Maybe you're right," he said, accepting the reproof with a lot more good humor than it deserved. "Let me see what I can come up with." He assumed his hard–thinking academic expression. "As I see it, our lines of investigation should begin to converge about now."

"How so?"

"I didn't say that they did converge—I said that they *should* converge."

"Ah."

He thought some more. "There's still that last letter that Uncle John Ward wrote to Aunt Daphine."

"Yes?" I said hopefully. "Do you have an idea of where we could find it?"

"No, I just thought it should be noted."

"You're a big help."

"Aren't we getting snappy?"

The conversation degenerated after that. By the time we got back to Aunt Maggie's house, we were both as ill as hornets. As soon as we got inside, Richard picked up his book and stomped out to the back porch, and I took my computer to the den and pounded on the keys. Aunt Maggie returned in the early afternoon, figured out that we were fighting, and went right back out the door. I didn't blame her. Richard and I don't fight often, but when we do, nobody wants to be around us.

It didn't last, of course. By mid-afternoon, we nodded civilly when we encountered one another getting drinks in the kitchen. About half an hour later, Richard came inside to read in the den, saying that it was getting chilly outside. A while after that, I offered to get him another drink since I was going upstairs anyway. From there we progressed to mutual apologies, and then hugs and kisses as we made up.

It had been a silly fight anyway, and we both knew it. The combination of pressure and frustration we had been putting up with for the past week just wasn't designed to make people happy.

We both decided that it was time to get away from it all, and called Carlelle, Odelle, and Idelle to find out a good place for listening and dancing to rock-and-roll. After arguing over which club was the best in Hickory, they decided to come along with us.

The five of us had a wonderful time, even if the ladies outnumbered the available gentleman. Richard ran himself ragged trying to make sure that we all got to dance before we gave up and danced in a group. After our feet gave out, we went to an all-night drive-in for hamburgers and milk shakes. By the time we finally dropped the triplets off at their apartment, it was almost two o'clock and I had a feeling that the three of them were going to be calling in sick at the mill the next morning. Or rather, later that morning. Richard and I slept until nearly noon ourselves.

I guess I was hoping that we would wake up ready and raring to go after the blackmailer, that our unconscious minds would have been working overtime and would have come up with the solution. It just didn't work out that way. We were just as stuck as we had been the day before. In fact, we stayed stuck for the next three days.

It wasn't for lack of trying, that's for sure. We spent hours going over everything we knew, trying to come up with motives, means, or opportunity for just about everybody in Byerly. I spoke to Aunt Daphine half a dozen times, trying to get confirmation for crazier and crazier ideas, but getting shot down every time. Richard went back to the V.F.W. and he and Vivian went back over her computer files, trying to find out some connection between Uncle John Ward and anybody. Nothing. We ate over at Aunt Nora's again, and afterwards quizzed her for any gossip I might have missed before. Still nothing.

We spent time checking out suspects we had already eliminated, like the Honeywells and Larry Parker. It turned out that Sid Honeywell spent every Sunday afternoon at the Byerly Nursing Home visiting his father, so he was in the clear for Cooper's murder. His son, although just as nasty as Aunt Nora had said, spent the Saturday that Dorinda was killed in jail in Dudley Shoals for being drunk and disorderly the night before. As for Larry, if we had been thinking straight, we wouldn't have even bothered speaking to him again. He was at Vasti's party taking pictures of people when Dorinda was shot.

We saw Junior and her deputy around a lot more than coincidence would explain. I wanted to ask her if she was having any better luck than we were, but I couldn't. If she was hoping to find out anything from where Richard and I were going, she was certainly wasting her time.

In between our useless attempts at investigation, we spent a fair amount of time with various family members. I went shopping with the triplets after they called in sick on Thursday, and Richard and I went to an auction with Aunt Maggie on Thursday night, and I babysat for Linwood on Friday afternoon so he could go to the dentist. On Friday night, all of the cousins who were old enough went over to The Mustang Club with Aunt Ruby Lee to watch Roger perform, and Roger let Clifford come up on stage with him and play.

We had to drag Thaddeous along with us that night because he was still moping about Joleen, but Clifford and Richard made a determined effort to get him drunk enough that he would talk it out. By the time they were finished with him, he was ready to dance with every woman in the place, one at a time or all at once.

At one point, I did ask him about the Burnette tradition of marrying the person you take to the reunion, but he told me that he hadn't asked her, she had asked him. As far as he was concerned, that didn't count. He said that if breaking the tradition bothered anybody, somebody else could marry her. After that, he pulled me out onto the dance floor.

I should have been having myself a wonderful time, and I probably would have been if I could have stopped worrying about Aunt Daphine. She kept telling me that she knew I had done my best and that I shouldn't worry, but how could I not worry? The closer it got to Sunday, when she was going to have to either pay the blackmailer or take the consequences, the worse I felt. She had trusted me, and I was letting her down.

Chapter 35

Finally it was Saturday afternoon, and Richard and I still didn't have a clue as to who was blackmailing Aunt Daphine, or who had killed Small Bill and Dorinda. I wanted to put off telling that to Aunt Daphine, but I knew it wouldn't be fair to her. Richard and I met her at the beauty parlor at closing time. As soon as she let everybody else out, she turned to us and said, "Have you had any luck?"

I had to shake my head. "I'm sorry, Aunt Daphine, but Richard and I just haven't been able to find out anything. We've tried, but . . ."

Aunt Daphine nodded sadly. "That's all right, Laurie Anne. I know you and Richard have done the best you can."

I'd have almost rather she yelled at us. That way I could have got mad right back at her, instead of feeling so low.

Aunt Daphine said, "I never did come up with any more money, so I guess we'll just see what happens tomorrow."

As if on cue, there was a knock on the door. We

looked up to see Aunt Nora peering at us through the window and waving.

Aunt Daphine went to unlock the door. "Hey there, Nora. What are you doing out in this neck of the woods?"

"Hey there yourself. I'm glad I caught you," Aunt Nora said. "I wanted to drop this off for you." She handed Aunt Daphine a thick white envelope.

Aunt Daphine said, "What's this?" as she looked inside. Then she looked back at Aunt Nora. "Nora, where did this money come from?"

"From all of us. From Aunt Maggie, and Ruby Lee and Roger, and Edna, and Nellie and Ruben, and me and Buddy. We want you to have it." She put her hands firmly at her sides, as if to emphasize that she wasn't taking it back. "We know that you're in trouble, and we know you need money. Now if that's not enough, you just say so."

"Nora, I can't take this."

"Yes, you can. If you don't, Aunt Maggie said she was going to come make you."

"But Nora—"

"Is it enough?"

I could tell that Aunt Daphine wanted to keep arguing, but maybe she could tell from Aunt Nora's expression that there wasn't any use. Instead she thumbed through the bills. "Yes, it's enough."

"You're sure?"

"Yes, Nora."

Aunt Nora nodded. "That's fine. I'll be getting back to start Buddy and the boys' dinner now."

"Nora," Aunt Daphine began again, but she satisfied herself with, "Thank you, sister."

"You're always welcome to anything we have,

Daphine. Don't you ever forget that." Aunt Nora nodded at me and Richard, and then left.

Aunt Daphine just stood there for a long time, staring at the money. Finally she said, "I just can't do it."

"You can't do what?" I asked.

"I can't hand this money over to that son of a bitch!"

I think that was the first time I had ever heard Aunt Daphine use that kind of language.

"Nora and the others will never admit it, but I know how hard it was for them to come up with this money, and I'll be damned if I'll just give it away to that miserable excuse for a human being. It just wouldn't be right."

"But Aunt Daphine," I started to say. Then I stopped. I had never thought she should be paying him off in the first place.

"I know what you're thinking," Aunt Daphine said. "What about Vasti and Arthur? Well I don't know what's going to happen with them. The *Gazette* won't come out again until Wednesday, so even if the blackmailer goes straight to Larry Parker, people might not even hear about it until after the election. Isn't that right?"

"Maybe," I said, but I didn't really believe it, and I didn't think she did either. The news would get around, all right. If the blackmailer called the right people, it would be all over Byerly in a few hours, which would be plenty of time to ruin Arthur's chances.

"If the people in this town let something like that keep them from voting for Arthur, then they don't deserve him as city councilor. I don't think it's going to make a bit of difference in this campaign, not one bit."

I nodded, mostly because she was expecting me to,

not because I thought that what she was saying was true.

She stood there all determined for a minute, and then I could almost see her deflate. "Who am I trying to fool? If I don't pay this money, Arthur is going to lose. Maybe it won't make any difference to some people, but there are as many fools in Byerly as there are anyplace else, and they're the ones who are going to vote against him. And what is Vasti going to say? She'll never forgive me, I know she won't." She looked at me. "If it were just me, Laurie Anne, I wouldn't mind so much, but it's not right to ruin everything that Vasti has ever wanted for her and Arthur." She hefted the envelope of money. "I've got to do it, I've got to. I'll pay back Nora and the others somehow, but I've got to pay that . . . that bastard. And I don't know that he won't tell people anyway, once he's got the money."

I didn't know what to say to her. Neither choice seemed right to me, and I couldn't try to talk her into something I didn't believe in myself. If only Richard and I had been able to find out who it was.

"I've got an idea," Richard said slowly. "Pay the money tomorrow, but let me watch for the blackmailer." I started to object, but he said, "Isn't it worth trying?" He looked back and forth between me and Aunt Daphine.

"And if you catch him," Aunt Daphine said, "we'll get the money back so I can give it back to Nora?"

Richard nodded. "That's the general idea."

"Won't he tell about me once he's arrested?" Aunt Daphine asked.

"Maybe Junior can do something about that," I said. And let's not forget that if we're right, this person is a murderer, too. Who's going to believe him?"

Aunt Daphine thought about it for a long time, and then nodded. "All right, then. That's what we'll do."

"We don't have to take the chance if you don't want to," I said.

"No, I think Richard's got a good idea, and you've just reminded me that this person is a murderer. Even if I was willing to let him get away with what he's done to me, I can't let him get away with killing Small Bill and Dorinda." This time she had really made her mind up. This was the Aunt Daphine I had known all my life.

Chapter 36

We stopped at the grocery store to get something to fix for dinner and then went over to Aunt Daphine's house to make our plans. Then Richard and I ran a few errands before we drove back to Aunt Maggie's and went to bed. Our plans didn't include much time for sleep.

I was so nervous that I hadn't expected to get any rest at all, but the alarm woke me at four in the morning. I nudged Richard awake and while he got dressed, I tiptoed downstairs to make coffee and pour it into the Thermos Aunt Daphine had loaned us. Then I made up a batch of sandwiches. Richard was going to be staking out the graveyard for at least several hours, and maybe most of the day.

I had that trembly feeling that I usually associate with the first day on a new job, but I thought I was acting pretty calmly up until I realized that I had made Richard twelve ham sandwiches. I packed them into a bag anyway, and threw in some of Aunt Maggie's cookies and some fruit. A cooler with canned Cokes rounded up the menu.

Richard came into the kitchen and he whispered, "How do I look?"

He was wearing navy pants, a black sweatshirt, and dark blue sneakers.

"Like a cat burglar. Very dashing."

He checked the clock. "I better get going. How about a kiss?"

"You bet," I said, and kissed him thoroughly. "You remember the way to the graveyard, don't you?"

"Of course."

"You don't have any books in there, do you?" I asked, patting his pockets.

"Of course not."

Convincing him not to carry a book had been tough, but he eventually admitted that he did tend to immerse himself in what he was reading, and that would seriously limit his usefulness as a spy.

I walked him to the back door, and hugged him hard. "You be careful."

"I will be," he promised. "I'll see you later."

I watched him as far as I could, then sat down at the kitchen table to wait. We had decided that Richard would have to walk, because we didn't want to risk leaving a car parked anywhere nearby and we didn't want anybody to see me dropping him off. It wasn't far, and I had given him detailed directions.

Leaving that early had been necessary for a couple of reasons. First, this way no one would see him arrive and get himself settled. Second, we wanted to make sure to get our arrangements in place before anybody who might be watching us started the morning shift.

These arrangements included the next step, which was a tap on the kitchen door. I looked outside to see who it was, and then let Linwood in.

"Is Aunt Maggie still asleep?" he asked.

"Yes," I said, but from behind me I heard Aunt Maggie say, "No, I'm not." She looked at us with both eyebrows raised and said, "Do you need me to do anything?"

"Just try to pretend that I'm Richard," Linwood said with a grin. "Only I don't talk funny like he does."

"Richard had to go out," I said, "but we don't want anybody to know he's gone. Linwood's going to stay here and let himself be seen from a distance, dressed like Richard." It was Linwood and Sue's trick that had given me the idea, though I didn't tell Aunt Maggie that, and when we called him the night before, Linwood had said he'd be glad to help.

Aunt Maggie just shook her head, and said, "I wonder if other families have to put up with this foolishness."

I started to explain further, but she held up one hand. "Don't even bother. If you want Linwood to be Richard, that's fine with me." She went past us and started to make coffee.

Linwood yawned. "Do you mind if I get some more sleep?"

"Go ahead. I don't need you as Richard for a while yet."

He went up to one of the spare rooms, and I went back to my own. Again, I hadn't expected to sleep, but again, I was wrong. The alarm woke me in time to get showered and dressed for church. Aunt Maggie had already left for the flea market, and I got Linwood up and dressed in one of Richard's shirts. When I started out the door toward church, I turned to wave and Linwood waved back. Unless somebody had had a telescope trained on the house, no one would have been able to tell who it really was. "You take an aspirin and go back to bed," I called back to him. "I'll give your apologies at church."

We probably could have gotten away without Linwood's presence. I could have just yelled back at an empty house. Still, both the murderer and Junior were smart, and we didn't want to take any chances we didn't have to.

I started out across the field toward the church. It was a nice day, I was glad to see. I would have hated it if Richard had been sitting out in the rain all day. Aunt Nora, Uncle Buddy, Thaddeous, and Willis drove up just as I got to the door, and I went in with them.

"Where's Richard?" Aunt Nora wanted to know.

"He's not feeling very good," I said louder than was strictly called for, "so I told him to go back to bed. Sometimes he gets hay fever at this time of the year, so I'm hoping that that's all this is."

Aunt Daphine arrived shortly after that, but she and I made a point of not sitting next to one another or talking about anything in particular. I knew she was thinking about Richard, just like I was, because she and I both kept missing the places to stand for hymns and prayers during the church service.

I must admit that I didn't pay much attention to the sermon because of wondering if the murderer was right there in church with me. Not everybody in Byerly goes to that church of course, but I couldn't help but look at people and try to see if I could tell from their faces. I couldn't.

The plan was for Aunt Daphine to go to the graveyard straight from church, so she politely but firmly turned down Aunt Nora's invitation for Sunday dinner. I did, too, using Richard as an excuse. Both Aunt

Daphine and I were nearly out the door when Vasti loudly called to her from the front of the church.

"Mama! Thank goodness I caught you! Where on earth are you off to in such a hurry?" She clattered toward us.

"I've got something I need to do," Aunt Daphine said tersely.

"Can it wait? I need your help typing position papers for Arthur."

"I don't think so, Vasti. Maybe tomorrow."

"But they've got to be done right away," Vasti wailed, "and you know I can't type. Mama, Arthur could lose the election if you don't come right now."

"Can I help?" I put in quickly. "I'm a pretty good typist." It was a side effect of being a computer programmer. "I don't have any plans for this afternoon."

"What about Richard?" said Aunt Nora, coming up behind us.

"I'll check on him before I go," I said, forcing a little laugh. "If it's hay fever, all he's going to want to do is sleep anyway."

"There you go, Vasti," Aunt Daphine said. "Laurie Anne can help you. Bye now!" She was gone before Vasti could object.

"I guess you'll be all right," Vasti said unenthusiastically.

I said, "Glad to help. Let me go check on Richard and change out of my good clothes, and I'll be over at your place in forty-five minutes."

"Can you make it faster? We've got an awful lot to do."

"I'll try." As soon as I got back to Aunt Maggie's, I explained the situation to Linwood.

"Sorry about leaving you here alone all day," I said.

Linwood snorted. "Are you kidding? This is the most rest I've had in weeks. I'm going to set myself in front of the television and watch the ball games all day long."

"Just be sure to stay away from any windows," I reminded him. "And don't answer the telephone."

"I know, you told me already. Hey, does Aunt Maggie keep any beer in the house?"

She didn't, but he seemed satisfied with a Coke. I left him in the den with a note for Richard explaining where I was, and changed into jeans so I could drive to Vasti's house.

Even though I had taken a little less than half an hour, Vasti was alternating between looking out her window and looking at her watch when I arrived. She wanted to put me to work right that minute, but Arthur insisted that I eat a sandwich first. I had to make it myself, of course, but I didn't mind that. Then I got to work trying to make sense of Vasti's notes.

It wouldn't have been so bad if Vasti hadn't kept changing her mind, but I tried to keep telling myself that that's how Vasti works. Fortunately she had a PC with word processing software for me to use, or I probably would have strangled her. As it was, I could just keep smiling and making the changes she wanted.

I suppose I should have been grateful for the distraction. If it hadn't been for Vasti, I would have been stuck at Aunt Maggie's with Linwood all day, and I hate watching football. Time went a lot faster this way, and I only glanced at my watch every five minutes or so instead of staring at it constantly.

I kept telling myself that there was nothing to worry about. Aunt Daphine was going to deliver the money just like before. She was to spend a few minutes at Uncle John Ward's grave, put fresh flowers out, tuck the envelope into the flower pot, and then leave. The toughest part would be not looking around to see if she could spot Richard.

Richard had suggested leaving a packet of fake bills rather than real money, but Aunt Daphine and I vetoed that idea. The blackmailer would know something was up if he opened the envelope and found newspaper clippings. He might realize he was being watched and come after Richard. Or he might go straight to the phone and tell anybody who would listen about Aunt Daphine. Or he might make a run for it, and we didn't want to risk his getting away.

Anyway, once she left the money, Aunt Daphine was to go home and wait for word from me or Richard. I suppose she could have come to Vasti's, but I think she was too nervous to try to act normal. Besides, if the blackmailer did spill the beans about her and Uncle John Ward, she didn't want Vasti to be there when she found out.

Of course, I wasn't nearly as worried about Aunt Daphine as I was about Richard. I kept trying to tell myself that that was silly, too. He had assured me that he'd find a secure hiding place, and I had made him promise that if he did see the blackmailer pick up the money, he was not to approach him. All he was supposed to do was to make sure that he could identify the person, and as soon as the coast was clear, get to the nearest phone and call for help.

What danger could there be? The only thing was, I was sure that having killed twice already, the blackmailer would likely do it again if provoked.

Vasti's phone rang a lot that day, but it was never Richard calling. Aunt Daphine would have delivered the money at about the time I got to Vasti's. Of course, we had no way of knowing when the blackmailer would come to get the money. We were pretty sure that it would be before dark, because there aren't any lights in the graveyard, but that was as close as we could get. All I could do was wait.

Chapter 37

I finally got everything typed to Vasti's specifications at about five-thirty, and I drove as fast as I dared to Aunt Maggie's house. It was completely dark by the time I got there.

"Richard!" I called out as soon as I opened the door.

Aunt Maggie was in the kitchen. "Which one do you want? The real one or Linwood?"

"I'll settle for either."

"Well, Linwood left a few minutes ago. He said he'd make sure nobody saw him."

"Had he heard from Richard?"

Aunt Maggie shook her head.

"Damn!" I reached for the phone and dialed Aunt Daphine's number.

"Aunt Daphine, this is Laura. Have you heard from Richard?"

"No. You mean you haven't either?"

"Not yet."

"Do you think something's wrong?"

"Of course not," I said, trying to convince myself. "It's just now gotten dark, so he's probably waiting a while to make sure nobody sees him. You haven't heard anything else, have you?" Meaning, had she heard from the blackmailer?

"Not a word."

"You just sit tight. I'll call when I know something."

I hung up the phone, and then looked out the door in the direction from which Richard should be returning.

"Trouble?" Aunt Maggie asked.

"I don't know," I said. "He should have been back by now." I checked my watch. I didn't want to rush over there just in time to scare the blackmailer away and ruin everything.

"Where is he anyway?" Aunt Maggie asked.

"At the old graveyard," I said. I was thinking about the graveyard, dark and secluded and suddenly very dangerous.

"Has he been there all day?"

I nodded. "How long has it been dark?"

"It was nearly dark when I got back half an hour ago."

"Aunt Maggie, how long would it take to walk here from the graveyard?"

"Maybe ten, fifteen minutes."

That meant he should have been back at least fifteen minutes ago. "Something's happened," I said. "Something's wrong."

"Now, don't get all upset. I'm sure everything is all right," Aunt Maggie said.

"I'm going out there," I said. "Do you have a flashlight?"

"There's one in my car. I'm coming, too," she said, leaving no room for argument. "You write him a note in case he comes home while we're out looking for him."

I did so and we left it taped to the front door. Then

I let her drive while I stared out the car window into the dark. I had never been to the graveyard at night, had never realized how far it was from everything else in Byerly.

"There it is," I said. We parked at the gate, and ours was the only car around. With the surrounding trees, it was pitch black inside the gate.

"Richard!" I yelled. "Are you in there?"

There was no answer.

"Come on," I said, lighting the way with the flashlight.

"Which way?"

"Over by the Marstons's plot," I answered. She looked at me funny, but she didn't ask any questions. As we trudged through the graveyard, I was grateful for all the time people spent tending to the graves. Aunt Maggie's flashlight wasn't much of a help, and the place would have been impassable if it had been grown-over. We finally found Uncle John Ward's grave.

Aunt Daphine's flowers were there, and I lifted the pot to look for the envelope of money. It wasn't there. So where was Richard? "Richard!" I yelled, and Aunt Maggie joined in.

"Are you sure that this is the right place?" she asked.

"I'm sure. He's got to be around here somewhere. Richard!"

"Well, he's not answering, so we better start looking. Come on." Aunt Maggie took the flashlight from me and led the way. Using Uncle John Ward's grave as the center, she started us in a slowly expanding circle. We had been looking for about fifteen endless minutes when we found him, curled up in a ball next to a tombstone.

"Richard!" I said, and reached for him.

Aunt Maggie held me back. "Careful, now. He's hurt."

That's when I saw the blood crusted on his shoulder. We knelt on either side of him, and Aunt Maggie trained the flashlight on him. I touched his arm, afraid that it would be cold, but he stirred a tiny bit and mumbled something.

Aunt Maggie knelt and aimed the flashlight so she could get a better look. "Laurie Anne, he's been shot."

Did I answer her or did I just stare? I'm not really sure. I was halfway convinced that I had to be dreaming, because this couldn't possibly be real. Aunt Maggie, thank goodness, didn't waste time on such thoughts.

She said, "I don't think we should move him, not knowing how bad off he is. I'm going to have to go find a phone and call for help." She pulled off her sweater. "Put this around him, and you lie down next to him to keep him warm as you can. He might be in shock." She started to hand me the flashlight.

"You take it," I said. "You'll go faster that way."

She didn't argue. "I'll be back as quick as I can." She was out of my sight in seconds.

I never did figure out how long I was there waiting in the dark. As soon as Aunt Maggie was gone, I lay down next to Richard as gently as I could, and pushed myself close to him. I whispered to him at first, telling him that it was going to be all right and that I loved him, knowing that the words were as much for me as they were for him.

My eyes quickly adjusted to the light, but there wasn't much to see. Not much to hear, either, though I jerked at every cracking branch. There was plenty for me to think about, once I made myself stop crying and decided that being sorry wasn't what was needed. That's when I got mad, and I think best when I'm mad.

I started out remembering the way Small Bill had stayed with Uncle John Ward when he died. The circumstances were all too much alike.

Of course Richard wasn't going to die, I told myself over and over again, so I wasn't going to have to carry out any last wishes. But if he had asked me to do something, I would have done it no matter what. Of course, Richard was my husband, but Small Bill and Uncle John Ward had been best friends for a long time.

Small Bill made a promise to Uncle John Ward that night in Vietnam, and from everything I had learned about that man, I no longer believed that he would have rested unless he thought that his promise had been kept. That meant that he thought that Uncle John Ward's last wish had been carried out.

But it hadn't been carried out. Was that why Small Bill had come back to Byerly? Had he finally found out that Uncle John Ward's gift was never delivered? What gift could have been so important that Small Bill would risk his own secret? There was only one thing I could think of that could possibly be worth everything that had happened.

By the time Junior Norton and Aunt Maggie got there with the ambulance, I had it all figured out. I knew who had been blackmailing Aunt Daphine, and who had killed Small Bill and Dorinda, and who had tried to kill Richard.

Chapter 38

Of course I put all of that out of my mind while we got Richard safely out of the graveyard. A doctor was waiting for us at the hospital emergency room in Hickory, and she quickly examined Richard while I stood by. After what seemed like an eternity, she turned to me and said, "Your husband is one lucky fellow. The bullet missed everything important. He's lost some blood and we have to get that bullet out, but he's going to come out of this with nothing more than a scar."

I must have looked like I was going to pass out about then, because suddenly Aunt Maggie had one elbow and Junior had the other. "Let's us get out of the way so they can get to work," Aunt Maggie said, and they led me to a chair somewhere.

Though I didn't think about it at the time, I realized later what an effort of will it must have taken for Junior to keep herself from asking me any questions. All she did while we were waiting was to get me a Coke and a package of crackers and make sure I ate them. Finally the doctor finished with Richard, and we followed along as they wheeled him to a room.

He was still unconscious, but I kissed him and held

his hand. The doctor again assured me that he was going to be all right, and after she left, I guess Junior decided that I was finally fair game.

"Well, Laurie Anne," she said, "are you going to tell me what's going on now?"

Aunt Maggie said, "I think you better, Laurie Anne."

I nodded. It was time to tell the story, or at least most of it. I wouldn't tell either of them what hold the blackmailer had on Aunt Daphine, and they finally resigned themselves to that. Of course I knew that they, and everybody else in Byerly, would find out once the blackmailer was arrested, but there wasn't anything I could do about that. I was going to keep my promise to Aunt Daphine just as long as I could.

I also managed to avoid telling them that Leonard Cooper was Small Bill Walters, because I didn't want to break my promise to Burt Walters either. I was pretty sure that Junior knew it already, since she had seen Michael Cooper, but that didn't matter as long as it wasn't official.

I finished up with the conclusions I had come to while waiting with Richard in the graveyard and asked, "Is it too late for Vivian to check it out on her computer?"

"Laurie Anne, it's only eight o'clock," Junior said.

I didn't believe her at first. Surely it had to be after midnight. But when I looked at my watch, I saw that she was right.

Junior made the call, and fortunately caught Vivian at the V.F.W. I was starting to think that the woman lived there. Vivian checked it out while we waited, and confirmed the first part of my suspicion.

"Well, it's possible," Junior said when she got off of the phone.

I asked, "Do you think we can get a search warrant by tomorrow morning so we can make sure?"

"Search warrant my tail end," Aunt Maggie said. "I'll find it if I have to tear the place apart with my bare hands."

"No need for that," Junior said. "We can get a warrant. I have a hunch that Laurie Anne has planned out exactly what she wants to do with what we find."

I nodded, and started to explain. We were ironing out the details when Richard said in a weak voice, "How now, you secret, black, and midnight hags!" I kissed him on the forehead, whispered that I loved him, and he drifted back to sleep.

"What did he say?" Junior said.

"That was from *Macbeth*," I said. "If I'm not mistaken, Richard just compared us to the three witches."

Junior thought it was funny and Aunt Maggie was a little bit put out, but I couldn't have been happier. Richard was going to be all right.

Chapter 39

Aunt Maggie and I stayed at the hospital all night, and tried to get a little sleep while Junior chased after the paperwork we needed. She was at the judge's house at eight in the morning, and after getting his signature, picked up the two of us so we could use the search warrant. Then we went to La Dauphin. As we had arranged, Junior stayed outside while Aunt Maggie and I went in. Junior didn't like it, but I had convinced her that the murderer wouldn't say anything if she was there.

We got there at about nine-thirty. They didn't open until ten, but we knew Aunt Daphine and most of the other stylists got in early so they could share a cup of coffee and arrange their hair brushes and curling irons for the day.

Aunt Daphine was at the front desk waiting for us. I had called her the night before to tell her about Richard, and to warn her that we would be there in the morning to finish things. Of course, she had wanted to hear it all right then, but I put her off. I couldn't have explained it all without Junior and Aunt Maggie hearing, and I was still bound by that promise.

"How's Richard?" she asked when we came in.

"He's fine," I said. "Aunt Daphine, I had to tell Aunt Maggie and Junior Norton that you're being black-mailed, but I didn't tell them why."

"That doesn't matter now, Laurie Anne, not after what happened to Richard."

I nodded. I had thought that she would feel that way, but I had to be sure. "Then you understand why I can't keep your secret anymore?"

"Of course I understand," she said, chin held high. "Don't you worry about me."

I nodded, relieved that that part was over, but dreading the rest. "Are all of the hair stylists here?"

Aunt Daphine said, "Yes. Why?"

I didn't answer her. "Call Gladys out here."

I knew she wanted to ask me why, but she obligingly called, "Gladys! Can you help me a minute?"

Gladys came out, saw me and Aunt Maggie, and said, "Hey Laurie Anne, Miss Burnette."

Aunt Daphine was looking back and forth between me and Gladys, but didn't say anything.

"Gladys," I said, "I need for you to get the other women out of the shop. Right now."

"Is there a gas leak?" Gladys asked.

I shook my head. "No, nothing like that, but we need them out of here. I can't explain right now."

Tell them that you'll treat them to a biscuit," Aunt Maggie suggested.

"Is that all right?" Gladys asked Aunt Daphine. For an answer, Aunt Daphine reached into the cash drawer and handed her two twenty-dollar bills.

Gladys went back into the main room and we heard her say, "Hey everybody! I've got good news for you."

"What?" somebody wanted to know.

"I don't want to tell you here. Let's go over to Woolworth's and get us a biscuit so we can celebrate. I'll treat, and Daphine says it's okay."

There were more questions, but Gladys added, "Come on, or we won't be able to get back in time to open."

It took a few minutes for them to get their coats and pocketbooks from the back, but soon enough they came on through and out the front door. Aunt Maggie and I stayed back by the wall, so I don't think most of them even saw us.

"Aren't you coming, Daphine?" somebody called out, but Aunt Daphine said, "No, I better stay here and keep an eye on things."

Clara McDonald was the last one in line, and I whispered, "Keep Clara here," to Aunt Daphine.

"Clara, would you mind staying with me," Aunt Daphine said. "I need your help mixing up some color for my first appointment. Gladys will bring you back a biscuit."

"All right," Clara said, and turned back.

As soon as the others were gone, Aunt Maggie locked the door and we joined Clara in the main room. I noticed that now her hair was chestnut. She looked uneasy when she saw me and Aunt Maggie, but all she said was, "What color did you want, Daphine?"

"She doesn't need any hair color," I said. "We just wanted to talk to you alone."

"What about?" Clara asked.

Without saying anything, Aunt Maggie walked past her and into the back room. A minute later she came back out and nodded at me.

I took a deep breath. That nod meant that Clara had

left her gun in her purse, but that Aunt Maggie had it now.

"What's all this about?" Clara asked, her voice rising. "What do you want?"

I ignored her questions and pulled a folded piece of paper out of my pocketbook. "We found this in your house, Clara."

"What were you doing in my house? That's illegal!"

I went on. "It's a letter from my uncle John Ward Marston to Aunt Daphine."

"A letter to me?" Aunt Daphine said. "What on earth was Clara doing with a letter to me?"

"It's a long story, and you may as well sit down." Aunt Daphine and Aunt Maggie did so, but Clara kept standing and so did I.

"Aunt Daphine, when Uncle John Ward wrote to you, he said that he had bought something for you. Remember?"

She nodded.

"Burt Walters showed us a letter that he got from his brother Small Bill during the war, just before his death. Small Bill was there while Uncle John Ward was dying. The last thing Uncle John Ward did was to write you a letter, and to ask Small Bill to deliver it and the gift he had for you."

"But I never got them," Aunt Daphine said. "Small Bill never came back."

"I know you didn't, but the letter and the gift did make it back to Byerly." I hesitated, because now I was going to have to break my promise to Burt Walters, but he had said to go ahead if it would help catch Small Bill's murderer. "After Uncle John Ward died, Small Bill became friends with a man named Leonard Cooper. When Cooper was killed in battle, Small Bill decided to trade places with him. He didn't want to come back to Byerly. He wanted to make his own life somewhere new, and he thought that this was his only chance. There was only one thing holding him back: the promise he had made to Small Bill."

"I'm leaving," Clara announced. "None of this has anything to do with me."

"I don't believe you will," Aunt Maggie said quietly, and Clara blanched and finally sat down.

I went on with the story. "Small Bill wanted to make sure that Uncle John Ward's letter got back to you, but he didn't trust the mail. That meant that someone had to bring it back. By now he was in an Army hospital under the name of Leonard Cooper, and who should he see being carried in but Ed McDonald, his old friend from Byerly. I checked, and found out that Small Bill was there when Ed was treated for those two fingers he lost. Small Bill thought he could trust Ed, so he told him he didn't think he was going to make it, and he gave him the things from Uncle John Ward and made him promise to carry them to Aunt Daphine."

"When Ed got better, he went back to the fighting, and by the time he got back to Byerly, everybody knew that Small Bill was dead. Ed must have assumed that he had died in the hospital after he saw him."

"Why didn't Ed give me my letter?" Aunt Daphine asked.

"I imagine he intended to, Aunt Daphine, but something happened before he could. I can only guess what it was, but I started supposing what it was like when a soldier came home. Probably the first thing he wanted to do was be alone with his wife. Then he'd probably sleep for a week. Isn't that right, Clara?"

Clara didn't say anything. She just stared at her finger, and twisted her diamond ring round and round.

"Of course, Clara wouldn't have been sleeping all that time. She'd want to unpack his bags and do his laundry, make him feel at home. That's when she found it."

"Found what?" Aunt Daphine asked.

"The gift Uncle John Ward had sent for you. Only she didn't know it was for you—she thought it was for her. I can't blame her for thinking that because I probably would have thought the same thing. By the time Ed woke up, she had probably told everybody in town that he had brought it for her. Ed couldn't stand the idea of taking it away from her, so he didn't. He just kept quiet."

"What about the letter?" Aunt Daphine said.

"He must have been afraid to give it to you because he figured it mentioned the gift he couldn't give to you. Maybe he read it. I don't know for sure, and I don't know why he didn't just throw it away. I'm guessing that he always felt guilty about it, and maybe he hoped he'd think of a way to make it right someday. He never did. Then he died.

"Afterwards, Clara must have gone through his things, and that's probably when she found that letter. And she read it. And she finally found out that the gift she had been so proud of for all these years was never meant for her at all. Isn't that right, Clara?"

Clara still wouldn't answer.

"I apologize for reading this letter, Aunt Daphine," I said, "but I had to make sure that I was right." I handed it to her.

Aunt Daphine unfolded it carefully, as if afraid she'd break it. Then she read it out loud.

Dear Daphine,

By the time you read this, I'll be gone. Bill keeps trying to tell me that I'll be all right, but I know better. I can tell the difference between a hurt you can walk away from and one you can't. I won't be walking away from this one.

I'm writing this to tell you how much I love you, and that you were the best thing that ever happened to me. I wondered before if we should have waited to make love to one another, but now I am so glad that we didn't. I thought we'd have our whole lives together, but I guess it wasn't meant to be that way.

Don't ever forget me Daphine, or how much I love you. I'm sending something to you along with this letter, something I wanted to give you myself, down on one knee to ask you proper. Always wear it for me, Daphine. Maybe we weren't married in the eyes of the law, but I know that we were married in the eyes of God, and that's all that matters to me.

I love you Daphine, and I'll be watching over you.

Love,
John Ward

Aunt Daphine carefully folded the letter, and softly said, "He bought me an engagement ring. He was going to ask me to marry him." Her eyes were brimming with tears, and I hated to interrupt her memories of Uncle John Ward, but I wasn't done yet.

"I was pretty sure what the gift had to be even before I read that note," I said. "I knew it had to be so important that Uncle John Ward wouldn't trust the mail, and it had to be so important that, even after all this time and all that had happened, Small Bill would come back to Byerly to make sure it was delivered. It had to be an engagement ring. The ring that Clara is wearing, now."

"It wasn't fair!" Clara shouted. "The boys always liked Daphine better, and I know that Ed would never have married me if Daphine had ever given him the time of day. But when he brought me my ring, I knew he really loved me. Me! I didn't mind it when he talked to Daphine all the time, and offered to help out with her yard and all. I had my ring, and I had Ed. Then Ed died, and I found that letter. Ed never bought me that ring, never bought me anything. Do you know how that felt?"

I said, "Maybe I could understand your not giving Aunt Daphine the ring back, and maybe I could understand your resenting her for it. But I can't understand blackmail and I can't understand murder."

"Oh my Lord," Aunt Daphine whispered. "It was you, Clara?"

Clara smiled, and it wasn't pretty. "When I first looked at that letter, all I thought about was that the ring wasn't meant for me. Then I realized what it meant, that Daphine was never married. That she had been lying all those years, and that Vasti was a bastard. You lied, Daphine."

"Yes, I did," Aunt Daphine said.

"All this time everyone in Byerly thought you were so wonderful for raising your daughter alone, and for starting this shop and all. And it was all a lie," Clara said. "I didn't have anything. All I had was the ring, and it wasn't even mine! You owed it to me. When Ed died so sudden like that, there wasn't any money. You owed it to me, every bit of it."

"So you blackmailed her," I said, wanting to draw her attention and her hate away from Aunt Daphine. "You worked with her every day, and you could see what it was doing to her, and you still blackmailed her. And you kept her ring."

"It's *my* ring!" Clara shouted. "I won't give it up."

"Is that what you told Small Bill Walters when he came to see you?" I asked, and she looked away. I turned back to Aunt Daphine. "When Junior searched Small Bill's hotel room, she found a *Byerly Gazette* from the Wednesday before he died. At the time she figured he picked it up in town, but then we found out that he had a subscription. It was mailed to him Wednesday afternoon, and he received it Friday. Do you remember what was in that paper? It took us a while to spot it. That's when they ran that full-page ad for Arthur, the one with a picture of Arthur and Vasti, his parents, and you. It's a wonderful picture of all of you holding hands, and looking proud. And your finger is as bare as it can be. That's the first time that Small Bill realized that you never got the ring Uncle John Ward had trusted him to deliver.

"He came to Byerly to try to find out what happened. He probably already knew that Ed was dead, since it would have been in the paper, so he went looking for Clara. Maybe he didn't immediately suspect that Clara had the ring, but when he asked her if she knew what had happened to it, there it was on her finger."

"That Small Bill thought he was so smart," Clara spat out. "He said he was an old war buddy of John Ward Marston's and gave me that phony name, but I knew he was Small Bill Walters all along. He threatened me, said he was going to take my ring away, but I wasn't about to let him. I found out where he was staying, and I went to his hotel Sunday to talk to him some more. He was leaving, so I followed him up to the mill and through the hole in the fence and up to Burt's office. When I caught up with him, I told him that if he told my secret, I'd tell everybody his. Then he tried to play rough, tried to grab my hand and take my ring away from me. Only I had my gun in my purse and I pulled it out. He shouldn't have grabbed for me like he did. I didn't mean for him to get shot like that, but he kept reaching for me. Even after the first shot." She shrugged her shoulders. "After the second shot I could see that he was dead and there was nothing I could do, so I left."

I hope I never hear anything so awful as that woman casually admitting that she had shot a man twice. "What about Dorinda? You killed her, too, didn't you?"

"She was here when Small Bill came looking for me," Clara said. "When they put that picture of him in the *Gazette*, she remembered seeing him with me and she threatened to tell Junior Norton. She said she'd keep quiet but only if I'd give her my ring." She clenched her fist around the diamond ring.

"So you shot her," I said.

"I had her meet me here at the shop and after I made sure that no one knew that she had come to see me, I pulled out the gun." She shrugged again. "She should have known that I would shoot her, too, but she didn't think that I would do it. She wasn't as smart as she thought she was."

"What about Richard?" I said coldly.

At least Clara had enough decency left to look embarrassed. "I felt bad about that, but I didn't know what else to do. I thought that you and he might be trying to pull something, so after I picked up the money, I hid and saw him start to pack up and leave. It was getting dark, so it was easy for me to come around behind him."

"Didn't you check to make sure he was dead?" I said, making myself keep my voice flat despite my anger.

"I should have, but I was afraid someone might have heard the shot. He didn't move, so I went on."

I nodded as if I understood, but there was no way that I could understand this woman. Aunt Daphine's eyes were wide in horror, but Aunt Maggie had no expression at all.

Clara looked around at us and asked, "What are you going to do now?"

"What do you think?" Aunt Maggie said. "We're going to put you in jail! Which is where you damned well belong!"

"You can't!" Clara said, looking around wildly. "If you do, I'll tell about Daphine and John Ward."

"You just go right ahead and tell," Aunt Daphine said firmly. "I might have forgiven you for keeping the ring, after all these years. I might even have forgiven you for blackmailing me, Clara, but you killed two people. You tried to kill Richard. Do you really think we'll let you get away with all of that?"

I was relieved that Aunt Daphine had been the one to say that. I knew that it had to happen that way, too, but I was glad it had been her decision.

"And after you spread your dirt," Aunt Maggie said, "you're going straight to jail. We in Byerly are going to forget you even exist, and you're going to be there for the rest of your miserable life. If you're lucky, you'll get the death penalty. If not, there's no telling how long you'll last in there, with all the drug addicts and thieves and whores. And murderers."

I had never heard Aunt Maggie talk like that, and

even though it was directed at Clara, I felt chilled to the bone.

Clara took a couple of sobbing breaths, and then said, "I suppose you've already called the police."

"Junior Norton is waiting inside," I told her. Now that she had confessed, I didn't try to keep the revulsion out of my voice.

She nodded. "I better go get my purse." She started shakily toward the back.

I was going to let her go, because I knew there was no back door, but Aunt Maggie held an open hand out in front of her. "We'll take that ring back now," she said matter-of-factly.

Clara looked right pitiful taking it off, and I almost felt sorry for her. Then I remembered how little feeling she had shown when talking about killing Small Bill and Dorinda, and about trying to kill Richard. She hadn't even asked if Richard was alive or dead. After that, I just felt sick to my stomach.

She held the ring up to look at it just for a second, then placed it carefully on Aunt Maggie's open palm before walking into the back room.

It wasn't but a few seconds later when we heard the gunshot. I knew that I should go see, but I couldn't make myself move. Aunt Daphine started to go, but Aunt Maggie shook her head and went back there herself. When she came back, she was nodding grimly. She said, "She's dead."

"I thought that you got her gun," I said.

Aunt Maggie ignored me. To Aunt Daphine she said, "I think this is yours," and held out the ring.

Aunt Daphine stared at it for a minute, and then reached out and took it. "Maybe I shouldn't want it after all that's happened," she said slowly, looking down at it, "but John Ward's dying wish was for me to wear it for him. Small Bill died trying to get it to me." Then she slipped it onto the ring finger of her left hand. "John Ward meant it for me and I'm going to have it."

I had expected Junior to come running when she heard the shot, but instead she took her time. When she came into the shop, she didn't speak to us, just went into the back room for a few minutes.

When she came back out, she said, "I should have known. Miss Burnette, I thought you were going to get the gun out of her purse."

"I must have checked the wrong purse," Aunt Maggie said evenly. "There wasn't any gun in the purse I looked in."

Junior nodded. "I see. What would you have done if she had tried to shoot one of you?"

"I could have handled her. Besides, there wasn't but one bullet."

"In this gun you didn't see?" Junior said.

Aunt Maggie nodded.

"Did Clara tell you why it was she was intending to shoot herself?" Junior asked.

"She confessed to killing Leonard Cooper and Dorinda Thompson," I said.

"Did she say why?" Junior asked, scrupulously polite.

I looked at Aunt Daphine, and she looked at Junior. "Blackmail," I said. "Dorinda saw Clara with Cooper, and guessed that Clara had killed him. She said she'd tell you if Clara didn't pay up." That was true, though not the whole truth.

"And why did Clara kill Leonard Cooper?"

I hesitated, and Aunt Maggie said, "Who can tell?"

"I notice that Clara isn't wearing that diamond ring she was so fond of," Junior said speculatively.

Aunt Daphine started to answer, but Aunt Maggie said, "She gave it to Daphine, Junior, and I'll swear to that in court if you want me to."

Junior shook her head. "It probably won't come to that. If we can match the bullets from her gun with the ones that killed Leonard Cooper and Dorinda Thompson, that will most likely close the case. I have a hunch the town council, especially Big Bill Walters, will be happy to leave it at that." She looked Aunt Maggie in the eye. "Miss Burnette, you know that Clara would still be alive if you had done like you said you were going to."

Aunt Maggie said, "Well Junior, you know as well as I do that law isn't always the same thing as justice. For everybody in town to hear about Daphine's private affairs isn't my idea of justice."

"That may be true," Junior admitted, "but it's the law I swore to uphold."

"I know you did, Junior, but I didn't. I'm the oldest in my family, and I've got to look after my folks the best I can. I didn't do anything that I can't live with."

All Junior said was, "I better call the crime scene people."

While Junior was on the telephone, Aunt Maggie gave Aunt Daphine a thick envelope. "That's the money you left for Clara yesterday. I found it when we were searching Clara's house. I suppose the rest of it is gone for good, but at least you've got this much back."

"You didn't tell Junior about the money," I said.

Aunt Maggie shrugged. "I don't see that Junior needs to know anything about it, do you?"

I shook my head. "I guess not."

We were there for several hours after that, of course, answering questions and signing statements and such. But eventually Junior let us go, and I headed for the hospital to check on Richard.

Chapter 40

"How do you feel about it all?" Richard asked when I finished telling him the tale that afternoon at the hospital.

"I'm just not sure," I said. "Maybe I should be sorry about Clara killing herself, but I'm not. Not after what she did to Aunt Daphine, and Small Bill Walters, and Dorinda. And to you." I reached over to touch him, just to reassure myself that he was all right. "I don't doubt that she got what she deserved, but I couldn't have made the decision Aunt Maggie did. I hope I never have to." I shrugged. "It's over now, anyway, except for the clean–up."

"So did the doctor say how long they're going to keep me in here?"

"At least through the end of the week."

"Great. Just the way I wanted to end my vacation."

"Are you kidding?" I asked. "You should count yourself lucky. I'm the one who's going to have to spend every waking moment repeating all of this to the rest of the Burnettes. And I'm going to have to talk to Burt Walters to tell him that Aunt Maggie and Aunt Daphine know about his brother. And he and I are going to have

302

to come up with something to tell Michael Cooper. And I'm going to have to track down Joleen and try to explain how her mother tried to blackmail Clara. And I'm going to call your boss and explain how one of his professors got shot. And most important, I'm going to have to try and mend fences with Junior. You get to lie here in this nice comfortable bed and read Shakespearean scholarship."

"You're absolutely right," he said solemnly. "Next time, I'll let you take the bullet."

Normally I would have hit him with a pillow, but under the circumstances, I settled for a long kiss. "There's not going to be a next time," I said firmly. "Don't you ever scare me like that again."

Getting things sorted out was even more of a pain than I had expected, but I lived through it, even when Hank Parker cornered me for an endless interview.

Somehow Aunt Daphine's secret stayed a secret, and so did Small Bill Walters's. There was lots of speculation as to why Clara had shot Cooper, but Junior just kept telling people that all she cared about was who. *Why* Clara did it wasn't Junior's business.

There was some talk about Clara giving her ring to Aunt Daphine, but since she didn't have any children, I guess it wasn't considered all that odd. After all, people said, you don't expect a murderer to be rational, especially not when she's about to kill herself.

Come Tuesday, Arthur won the election by a landslide. Of course, that meant there was something else Richard got to avoid: the party Vasti threw to celebrate. As for me, I enjoyed it. Partially because I like noisy parties and partially because I was tickled to death that Arthur had won. But the main reason was because of how proud and happy Aunt Daphine looked when she stood there next to Vasti and Arthur, and how every once in a while she looked down at the diamond ring on her finger.